PUFFIN BOOKS

THE
NINE
NIGHT
MYSTERY

Sharna Jackson is an award-winning author and curator who specializes in developing socially engaged initiatives for children across culture, publishing and entertainment. She was recently the artistic director at Site Gallery in Sheffield and was formerly the editor of the Tate Kids website. Sharna's debut novel *High-Rise Mystery* received numerous awards and accolades, including the Waterstones Children's Book Prize for the Best Book for Younger Readers. Sharna lives on a ship in Rotterdam in the Netherlands.

THE
NINE
NIGHT
MYSTERY

SHARNA JACKSON

PUFFIN

PUFFIN BOOKS

UK | USA | Canada | Ireland | Australia
India | New Zealand | South Africa

Puffin Books is part of the Penguin Random House group of companies
whose addresses can be found at global.penguinrandomhouse.com

www.penguin.co.uk
www.puffin.co.uk
www.ladybird.co.uk

First published 2024

001

Text copyright © Sharna Jackson, 2024
Chapter headers illustrated by Arabella Jones

The moral right of the author and illustrator has been asserted

Set in 11.5/15.5 pt Baskerville MT Std
Typeset by Jouve (UK), Milton Keynes
Printed and bound in Great Britain by Clays Ltd, Elcograf S.p.A.

The authorized representative in the EEA is Penguin Random House Ireland,
Morrison Chambers, 32 Nassau Street, Dublin D02 YH68

A CIP catalogue record for this book is available from the British Library

ISBN: 978-0-241-52361-2

All correspondence to:
Puffin Books
Penguin Random House Children's
One Embassy Gardens, 8 Viaduct Gardens, London SW11 7BW

To those of us who leave before their time,
and the ones they leave behind.

Listen. I'm never doing favours for Mum again. If she tries it, I'm shutting her down with a hard no – the hardest no from Wesley Evans. She can send one of her other kids – or, better, do them herself because I'm not about that helping life any more. Favours can do one. Requests? What? Nah, I've retired.

Why?

Well, it's early morning, Easter holidays. I'm not at no holiday club. I haven't gone away with my mate Bobby. I'm not even in bed eating chocolate eggs.

I'm at our neighbour Rachel's house, in her room. I just dropped a paintbrush she asked me for on her floor, and she didn't do or say anything when it rolled under the bed.

Not because she's asleep or lazy.

But because she's dead.

Rachel Kohl. Dead in her bed.

I squeeze my eyes shut. Rachel's room is shrinking, and so's my throat. I scratch at my neck in straight fear. I'm trying to breathe, but suddenly I don't know how to. Bruh. It smells weird in here. Not like death – or what I *think* that smells like – but, like, I don't know, flowers and herbs, but sour. What I *do* know is that I'm gonna puke. Scary thoughts are Usain Bolting through my brain, and one idea is doing laps.

Someone's done this to her.

Someone we – my friends Josie, Margot and I – invited to her surprise fortieth party.

Just last night.

Five of Rachel's friends, including Mum, came and, yeah, they were a bit weird, but they didn't give 'murderer'. I was only with them for a few hours, though, so I ain't vouching for any of them. I'm not stupid.

That party was stupid, though. I well regret getting involved, but we couldn't help ourselves. It's what we do. We were doing a favour for Mum, who wanted to do something nice for Rachel.

We thought we were inviting friends over. Instead, we brought enemies to Rachel's door, and her life to an end.

You see now? No more favours.

Because this was our fault, kind of.

Oh my God. Warm tears roll down my face. I'm just straight-up crying. I can't handle any of this – evil people, my guilt . . . Rachel's ghost.

Ghosts are the worst.

I make the sign of the cross and promise God I'll start

going church more. I also ask Him to have a word with Rachel, persuade her not to haunt me. Rachel seemed cool in life – an actress apparently. Never saw her on TV, though.

But Rachel in the spirit realm? In death? Who knows how she rolls over there. Some ghosts not only move through walls; they move mad, very vengeful. They're not all like that Casper; they ain't all friendly.

I have to get out of here and do something before other-realm Rachel does something to me – but what? I don't know the process. I ain't a detective. I'm eleven, and this is *not* my area of expertise. Painting probably is. But now I don't even have my brush.

What would you do? Who do I tell first?

Do I run home screaming to Mum? Nah, can't. I've got to tell her properly, give her a fresh mint tea first. She liked Rachel. They were close – they met at their stomach ache support group thing. Since she moved here, to Copsey Close, they've been besties, living in each other's pockets. Mum even has a key for Rachel's house, and you don't just dish those out to anyone. But Mum's been busy lately, distracted – it's why she wanted to throw Rachel a party in the first place.

Don't suggest calling Craig – that guy's my dad in name and biology only. I haven't even seen that fool for years anyway, so that's pointless.

Ask my sibs – my twin brothers and sister – for help? No, they'd offer none – plus, they're younger than me; they know nothing. They do my head in sometimes, but I don't want them near dead bodies.

Yeah, best thing to do is keep it cool, text Josie and Margot, and figure this thing out together. Those girls are my best friends – well, Josie is. Margot's getting there. They both live on the close too, so they can get here in seconds.

Josie spends half her life on Google, searching for ways to change the world, or different ways to tell me what to do, so she'll have ideas. Margot will go into secret-agent mode. She says she wants to be a writer, but I swear Margot's a baby spy – she's loaded and too fancy to live here. Listen, I love my town, but, like, you have a whole big house in London, why live in a little one in Luton? Make it make sense. Margot will start coming up with theories and plots. That or she'll cry – which, fine, this is the worst thing to happen, ever – but she won't be that sad. Nah. She'll weep about the beauty of the circle of life or some crud like that.

But you know what? I'd rather listen to that, and be with them, than be here.

We make a good team and we've actually done decent things as a trio. A few months ago, Josie set up what I thought was a well cringy club. She called it the Copseys, after where we live, but also because it sounded professional. The Copseys is kind of a second-hand Scout troop, but you know what? It's good. We help people.

Now we have to help Rachel.

Yeah, scratch what I said about forgetting favours.

It's time to go and I need my brush.

I open my eyes and look at Rachel. Her wide-open eyes stare up at the ceiling. Her mouth is twisted. She's not smiling.

She's not acting. It's not nice. It's awful. I look away from her face and down by her side. A book – one she got gifted last night – lies next to her. On top of it is a bitten cheese-filled potato skin.

A breath catches in my throat. Mum made those, and she wouldn't let anyone except Rachel eat one.

I stare at the skin as I squat down and inch my fingers forward, patting the thin, worn carpet. It's damp. I'm frightened to look at my fingers – I'm not the biggest fan of blood. I wave my hand near my face and smell spices.

Another present, another guest.

I lie on my stomach and tap under the bed, past a scrap of paper, until I can feel bristles. When I do, I yank the brush towards me. I run out of Rachel's room, slamming her door behind me, and scramble, whimpering, down the stairs. At the bottom I let out a cry and burst into sobs. I pull Rachel's front door open and run into the close, right into Josie.

LAST NIGHT
SUNDAY 9 APRIL

RACHEL'S SURPRISE PARTY

1

Josie peered round Rachel's yellowing net curtains. She pressed her brown cheek against the window and looked out over the close. 'Yeah, I reckon we've done a good job – Copsey party-planning badges for everyone. But you know what? *I* wouldn't want a surprise party.'

'Why not?' Margot asked, smoothing creases out of a red-and-white-checked tablecloth. 'Friends, family, cake, presents? I'm not getting the problem.'

I looked up at the girls, paintbrush in my hand, Rachel's birthday banner in front of me. I've known Josie my whole life, but Margot's new. She moved to the close almost a year ago now. First, I was like, meh, then grrr, but she's actually all right. 'Me neither, Margot – Josie's always said she hates surprises and I'm all . . .' I raised my arms and made a confused face.

Josie shrugged. 'You're right. I don't.'

'Why, though?' asked Margot. She twirled a long dark curl round her finger. She does that when she's thinking. 'OK, bad surprises – not great, sure, but even they can be exciting, give you something to write about. But good ones, ones like this? What's the issue?'

'They're just not for me,' Josie said. 'I can't explain it.'

'I can,' I said. 'I know what your beef is.'

'You do?' Josie put her hand to her chin. 'Go on, tell me. I did a Buzzfeed quiz about this once, but the answers felt off.'

Margot shuddered. 'A robot wrote it probably.'

I popped my paintbrush on the plastic bag next to me and put my pinkie on it to stop it rolling. Rachel's carpet was tatty, but I wasn't gonna put paint on it, and make it worse. 'Josie, you ain't about surprises cos surprises mean things going on behind your back. You're not in charge – *that's* the problem. If you ain't the boss, you're lost.'

Margot laughed. 'Pure poetry! I'm stealing that.'

'Take it. It's yours and it's true. You know I'm right.'

Josie stood still. For a hot second I thought she was heated. Mad with me. 'Hmmm. You might be on to something.' She picked up a red balloon and began to blow it up. 'Interesting.'

So far so Josie.

'Tell you what, I'll make you a deal,' I said. 'I'll never, ever throw you a surprise party.'

Josie laughed. 'Promise?'

I bowed my head slightly. 'Swear down. I swear on the Copsey Code.'

'Don't make promises you can't keep, Wes,' said Mum as she swept into the living room. Her long skirt flowed around her ankles and her long locked hair swung against her back. 'It never ends well.' She held a plate of potato skins in front of her, while their delicious smell trailed behind. I got up and followed the scent like an untrained terrier. As soon as she placed them on the table, I reached for one. Mum slapped my hand away.

'No!' she said sternly, but with a slight smile. 'These ones are for Rachel and Rachel only, OK? Vegan cheese, so they're good for her gut. And they're her favourites.' She looked down at the plate. 'At least I think they are.'

'*Think?* You don't *know*?' I shook my head. 'What kinda bestie are you?'

Mum laughed. 'Not a very good one, clearly.' She put her hand on her hip. 'It's just that sometimes Rachel says one thing one day, then a completely different, conflicting thing on another. Can't keep up sometimes.'

'Sounds confusing,' said Josie.

I nodded. 'And annoying.'

'Ah, maybe it's all the acting she does,' said Margot.

I snorted. 'Acting where? You ever seen a film, TV show or play with Rachel Kohl in it? A TikTok even? Cos I know I haven't.'

Margot and Josie shook their heads. 'She's not on IMDb either. I had to look,' said Josie.

'Ah, well, it all takes time, I think. You have to start small to get the big roles, don't you? Anyway, the confusion's part of the fun. Sometimes.' Mum sighed. 'Besides, I haven't seen much of her for a few weeks. I've been busy, other people to see.' A smile danced on her lips. 'So this party's an awesome way to reconnect, and I'm seriously grateful for your help. Couldn't have done it without you.'

'You're *so* welcome, Ella,' said Margot, beaming at Mum.

I looked over at Josie, who stifled a laugh. Margot well likes Mum. Always calling her Ella, always answering her questions, always begging for friendship. I get it – Mum's decent, but Margot's desperation was heavy.

'Remind me, Josie,' said Mum, 'what time did you tell everyone?'

'By seven fifty,' said Josie. 'The sun sets at seven forty-eight today –'

'Wow, specific, OK,' Mum muttered.

'It should be dark when they get here. They can sneak in or hide outside if Rachel's early. She's still due back at eight, right?' Josie looked at her phone. 'In fifteen minutes?'

Mum nodded. 'Yep, she just thinks we're catching up, so she went for her daily walk round the park, and to pick up a picture frame she bought off eBay.'

I looked down at my banner then up around Rachel's living room. Besides the decorations we had already put up, yeah, it was pretty bare and basic in here. Thin beige carpet, scuffed white walls and a ceiling I swear was sagging. A tatty two-seat blue-and-green tartan sofa was pushed against the bay window. Another sofa – also tartan, but not matching, clashing red and mustard – sat against the long wall. There was a mantelpiece opposite this sofa, with a large dirt-flecked mirror hanging above it. Her small rectangular dining table, covered by the tablecloth and decorated with glitter by Margot, had its four chairs tucked underneath. This set-up was by the patio door, which opened on to her yard. 'Yeah, she could definitely do something in here.'

'It is a little bleak,' said Margot. 'The picture frame would help.'

'It depends on what's in it, doesn't it?' said Josie.

I leaned back. 'It's funny, though. Rachel's always getting packages –'

'How do you know?' asked Josie, an eyebrow raised.

Margot put her hands round her eyes to make binoculars and peered around the room. 'Who's the spy now, eh?'

'Nah!' I tugged the hem of Mum's skirt. 'Innit, Rachel's always getting parcels?'

Mum nodded. 'We take most of them in. Like her personal depot, we are.'

'All those deliveries and nothing to show for it. It's weird. Like, I'm sorry – I know she's your mate, Mum,' I said with a shrug. 'But you know I'm right, though.'

'Right is letting people live how they want,' said Josie.

'I'm with you there,' said Mum.

I looked at Margot. 'Girl, back me up!'

She paused. 'They're both right, Wes, but, I agree, it is . . . interesting.' Margot leaned forward, like she was letting us in on a secret. 'So earlier, when I went to use the bathroom, I noticed her main bedroom – the big one, well, biggest one – at the front? It has a lock on it! She must sleep in a smaller room at the back. Why?'

'Because it's a free country. Kind of,' said Josie. She looked at her phone, then at my banner. 'We've got to get that up.'

I dabbed it with my finger. 'It's still wet, though.'

'You started late, so of course it is,' Josie said. 'I told you about time, so this is what we get. Lift it anyway. If these people are punctual, they should be here any second.'

Together we hoisted the damp, crinkled paper like a floppy flag. The reds, blues, greens and yellows I'd used to shout 'HAPPY 40TH RACHEL' began to run together and drip.

'Well,' Mum said, 'it's . . . something.'

'Something out of a horror film, yep.' Margot grinned. 'Let's hope no one dies at the end!'

I glared at her. 'Don't jinx it, Margot. Don't be bad vibes.'

She laughed. 'Don't be silly.'

Rachel's doorbell rang. Our guests had arrived.

Margot squealed and wriggled her fingers. 'Do you think they'll recognize me?'

2

Mum bounced to the door with a spring in her step. 'Coming!' she trilled. She seemed excited. She's been super happy lately, in a real good mood. Probably glad to be away from my sibs, who are the founding members of Team Too Much.

Margot craned her neck round the doorway, eyes on stalks, eager to see who was here.

'What you on about, Margot? Recognize you?' My eyes narrowed. 'What did you do? You had two jobs – make a Facebook and message Rachel's friends –'

'And not use a real photo or name!' Josie added. 'I know that's what you've done.' She shook her head. 'Should have done it myself. It would've been safer.'

'Relax, relax,' Margot said, reaching into the back pocket of her jeans. 'I layered loads of filters on top. Voila!' she said proudly, turning her phone towards us to show us a figure that didn't look all that human honestly. Picture something between anime and *Avatar* and you'd still be nowhere near.

'Thank God,' Josie said. 'It looks nothing like you.'

'You don't think it captures my spirit?' She tossed her long curls behind her back and twirled.

'You ain't right, Margot,' I said, laughing. 'All wrong.'

She shrugged and laughed too. In the hallway a man with the loudest voice said – screamed would be more accurate – 'What time she a come?'

'That's got to be Whisper . . .' I said.

Margot grinned. 'I'm sorry, but that's the best, most ironic, highly iconic nickname ever. Much better than Fitzroy Jenkins or whatever his actual name is.'

I laughed. 'Right? I could hear him down the phone when Mum called him. It was like he was in the room, and he wasn't even on speaker!'

Josie nudged Margot. 'So, come on, who did you message? Not sure I trust you now, not after seeing that profile.'

Margot handed her phone to Josie. I leaned over her shoulder to look. 'I, as Morgana Foxley, my nom de plume –'

I sighed. This girl. So bougie.

'– reached out to four friends. In addition to Ella and Whisper, we are expecting a Miss Lauren Roberts, a Mrs Hazel Wilson and one Mr Apollo Fortune –'

'Apollo Fortune? He's gotta be running scams with a name like that,' I said. 'Ain't no one born into this world as Apollo Fortune.'

'You think everyone's a scammer,' said Margot. 'I mean, you thought I was sus for the longest time.'

'Honestly, Margot? I still do,' I said.

Margot smiled and rolled her eyes.

'It could be his stage name?' said Josie. 'Makes sense. Protects your privacy. I'm for it.'

'If you say so. I don't believe it, though. I'm keeping an eye on that one. Who's the fourth?' I asked. 'That's three people.'

'A Ms Caroline Nicholls.' Margot took her phone back and found her profile. 'Look.'

The woman with long blonde wavy hair held up a huge flag with a red leaf in the middle of it.'

'Canada,' I said. 'Such an elite flag.'

'Not as elite as Japan's, but whatever. Caroline didn't even reply to Morgana's message!' Margot pouted. 'Rude.'

'Could be the time difference,' said Josie. 'Canada is – let's assume she's in Toronto – at least five hours behind us.'

I stared at her. 'How do you just know stuff? Like, random facts?'

She shrugged. 'Someone's got to know things. You never know when you might need an answer.' She leaned forward. 'Plus, I really want to win *Pointless* one day and I need knowledge for that.'

'That's right, young miss. Knowledge is power!' said Whisper, as he walked into the living room, wagging his finger. He nodded at the three of us, took off his flat cap and waved it at us. He wore a smart suit-like jacket with grey tracksuit bottoms and white trainers. A bright blue backpack dangled from his right hand.

Margot leaned over. 'He confuses me visually, but I'm into it,' she muttered.

'What you say?' Whisper shouted.

Margot winced at the volume of his words. 'I like your outfit,' she said, matching his volume.

'Ah!' he said, putting his finger in his ear. 'Thank you, thank you. No need to shout, though.'

I tell you, I almost bit my bottom lip off, trying to stop myself creasing up over the cheek of it. I didn't dare look at Margot or Josie because I knew they'd be doing the same. I glanced up at Mum, who choked back a laugh and spun in the other direction.

Whisper stepped forward. 'Westley?'

'Wesley, yeah.' I put out my hand and he shook it vigorously.

'These two are your girlfriends, Margot and Josie?'

'My *girlfriends*? Nope,' I said firmly.

'They put you up to this?' he replied, nudging me in the ribs.

'Put me up to what?' I raised an eyebrow.

'Doing this function?'

'It was a joint effort actually,' said Josie.

'Hmmm,' said Whisper.

'Hmmm?' Margot replied. 'We wanted to help Ella celebrate Rachel.'

Whisper stared at us. 'You ain't regular kids.'

'We're not,' said Josie proudly. 'We're Copseys!'

I'm telling you, I could have collapsed on the spot. Cause of death? Cringe.

'You're what-sies?' asked Whisper, understandably confused. Mum returned to the living room, this time with a tray of garlic bread. He turned in her direction. 'Gluten free?'

'Of course,' she said. 'Everything is.' She patted her gut. 'No stomach aches today. Not for us or Rachel.'

'Good, good,' said Whisper. 'My memory's not what it was, you know, but I tell you I saw Miss Rachel eating biscuits in the park? Chocolate digestives?' He stuck his tongue out.

'Chocolate digestives?' I asked. 'A top-three biscuit, that is. I'm not seeing the problem.'

'Gluten and dairy are the problem,' said Whisper, wagging his finger. 'She's not supposed to touch either, but what do I see? Rachel scoffing them in Wardown Park, straight from that packet into her mouth. She was parked up on the bench, but her mind was on Mars. Me a call out, "Rachel! Rachel!" But she just –' Whisper mimed mechanical, robotic eating – 'so I pedalled on. I tell you this, Ella?'

Mum sighed. 'Yeah, you said.'

'I know that packet from a mile off. Always kept them in stock.' Whisper shook his head. 'I'm telling you, Ella, Rachel don't have no irritable bowel.'

'Why waste time going to IBS club then?' I asked.

'Exactly!' said Whisper.

Outside, on the driveway, two voices grew louder as they approached Rachel's front door.

'Unbelievable! You didn't see me reversing?' a woman shouted.

'I didn't! I'm truly sorry,' replied another. She sounded older.

'You will be.' That sounded like a threat.

The force of three knocks shook the house.

3

The three of us stood behind Rachel's front door, listening in to the argument unfolding on the other side, watching the taller woman wag her finger at the other through the frosted glass.

'You'll pay for this,' the younger voice growled, pure menace in her tone. She had one hand on her hip, the other on her head.

Josie gently kicked my ankle. 'Open the door,' she said quietly. 'We should break it up.'

'Should we?' Margot whispered. 'It sounds like it's getting good.'

I pulled the door open to two women, the younger one glaring down at the older one.

'It's gonna cost me thousands!' said the younger one. Her, I'm guessing, once white face was now tomato red, her nostrils flared. 'Thousands I don't have!'

'I'll cover it, I promise – it's no problem.' The older woman placed a hand on the angry one's arm. She looked over at us apologetically. 'Sorry, sorry – we had a minor bump. We're here for Rachel's party?' She began to step inside the house with her green-wellied foot. 'We're not late, are we?'

Margot blocked her with her body and looked down at her phone. In Margot's mind this was a VIP party and she was head of security. She looked up at the younger woman, whose face was fading to a hot pink. Her blonde hair was scraped back into a tight bun on top of her head, pulling her face tight and her eyebrows high, right by her hairline. She put her hands in the pockets of her grey hoodie and tapped her white trainer impatiently.

'Lauren Roberts?' asked Margot.

'Yeah.' Lauren nodded and pushed her way into the house and headed up the stairs. 'I need the loo.'

'And you're Hazel? Hazel Wilson?' said Margot.

'That's me,' Hazel replied. She shifted the gold-wrapped box she was carrying towards her armpit and tucked her brown bobbed hair behind her ear with her free hand. She studied Margot. 'You're the young lady that reached out?' She smiled broadly when Margot nodded. 'What a nice thing to do! I haven't seen Rachel in, oh, a while now, so this should be . . . wonderful.'

She giggled, then gently but firmly pushed her way into the hallway, where she paused. She looked up the staircase after Lauren, then wiped a finger down the banister. Then, gross, she rubbed her thumb on her fingers and

22

brought them to her nose. Hazel winced at the smell but chuckled at us. We heard her say hello to Whisper and Mum in the living room.

'See that sniffing?' I asked quietly. 'These people are weird.'

'We haven't even met Apollo yet,' said Josie. 'Hazel,' she mouthed. 'Landlord?'

I shrugged to say maybe.

Margot nodded. 'Could be. A weird mix of friends, right? Very strange.'

'Strange?' said Lauren, from the top of the stairs. Hood up, eyes burning down, a real jump scare. 'Nice. Welcoming. Thanks.' She wiped her nose and her eyes, which had switched from bright blue to soft pink, matching her cheeks. She'd been crying.

Margot clocked this immediately too. 'Oh, strange? Yeah, "strange" means . . . it means . . . cool these days,' she lied. 'But more importantly –' she lowered her voice – 'are you all right?'

Lauren's eyes softened for a split second but quickly hardened. 'Fine,' she snapped, sniffing and shaking her head. 'Yeah, I'm fine.' She joined the party.

'"Strange" means cool now, does it?' I raised an eyebrow.

'Words mean things,' said Josie. 'Or at least they're supposed to.'

Margot waved her hand. 'Please, language changes all the time. It's all good; she bought it.'

'No chance,' I said.

'No way,' added Josie. 'I'm nervous now. Are these people going to get along? Hazel and Lauren clearly don't.'

Margot shrugged. 'It'll be fine – and if it's not, it'll be fun to watch it go wrong anyway. It will be an emotional experience.'

'And that's what counts, right?' I asked. 'As long we feel something, it's all good?'

Margot laughed. 'Leave me alone – I'm trying to be positive.'

A figure approached Rachel's front door. 'Apollo,' Josie whispered.

The shadow crouched down and the letter box flipped up. 'Hello?' the voice trilled from the other side. 'Am I late late or just, you know, cool?'

'Late,' Josie replied flatly.

Margot nudged Josie out of the way and leaned towards the letter box. 'Apollo Fortune?'

'The one and only! And you – I can tell by your energy that you, you, my dear, are Morgana Foxley. Be a love and let me in, Morgana – my knees and back can't take much more.'

Margot grinned and opened the door. Apollo stood there in a vivid floral shirt and smart black trousers. He wore a smooth leather bag across his chest. His thick silver hair was perfect. I mean, perfectly pushed and swept to the side. Honestly, it looked well cool. Too cool. Too slick for this town. He held two helium balloons in his hand: a

24

golden four and a golden zero. He stepped into the hallway and looked around.

'Really, Rachel?' he muttered. He closed his eyes, took in a deep breath and turned to face us. 'Morgana,' he said, tapping his chin, 'you're much younger than I thought you'd be.' He let go of his balloons, which bobbed against the ceiling. He crossed his arms and tutted, pretending to be mad. 'Now, now, catfishing is naughty and extremely dangerous.'

'It was for our protection, actually,' said Margot. She extended her hand. 'I'm Margot; this is Josie and Wes.'

'Co-party planners,' added Josie, always craning that neck for credit.

I said my hello. 'Good to meet you.'

'And you,' he said. 'Am I the last one?' We nodded. Apollo leaned forward and fiddled nervously with the buttons on his shirt. He lowered his voice. 'What are they like? Are they good people?'

'Well,' I said, 'they seem . . . OK, but we don't know them – or you – do we?'

Apollo stepped back. 'Hmmm.' He nodded and smiled. 'Well, I'm going in – wish me luck!' He reached up for his balloons, threw his shoulders back and began to walk into the party. Before he stepped into the living room, he looked back at me with narrowed eyes.

4

Mum looked down at her phone. 'Rachel's five minutes away.' She grinned at everyone in the room. 'She thinks it's just going to be us.' Mum clenched her fists and laughed. 'She'll die of shock!'

'Ha! Let's hope not!' said Apollo from the red-and-mustard sofa. He clapped his hands together and laughed. 'Places, people!'

Like we were in a play. This dude was Cheddar cheesy.

'We're not in a play, mate,' Lauren muttered, reading my mind. She reached into a bowl on the table and nibbled on a crisp.

'But all the world's a stage, my love,' said Apollo with a smile. 'Isn't it?' He looked around the room for support.

He found it in Margot, of course.

'I think so! And since it is – what . . . role do you all play in Rachel's life?' Margot looked well impressed with her wordplay. 'How do you know her?' She didn't wait for an answer. 'We'll go first. So we – Wesley, Josie and I – all live here on the close. Ella is Wesley's mum. Ella and Rachel are best friends –'

'They are? Since when?' asked Apollo. 'That's news to me. Sorry, love, but I haven't heard of you. Rachel's never mentioned you.'

'She hasn't? Oh.' Mum scratched at her neck. 'Well, I wouldn't say best friends.'

I disagreed. 'Up until the last few weeks you saw her every day, Mum. Now, if that's not besties, I dunno what is.'

'Yeah,' said Mum. 'Yeah, we're close – we met at our IBS support group at the hospital.' She looked at Whisper. 'That's where we met this one.'

Whisper raised his glass then took a sip.

Hazel sat forward on the sofa next to Apollo, her face full of concern. 'I never knew Rachel had IBS. Gosh.'

'Why would you know?' said Lauren. 'That's private –'

'Or it's not the truth!' Whisper wagged his finger. 'I have my suspicions.'

'You really project that voice, don't you?' Apollo laughed. 'You're wasted here, darling. Theatreland needs you. But, yes, to your point, Hazel, I didn't know that either. Curious.'

Lauren sighed and folded her arms on the table. Her lips trembled. 'Like I said. Private. Information.'

'No, you're right,' said Apollo, putting his hands to his chest. 'Privacy's a basic human right.'

'Is that why your name's Apollo then?' I asked. 'For privacy?'

Whisper chuckled. 'Hehe, good question, Westley.' He raised his chin at Apollo. 'I know your parents didn't give you that.'

Apollo shifted in his seat. 'And that matters why?' He sniffed. 'We don't have to accept every gift, do we? But, yes, Apollo Fortune is my . . . chosen name.'

Or a criminal's alias, I thought. *And/or*.

'How did you come up with it?' asked Josie, shifting her weight. 'That must be an interesting process – where do you start?'

'Ah! Indeed. Well, I renamed myself after two of my favourite theatres in London. I'm a playwright and theatre director, you see? It's fitting, I think,' he said proudly.

'Oh, you're one of Rachel's successful friends?' said Hazel, turning to face him. 'How nice to meet you!'

'Well –' Apollo smiled smugly – 'that's not for me to say, but yes, I did sell quite a few tickets to my last show, *Apollo After All*.' He sipped his drink.

'How many?' I asked.

'How lovely!' said Hazel. 'I'll make a note to look out for it.' She looked around the room. 'It's funny – and please, I mean no offence, not to anyone – but I did wonder, what with her new role in that play, and that she's famous in London –'

'Famous?' Apollo laughed into his glass. 'She's not famous in London. She's not famous anywhere.'

'What play?' said Mum. 'She's never said anything about a play.'

'– that, well, this party would be livelier,' said Hazel. 'With more people.'

'Oh, we're not enough for you?' said Lauren, throwing daggers at Hazel.

'You were the only people connected to her Facebook,' said Margot with a slight shrug. 'We did our best.'

'No, I know!' said Hazel. 'That's not what I meant. I . . .' Her voice trailed away in shame.

Margot nodded. 'It's fine. Honestly, I thought I'd find more of her friends.'

Apollo shook his head. 'I wouldn't have thought so. The Rachel I know is quiet, bit shy, keeps herself to herself.'

Mum laughed. 'Quiet? Not any more. She never stops talking – it's a mile a minute. It's like she's in a rush all the time.'

'Is that so?' said Apollo. He jerked his chin towards Hazel, then drummed his fingers against it. 'What's this about a play? Which play? Where?'

'I know of the play, yeah,' said Lauren, cutting in. 'No details, though. She has to keep it under wraps, she said.' Lauren took a deep breath. Her voice wobbled. 'I hope it happens.' She sighed and stood up. 'I need the toilet.'

Again? Instead of going to the bathroom, she should go to the doctor's.

The room fell silent.

Above us, the living-room light flickered.

'This place needs rewiring,' said Hazel. 'It's on the list, I promise.'

'You're the landlord?' asked Whisper.

Hazel nodded. 'I am, yes.'

Josie smiled smugly in my direction.

Whisper looked around the living room then stared at Hazel. 'Rachel a good tenant or not?'

She paused before speaking, finding her words. 'Great,' she said, her gummy smile glued to her face. 'Yes. She's . . . excellent.'

I wasn't buying it.

Mum's phone beeped and she sat tall. 'She's coming!' She bit at her nails in a funny, dramatic way.

'Oh!' said Apollo. He wriggled his fingers. 'Places, people – for real!'

Josie jumped up and switched off the light. 'Everyone, crouch! Hide!'

'What about Lauren?' whispered Hazel in the dark. 'She's still upstairs.'

'She'll have to stay there – there's no time!' Josie hissed.

Rachel got louder as she approached the front door. 'I'm going to keep going – whether you like it or not!'

She put her key in the door and stepped into the house. She raised her voice. 'Will you just listen to me?'

Oh, we are listening, Rachel.

She slammed the front door behind her. 'You know what? I don't care! I don't care what you think. It's too late now! It's nearly over!'

When she flicked on the living-room light we all stood up.

'Surprise?' I said beneath everyone else's happy shouts.

5

Rachel dropped her phone to the floor. She stepped backwards and bounced off the door frame. She clutched at her chest, then held her stomach tightly. As she bent at the waist, her long black hair hung forward. Her wide eyes scanned the room, and she looked at each one of us, confused, as she tried to work out why we were all up in her house without permission.

'Rachel?' Apollo asked, clicking his fingers in her face. 'You in the room with us, darling?'

She didn't respond. Rachel looked up at my dripping banner, then at Mum.

'You did this?' she asked breathlessly. 'For Rachel?'

Mum squirmed on the armrest of the sofa. 'Yeah, who else?'

'I-I thought you were busy. I haven't seen you . . .'

'Not too busy to celebrate you,' Mum said gently.

Rachel's smiled. 'Oh, damn!' she said. Her brown eyes filled with tears.

'Happy birthday!' Mum shouted. We all joined in in a raggedy, overlapping way.

Rachel put her hands together, then touched her chest. 'Thank you!' She paused. 'Wow,' she whispered. 'I . . . this . . . wow, just wow. A dream come true for old Rachel.'

Whisper gently rolled his eyes. 'There she goes again, talking about herself like she's someone else –'

'Ah, the old third person,' said Apollo. 'She's always done it, hasn't she?'

Hazel laughed. 'I do find it funny.'

'That's what happens when you hang around theatres! Apollo thinks it's charming.' Apollo laughed.

'Bet you do,' muttered Whisper.

Apollo opened his mouth to clap back, I guess, but Rachel put her hand on his arm to stop him. He tutted, turned away and bit into a potato skin that he quickly spat into his hand. 'Bitter,' he said quietly. 'And rubbery.'

Oi, nah, rude. Mum made those! I glanced over to see if she'd clocked that and thankfully she hadn't.

'So, Rachel –' Whisper smiled – 'who were you just chatting with?'

This man was something else. Yeah, a good question, but bad time. It was supposed to be a party.

'Why you so stressed?'

Rachel blinked twice then grinned. 'Ah, oh, that? That was Lauren – the lovely lady who does my massages. She has the *softest* hands. I was just with her, you know?

Before this. Yes. At the park? We were running lines for my new role.'

The room fell silent. Hazel shifted in her seat and coughed at the floor.

'What?' Rachel asked with a laugh.

Lauren appeared in the doorway, eyes red, lips pursed. A look of fear ran across Rachel's face. She shook it away and smiled. 'Oh! Ha! You're here too!' She laughed and slapped her thigh. 'I-I was talking about *another* Lauren.' She waved her hand.

'Sure you were,' Lauren said. 'Cheating on me with another masseuse? Also called Lauren? Wow, what a coincidence. What loyalty. Happy birthday.'

'Thank you!' Rachel said brightly, ignoring or not noticing Lauren's shade.

But Mum felt it get chilly and tense, and she clapped her hands to cut the tension. 'Rachel,' she said, 'take your coat off, get comfortable.'

Hazel pointed down to her gold gift. 'Yes, open some presents!'

Rachel nodded. 'Great! I have something to show you anyway.' She turned round and began removing her black quilted jacket. Her slim brown arms poked out from her baggy white T-shirt.

Apollo gasped. 'Wow, Rachel! On a diet, darling? If so, stop immediately.'

'Just getting stage ready,' Rachel replied, punching the air, pretending to shadow-box. '*And* I quit smoking.' She pointed to a patch on her arm.

Lauren coughed.

'When did you even smoke?' Apollo laughed. 'It's . . . it's like I don't even know you any more.'

'Well, you'll know this,' she said. 'Ready?' Rachel jumped and turned round and pulled her T-shirt towards us. It had a picture of five ladies posing, throwing up peace signs. The adults in the room cooed and chuckled.

'Cool shirt!' said Margot. 'Vintage!'

'Am I . . . supposed to know who they are?' I asked.

'The Spice Girls!' said Mum, like I was an idiot.

'The best band ever, hello?' said Rachel. She turned to Mum. 'Ella, I don't know what you've been doing recently, but you need to school your boy.'

Mum laughed. 'They were great, Wes. Oh God, I loved the Spice Girls. Which one were you?'

'Allspice,' said Rachel. 'All of them!'

Mum sighed. 'The nineties . . .'

'Best decade, best era,' said Apollo solemnly. He bowed his head, like he was in mourning.

I didn't get it. It's only years. Numbers. Time. 'Why, though?' I asked. 'What's so good about the olden days?'

Rachel threw her hands up. 'Everything, Wes – mood rings, the Body Shop, *Top of the Pops*, Blockbuster Video –'

'Super Nintendo,' added Mum, clapping her hands together.

'Creating codes with your friends.' Rachel laughed. 'My favourite was "IDST". Rachel wrote it everywhere.'

'What does it mean?' asked Margot, putting down her paper cup.

'*If Destroyed, Still True.*' Rachel smiled but her lip quivered a little bit.

I was well confused, I tell you. 'OK . . . doesn't sound that great. Seems like you just liked the stuff.'

Whisper chuckled. 'The stuff wasn't that good, and neither were the days. Trust me.'

Rachel laughed. 'Nah, I don't trust you.'

'I don't trust you either,' said Whisper with a shrug. 'So we'll call it evens.'

Rachel bounded over and put her arm round him. 'You're a funny old coot,' she said, turning his flat cap backwards.

He laughed. 'That's rich, coming from you.'

'But I love you anyway.' Rachel stood up straight. 'Now what did you get me?' she said in a well-weird voice.

'Is that your Welsh accent, darling?' said Apollo. 'It's still good!'

Rachel bowed and smiled. 'I needed it once. For a little role.'

'*Welsh?*' I spat. It was a fair question, but the delivery was way harsh. 'My grandad was from there; he sounded nothing like that.'

'Might be a different region, though,' said Josie, trying to soften my words.

'Speaking of roles, Rachel, what is this new one I've just heard mutterings about?' asked Apollo. He put his hand to his chin, pretending to be chill and casual.

'Yes,' said Whisper, looking at her. 'You going on TV? You know, when I first met you up at the hospital, I recognized you, but couldn't place you.' He laughed. 'My memory's not what it was. That's what Thelma says anyway.'

Rachel paused, then smiled. 'Oh yes. You said. Anyway – can't say much about the role yet, but I know it'll make me rich!' She glanced sideways at Hazel.

Hazel nodded. 'Well, that would be good, wouldn't it? Everyone needs money, don't they?'

Rachel shifted on the armrest. 'Indeed.'

6

Mum did that hand-clapping tension-breaking move again. 'Presents then?' she said.

Margot turned to Josie. 'Oh my gosh, we forgot to get something!'

Rachel, now eating one of Mum's potato skins and not finding it bitter, waved her free hand and swallowed. 'No, stop right there,' she said. 'You helped Ella with this.' She reached up for Mum's hand and squeezed it tight. 'I *love* this; I won't ever forget it. Besides, your presence is my present, a gift that keeps on giving –'

'You a headache, yes.' Whisper laughed loudly.

I wasn't taking that from old Shouty McShoutyface. 'Oi!' I said. 'Nah, don't cuss us!'

'It's a joke.' Whisper kissed his teeth. 'You youngsters these days are no fun. This is what I brought.' He groaned as he leaned over to rummage through his backpack. He pulled out a flask and swung it near Rachel. 'Thelma made this just for you.'

'That's so kind!' Rachel said. She reached out as Whisper poured some liquid into the flask's cup. She breathed in the scent and paused before taking a sip.

'What's that?' I asked, sniffing the air. 'Smells spicy.'

'Smells great!' said Margot. 'What is it? What's the recipe?'

'Sorrel tea,' Whisper said proudly. 'Sorrel buds, some orange zest, fresh ginger – a really good concoction, great for the gut. We make this back home all the time. Want to taste?'

I eyed the flask. 'Nah, I'm good.'

'I do,' said Hazel.

Rachel passed the cup to her, and she took a gulp.

'Wait!' said Whisper. 'It's hot! Careful!'

Too late. Hazel coughed on the drink, while Lauren stifled a laugh. 'Oh, that's . . . fragrant!' Hazel said, smacking her lips together. 'Lovely. I must get the recipe from you, Mr . . . Whisper.' Hazel passed his cup back, then handed her gift to Rachel. 'For you,' she said.

Rachel tore off the gold paper with glee and grinned as she pulled out a black velvet horse-riding helmet.

'To keep you safe – that is, if you can take the reins.'

'Very funny, Hazel, and very kind too!' said Rachel.

'Horse riding?' said Apollo. 'But, Rachel, what about –'

Rachel put up her hand to speak, but quickly grabbed her stomach. 'Oh,' she said, wincing, her eyes shut tight.

'You all right?' asked Lauren, quickly stepping forward and reaching for her hand.

'Yeah, yeah,' said Rachel softly. 'Stomach just hurts a little.'

'You sure, Rachel?' I asked, and she nodded.

'These might help.' Lauren reached into her hoodie pocket and pulled out two small dark bottles. 'I didn't have time to wrap them. Marjoram and Roman chamomile – put a few drops in your burner and some in your bath. I hope they . . . do something to help.'

'I'm sure they will,' Rachel replied. She stared at Lauren and Lauren stared back, like they were in love or something.

'Well, I –' Apollo began – 'brought you a little something special too – apart from the balloons. Here.' He handed her a thin home-made book.

Rachel peered at the cover. '*A Life in Forty Scenes*?' She smiled. 'You finally finished it?'

'My opus, yes! I signed it for you.' He tapped the clear plastic cover. 'First edition.'

Rachel put her hand on Apollo's shoulder. 'You did it,' she whispered. 'You actually did it.' She opened the booklet, savouring the words on the first page. She then flicked to the middle and began reading. As she did, the smile on her face slowly fell into a frown. She looked up at Apollo and stared into his eyes. 'An achievement indeed.'

Apollo gulped and ran his hand through his silver mane. 'Thank you.'

'I've got something – or someone – coming for you,' Mum said. 'Molly, my sister,' she explained for those who didn't know. 'She's not back until Wednesday – I thought it was today. I really want you to meet her. You'd get along so well . . . really well!' Mum raised her eyebrows.

Look at Mum trying to matchmake. Rachel and Auntie Molly? Nah. I didn't see it for them. Too different.

Across the room, Lauren sighed loudly. 'I don't think Rachel . . . has time for that.'

Rachel smiled at her.

Whisper chuckled. 'What does Miss Molly do?'

'She works in cyber security,' said Mum proudly, smiling smugly like she knew what that actually meant. She didn't have a scooby really. 'Keep all your devices and important belongings safe – choose strong codes, make them memorable and don't share passwords now!'

'Good advice to live by.' Rachel nodded. 'Why couldn't she make it?'

'She's in America,' Mum replied. 'At a conference.'

'Oh, very jet set,' said Whisper with an impressed smile.

Rachel sighed. 'I always wanted to travel more.'

Whisper nudged her with his elbow. 'You're only forty, girl, not four hundred and forty. Go see the world!'

Rachel smiled. 'Yeah. One day.' She sighed and looked up. 'My favourite present has got to be this,' she said, pointing to my banner. 'Wesley, I know this is your work. Your mum's shown me loads of your stuff.'

'Yeah, thanks, thanks.' I scratched my neck, embarrassed, not wanting the attention on me or that dripping, damp disaster.

Rachel put her hand to her chin. 'It's amazing. Oh! I have a little project! I've been trying something and, well, honestly I don't have the range. Give me a hand?' She smiled. 'I'll pay you.'

Hazel coughed.

I glanced over at Mum, who nodded and begged me with her eyes to say yes. Eurgh, money is cool, but I like free time better, but fine. 'Yeah,' I said. 'When?'

'You still on holiday?'

'Yeah, we are.'

Rachel smiled. 'Tomorrow morning then? Bring your paintbrush!'

'What's the project?' asked Josie.

'Something nice to brighten up the place?' said Margot. 'Oh – are you doing something in your front bedroom? It's locked and I'm intrigued!'

'Nosy. She means nosy.' I had to make that clear.

Rachel sat up straight, her face serious. 'Did you go in there?'

'Of course not,' said Margot, looking guilty now. 'I-I was just wondering.'

'There are loads of cars behind there. Speeding vehicles,' said Rachel. She shook her head but smiled. 'Beep, beep! Very dangerous.'

Margot looked at Josie, then at me. 'Erm, right. OK . . .'

Rachel leaned over and winced in pain. 'Oh!' she said, short of breath. 'My stomach's on fire.' She looked up at us apologetically. 'Sorry, friends, I'm going to have to call it a night. Must be something I ate.'

7

'Right,' said Josie. She looked nervously over at Rachel, who had sunk into her red-and-mustard tartan sofa next to Apollo. 'Let's clean up. Most people have gone now.'

Rachel shook her head and waved her hand. 'No, no,' she said quietly. 'I'll do it.'

'OK,' Josie replied, 'but we'll at least cover the food so it doesn't attract flies and will still be fresh-ish in the morning.'

Rachel nodded. 'Thank you. I know it doesn't look like it –' she flicked her hands down her body – 'but this is *exactly* what I needed. I'm just . . . just so tired.'

Mum came down the stairs and popped her head round the living-room doorway. 'How you feeling?'

Rachel waved her hand. 'Meh.'

'I've made your bed, put some of Lauren's oils in your burner.' Mum's phone beeped. The blue light lit up her face as she smiled down at the screen.

'Who's that then?' I asked, my eyes narrowed.

'I-I've gotta pop home,' she said. 'The kids are playing up.'

'Then why are you grinning?' I said. 'If the sibs are on one, what's cute about that?'

'I can't smile, Wes?' said Mum. 'I smile at your texts too. Don't be jealous now.' She turned to Rachel. 'I'll pop back in a bit, make sure you're good.'

Rachel shook her head. 'Don't worry. I'll be fine.'

'Sure?'

She looked at Mum. 'Yeah, I've been learning to live without you these past weeks.'

Mum gulped. 'I'm sorry . . . I've just been busy.'

'You go. I'll keep an eye on her,' Apollo said gently.

'OK,' Mum whispered. She looked at the three of us. 'Good work today.'

'Thanks, Ella!' said Margot brightly.

'Wes, I'll see you at home.'

'Not if I see you first,' I replied.

'Look at my son the comedian!'

I watched her skip across the road through the crack in Rachel's curtains. Then I turned to the table to cover the party food, taking bites as I wrapped. 'Mum's up to something,' I said, my mouth full. 'Something's different, I can sense it. Always got the giggles. Always on her phone. Always doing up poses in the mirror.'

'Maybe she's got a boyfriend!' Margot sang.

'Nah.' I shook my head, then paused. Wait . . . Maybe Margot had a point. 'Do you think so, like, for real?'

Margot shrugged. 'Maybe? Would you be mad?'

I hadn't thought about it really. Mum's not seen anyone since Craig left, so I honestly didn't know how I'd feel. 'I don't think I'd be heated, no,' I said. 'Anyway, I'm keeping my eye on her. I'm noticing things.'

'Well, notice me cleaning quicker than you, and copy that,' said Josie. She turned to face the room, then quickly turned back. She nudged me, leaned forward to look at Margot, and put her fingers to her lips. She jerked her head behind her. Apollo and Rachel were deep in conversation.

'Why tell them you're famous?' Apollo said in low tones. 'I don't get it, darling.'

'It's not for you to get,' Rachel said. 'Honestly, I think you got enough out of me.'

Apollo paused. 'Do you need money? I can help.'

Rachel didn't answer.

'Come back to London,' he said gently. 'This is . . . this is not it. What are you *doing*?'

'Living a life. Tying up loose ends.'

'But this place, this town, it's all so dire, Rachel, so drab –'

People are so rude about Luton, I swear.

'So do one then,' she said firmly. 'Leave if you don't like it.'

That's right! Get him, girl!

'Oh my gosh,' Margot whispered. 'Awkward.'

Josie nodded, then coughed – her equivalent of Mum's hand-clapping thing. 'OK, Rachel,' she said, turning round brightly. 'We're done!'

Rachel smiled. 'You three are the best.'

Apollo looked at his phone. 'Oh, I must go to make the next train. It's been a pleasure, Morgana Foxley and friends.'

Margot grinned and bowed. 'Yes, it was, Apollo Fortune.'

He leaned over to kiss Rachel on the cheek. 'I will be calling in the morning. We have to do better, keep in touch more. I do love and miss you, you know?'

Rachel smiled. 'You too. Sort of.'

'You can keep the balloons.'

'Wow, so generous.'

Apollo laughed as he left the house.

Rachel sighed. 'Hugs for Rachel, please?' she said, opening her arms wide in our direction.

Josie went first. When Margot broke out of her hug, her hair became tangled in a necklace Rachel was wearing. As Margot pulled her hair from it – and out of her head – she looked at it.

I did too. A gold necklace with a pendant. This pendant was like . . . half a broken heart cracked in two. It had the word 'best' written on it in letters that kind of stepped down.

'That's cool,' said Margot. 'Who has the other piece?'

'Rachel,' said Rachel. 'I'm my own best friend,' she added, laughing.

8

The three of us huddled in our meeting place, the doughnut. It's what we call the circular road in the middle of our cul-de-sac.

'So that was weird,' said Josie.

'All of it,' said Margot. 'Strangeness from start to end. Where to begin?'

'I'll go first,' said Josie. She turned to me. 'Your mum was trying to set Rachel up with your aunt and I don't think that's a good match myself.'

I laughed. 'My thoughts exactly. Mum's way off the mark with that one. Anyway, carry on.'

'Something's up between them, Rachel and your mum, that is. Rachel thought your mum was over their friendship because she's been so busy.'

'Yeah,' I agreed. 'Plus, Mum said Rachel changes her mind about things. Maybe Mum is a bit over it.'

'Probably because Rachel keeps lots of secrets. That's what I was sensing,' said Josie.

'Right!?' said Margot, her eyes bright. 'Her friends couldn't agree on the most basic things about her.'

'Apollo was moving like he knew very little, but he's been friends with her the longest,' I added. 'Ooh! He did say she wasn't famous in London – you catch that?'

They nodded.

'Why say that then? Who you trying to impress, in Luton, with that noise?'

'Well, she only told Hazel and Lauren that,' said Josie. 'Maybe she owes them money?'

'Her landlord and her masseuse,' said Margot. 'Hmm . . . maybe. I quite liked Apollo.'

'That guy? Oof, nah. I saw him spit out Mum's food and I didn't like it.' I shook my head. 'I dunno about him.'

'I don't know about any of them,' said Josie. 'I sort of liked him, though. Nice hair.'

'Great hair,' added Margot. 'And he's really fun –'

'But shady,' I said. 'That stage name, the rest of that sofa chat? I'm sick of people cussing Luton.' I looked at Margot. 'You know how I feel about that first-hand.'

Margot laughed. 'Indeed I do.'

Yeah, she knew all right. When she moved here from London last year, she thought she was too good for this town, but she's calmed down now. I showed her some sights, gave her what for and now she's on code.

'But if you think he's shady,' said Josie, 'what's your verdict on Whisper? He was a bit suspicious –'

'Even Rachel said so,' said Margot with a nod.

'He doesn't buy her stomach issues,' said Josie. 'I mean, it seemed like she has them to me.'

'Maybe he put something in that tea to test his theory?' Margot and Josie silently stared at me. They're so dramatic sometimes. 'What?' I said. 'I'm just throwing out ideas. I'm just saying.'

'Just saying that Whisper's trying to poison Rachel?' asked Josie. 'That's a bit much.'

I wagged my finger. 'Nuh-uh. I never said that – don't be putting words in my mouth now. Anyhow, Hazel Thee Landlord drank it as well.'

'She seemed nice, but I felt they had a tiny bit of tension too,' said Josie with a sigh. 'Over money.'

I nudged Margot. 'And what's with the horse-riding helmet? Any guesses? Pricy posh hobbies is your department.'

She laughed. 'I guess she must ride horses. I don't know – leave me alone!'

I tutted. 'Imagine inviting her landlord to her birthday party? Wack. Sad.'

Margot playfully slapped my arm. 'I didn't know, OK!'

'I don't believe in landlords. It's not right,' said Josie. 'Everyone should have a home without someone else making a profit.'

'But your dad's an estate agent, Josie,' I said. 'That's like . . . the final boss of landlords. So now what?'

'Shut up,' she said. 'I'm talking to Dad about his choices. Go back to cussing Margot.'

Margot laughed. 'Stop it! I did my best.'

'OK, Morgana.' I nodded. 'I believe you.'

'You know who I believed, though?' Margot leaned in to whisper. 'Lauren. She looked so sad.'

'Because they're in love and Rachel's been creeping and cheating – and now Mum's trying to set her girl up with someone else? I'd cry too, honestly. Plus, that phone call as she came in definitely wasn't with the Lauren we met, was it? Sheesh,' I said. 'That was heated.'

'I don't believe she was running lines,' said Josie.

'I don't buy it for a second,' I said.

Margot nodded. 'Yeah, but she was sad before that.'

'Probably because Hazel had smashed her car up. I'd be mad too – if I had a car, could drive it, yada yada.'

'Yep. Maybe.' Margot looked back at Rachel's house. 'I just . . . want to know more. I want to understand her, get her connection to those people. I reckon we should do a proper deep dive into the opaque pool that is Rachel.'

I shuddered. 'What? Gross.'

'OK, wrong words, but what do you say?' Margot raised her eyebrows in my direction.

'I'm interested,' said Josie. 'It gives us something to do over Easter. It's been a while since we've had an investigation.'

'*An investigation?*' I laughed. 'Just say you're in the mood to snoop and keep it pushing, Josie.'

Margot tapped her foot. 'Are you in or not, Wes?'

'OK, touchy – I'm in.'

Across the close, a light came on in Rachel's front bedroom.

'Watch out now,' I said, lowering my voice. 'Speeding vehicles, beep, beep.'

'That was so strange,' said Josie. 'But, yeah, let's make a plan tomorrow?'

'After you've done painting with her, Wes?' Margot added. 'Get some gossip while you're there, please.'

I nodded. 'I'll text you. All right, I'm off. Night.'

'It was an experience; didn't I tell you?' said Margot as she skipped away.

'Party-planning badges for everyone!' Josie shouted as she let herself into her house.

9

Mum was sitting on the edge of her bed, looking at her face in the mirror, pulling the skin around her jaw. I stood by her window.

'Do I look old, Wes?'

'Oh yeah,' I said. 'Ancient and dusty. My mummy be mummifying.'

'Shut up, you.' She sighed. 'Wes? Can I ask you another question?'

'Depends on what it is, doesn't it? Go on. Wait, is it about you trying to set Auntie Molly up with Rachel, because that's a no go.'

Mum smiled. 'No, it's not that. It's more personal.' She fiddled with her hands in her lap. 'Do you . . . ever miss your dad?' she whispered.

My shoulders rose. 'After what he did to you?' He cheated, that's what he did. I shook my head. 'Nah.'

Mum sighed. 'Could that change?'

I snorted. 'Doubt it.' I paused. 'But if he's sorted his life out maybe.'

Mum's phone beeped beside her. She brought it close to her face. 'Aww, it's Rachel.'

'What's she saying? She still mad with you for ditching her? Yeah, we noticed.'

Mum stared at her phone and sighed again. 'Look, between me and you, sometimes she can be a bit much, is all – I still like her, but honestly I needed a bit of a break.'

'Yeah, I feel you,' I said, because Margot and Josie sometimes work my last nerve too. I nodded at her phone. 'Tell her to rest – she should be in bed.'

'I will. It's still earlyish, though, just gone ten. She says she loved the food, thanks again, and is nine a.m. OK?'

'Nine!?' I huffed. 'I'm supposed to be on holiday! This is giving gulag, Mum. Do I have to?'

'She would really appreciate it, Wes, and I would too. Go on, do me a favour.' She clasped her hands together.

'Don't do that.'

'Do it for me?' She opened her eyes really wide. I hated that begging face because even though it was well cheesy, it did its job.

Her phone beeped again. That wide smile – the one I just saw at Rachel's. She put the phone face down on the bed.

'Your bestie again?'

Mum didn't say anything. She just smiled and opened her eyes wider.

'Gah, fine! I'll do it. If it gets me out of babysitting the sibs at holiday club, then good.'

'It will. Plus, she said she'll pay you. Pocket money would be nice, right?'

'Yeah, I guess.' I gently pulled back the net curtain from Mum's window and looked at Rachel's house across the close. The light in her front bedroom was off. Hopefully she was resting now. Sitting up in bed, finishing off the food, wearing her riding hat, reading Apollo's plays, drinking Whisper's weird tea and smelling her aroma-therapy oils. Making good use of her gifts.

I looked down towards the street and narrowed my eyes. On the pavement in front of her house was a tall person, their head covered in a dark hood, looking up at her house. One hand on their hip, the other on their head. Maybe they sensed me staring because, as I did, the figure slowly turned to look at me and it didn't feel good.

I gasped and dropped the curtain.

'What's the matter?' said Mum, panicked. 'What's wrong?' She got off the bed and joined me at the window. Her eyes scanned the street. 'What did you see?'

'Nothing, nothing,' I replied. I took a breath and another look, and this time there was no one there.

I must have been seeing things.

I must have been hearing things too because later that night, when I got up for a wee, I swear I heard giggling, laughing and glasses clinking downstairs when everyone was supposed to be asleep.

DAY ONE
MONDAY 10 APRIL

THE AFTERMATH

1

'Ooh, careful!' said Josie. 'All right? You finished painting already?' She nudged me with her shoulder. 'Did you get any gossip?'

I quickly turned round and wiped my eyes. I could hear my pulse thumping and my blood rushing through my body. The vein in my temple twitched so hard I'm sure Josie could see it trying to break free from my face. I looked up at Rachel's house.

This was crazy.

Rachel upstairs, dead, me down here, alive, aware of everything my body was doing. I shook my head.

Josie peered at my face. 'Are you OK?' She looked down at my hands. 'Why are you clenching your fists so hard?'

I didn't know I was.

'Your knuckles are white . . .'

I swallowed hard, my throat desert dry. 'Text Margot,' I croaked. 'Get her.'

Josie shrugged and reached for her phone. 'Fine,' she said, as she typed. 'While I do, let me tell you what I did last night.'

'OK,' I said weakly. Her voice was growing distant, fading away; all I could think about was Rachel.

'I did a little bit of self-reflection – well, group-reflection – and made a list of the ways we could have improved the party . . .'

'Josie, it doesn't matter.'

She snorted, like I was a complete idiot. 'But you have to evaluate performance, duh.' If only she knew that snort would soon be a sharp gasp.

'Good morning, Copseys!' Margot shouted, arms outstretched, from number seven. Her long curly brown hair bounced behind her as she ran over. She put a hand on each of our shoulders. She looked at my eyes and immediately stepped back. Her face fell. 'Something's wrong. What's wrong? What's happened?'

I took a deep breath. 'She dead.'

'Who?' said Josie.

'Rachel! Rachel's dead!' I burst into tears and my shoulders just shook in despair, fear and sadness.

The air in Josie's body rushed out of her and floated above us in the doughnut. She stumbled backwards, unsteady on her feet. 'Can't be. We just saw her last night. Is this a prank?' She looked around the close. 'Is this . . . is this a trend?'

I shook my head.

'Where's the evidence? What are the facts?'

'Josie, I saw her!'

Margot stared at me. 'He's not lying. Oh my God, he's not lying. I feel sick. I'm going to be sick.' She leaned over and put her hands on her knees. 'God, I might die as well.'

'Please, not you too.' I put my hand on her shoulder.

Margot's back heaved as she gulped down deep breaths. 'But – but she was just here, celebrating her birthday, and the next day dead? It's . . . it's like some cruel, twisted amateur poem.'

'It's not poetic, Margot. It's wrong, just wrong,' said Josie, shaking her head. 'No, I can't have this. I'll fix it.'

Margot straightened up. She threw her head back and stared at the sky, her hands on her hips. 'We can't fix death, Josie,' she said. 'I wish we could.'

'No, we can't google our way out of this one,' I added.

Margot reached out for my hand and squeezed it. 'You good?'

I shook my head. 'Not even a little bit. It's mad. Beyond.' I looked up at Rachel's front window and lowered my voice. 'I'm scared of what's next.'

'Funeral planning?' said Josie.

I shook my head. 'No! Whether Rachel's gonna haunt me or not! I found her, so she's gonna wanna chat to me about it, you know, from the other side.' I saw them share a side eye. 'Listen, you might not think ghosts are real, but when Rachel visits you in your dreams, bringing the baddest of vibes, or when she's floating right through your house, through your bodies, remember I told you, yeah?'

'All right, Wes. We'll remember,' said Margot in a soft voice. She exhaled. 'First things first. Who have you told? Who knows?'

Josie wiped her eyes. 'Your mum or the police?'

'Not yet,' I said. 'I had to tell you first.'

'OK, good,' said Margot quietly.

'Good how?' Josie raised her voice. 'We need to call the police! Now.'

Margot glanced around the close. 'I . . . just think we need to . . . look into this ourselves – just for a little while – before we do anything, or bring anyone else in.'

'*Bring anyone else in?*' Josie said. 'Listen, you know me, I love taking charge. I can admit that –'

'That's growth,' said Margot. 'That's good.'

'But this is way beyond us. I know my boundaries. This is death, Margot. It's not . . . it's not . . . party planning.'

'Yeah, it's not,' said Margot. Her eyes flashed. 'It's murder solving.'

Josie gasped and took a step back. 'You think it's murder?'

'You *don't* think it's murder?' said Margot. 'Hmmm, I thought it was obvious.'

'She wasn't well!' said Josie. 'We know that.'

'We know she had a tummy ache. You don't die from those. All her friends? Sus,' Margot replied. 'We felt that.'

They turned to me, their eyes asking for my opinion, for me to choose a side. 'I . . . I dunno,' I said honestly.

'Was there anything odd about Rachel's room?' asked Margot.

'Her dead body not odd enough for you?'

'Her room, Wes?' said Josie.

I closed my eyes and thought of her room, while trying to block out the image of Rachel's body. 'Well . . .'

Margot's eyes widened. 'Well, what?' Josie put her hand on Margot's arm to steady herself.

'That drink . . . that tea Whisper gave her was all over her bed and the floor.'

Margot pointed at Josie. '*See?* The drink you suggested was poison last night!'

Josie took a step back and raised her arms in protest. '*Me?* That was Wes's theory, not mine.' She looked at me. 'Anything else?'

'It also smelled weird.'

'Well, that's to be expected,' said Josie. 'What else?'

I took a deep breath. There was something else, but I didn't like what it could mean or where this information could go. 'There . . . there was also a potato skin right by her hand.'

'Her favourite food? The ones your mum made?' said Josie.

'The ones we couldn't eat,' Margot whispered. She looked over at my house, then stared at me. 'You still have Rachel's key, right?'

2

We huddled in silence by the door. The living room was mostly like we'd left it last night. Curtains closed except for a small crack that let a little light in. Rachel's wooden picture frame leaned against the wall. The gold four-zero balloons had slightly deflated and just grazed the ceiling. The clingfilm-covered plates of party food sat on the tablecloth. All except one plate, Mum's plate, which was open.

Nah. It couldn't be. Could it?

I shook my head, getting that thought gone before it spiralled into a full-on panic attack. I turned to my birthday banner.

Margot was right – someone did die in the end.

I threw up in my mouth a little and Josie noticed.

'You OK?' she whispered.

I nodded and swallowed, but of course I wasn't. Why do people ask stupid questions? And why do others reply with lies?

I sighed and snuck another look at my banner. Other-realm Rachel better take up any haunting business with Margot, not me. She was the one who cursed the party. Now she scanned the room. 'So what now, Sherlock?'

'Hmmm. Good question. Take some pictures?' Margot leaned into the room with her phone out.

'Just don't touch anything,' said Josie. 'We'll be implicated.'

'We won't,' said Margot. 'Our fingerprints are everywhere from yesterday.' She looked at Josie, then me. 'Right, let's run through last night.'

'We left here at half nine, didn't we?' I said. 'Apollo left just before us to get his train.'

Josie rubbed her chin. 'When did you get here this morning?'

'Just after nine a.m. Why?'

'She's figuring out a time-of-death window,' said Margot.

'Oh, OK,' I said. 'Well, Rachel was in her front bedroom after we'd gone. I know that.'

'The locked room?' asked Josie.

'Yeah.'

Margot looked up. 'What time, spy?'

'I was just looking, all right?' I sighed. 'About ten because she'd just texted Mum and I . . . I . . .' I fell silent as I thought back to last night.

'You . . . what?' asked Josie.

'I-I saw someone on the street, looking at her house.'

'A suspect enters the chat!' Margot whispered. 'Who? Someone from the party?'

I shrugged. 'I dunno. I couldn't tell . . . but they did look kind of familiar.'

'How?' asked Josie. 'How tall were they? What were they wearing? Were they white, Black, South Asian, East Asian –'

'I dunno, Josie! The way they stood, I guess. They were tall, had on a grey hoodie –'

'Like Lauren?' Margot gasped. 'Lauren was wearing a grey hoodie last night. Was it her?'

'I said I don't know!'

'Lauren kept going upstairs last night,' said Josie, rubbing her lip.

'And that's why we're going up there. Clues.'

'I wasn't suggesting we do that, Margot; it was an observation.' Josie shook her head. 'Look, we shouldn't even be down here. I'm calling the police now. Enough.'

Margot put out her hand to stop her. 'Wait. Let's just see if that bedroom's still locked. There might be something there.'

Josie looked at her, lips pursed, arms crossed. 'I really don't like this.'

'I know, but we need to know. We need more,' said Margot. She turned round and walked up the stairs.

While my shoulders slumped, Josie's rose. She shook her head as she followed Margot, squeezing her phone in her hand.

It had three nines on its screen.

On the landing, I stood by the front bedroom door but kept staring at Rachel's room. While I'd be sick on the spot, projectile vomit, if she suddenly stood up, opened her door, and shouted at us for creeping around her house, what would be better than that right now? Nothing. Nothing apart from getting out of here.

'Nothing incriminating in there – just those arm patches.' Margot shut the bathroom door behind her.

'I can't believe she smoked,' said Josie. 'So stupid.'

'So old-fashioned,' added Margot. 'But she did like vintage things – her Spice Girls T-shirt?' She nudged me out of the way and tried to push the door to the smallest bedroom of the house. It wouldn't open, not easily.

'Be careful, Margot!' said Josie. 'You don't know what's behind there. Or who.'

'Don't say that, Josie,' I said. 'You don't think someone's here, do you?'

Margot shook her head. 'Nope, they would have killed us by now.'

Rachel's house started spinning around me. Nice one, Margot. I held on to the banister for support. 'I have to talk to Mum. We can't . . . I can't . . .'

'I'm sorry, Wes,' Margot said. 'I didn't mean it. Just two more mins, I promise.' She pushed the door again and it opened a little. 'OK!' She put her head in the gap between the door and its frame. 'Loads of opened Amazon boxes.' She dug into her pocket for her phone, held it above her and took a photo.

'Told you she got lots of deliveries,' I said weakly. 'She has loads of stuff.'

'Yes, but where is it?' said Josie. She was standing on her tiptoes, looking into the room. 'Those are empty; the house is bare.'

Margot pointed to the locked bedroom door, then reached forward to touch the small black combination lock. 'It might all be in there.'

'It would make sense,' I said.

'But what doesn't make sense is the lock; if you're the only person who lives here, why have it?' Margot turned to me. 'She is the only person who lives here, right?'

'As far as I know, yeah.'

She squinted. 'Hmmm. This lock has four numbers, and the combination is set to four zeros.'

'So?' I asked.

'Four zeros feels intentional,' said Josie. 'Like someone really tried to hide the code.'

Margot agreed. 'Yep, my dad uses one at the gym, and he only ever flicks one of the numbers to lock it. Setting it all the way back to four zeros is, like, a major effort.'

I leaned over. 'Try her birthday maybe? April the ninth. Zero, nine, zero, four.'

'It's worth a go,' said Margot. She flicked the numbers but nothing. 'This needs more thought.'

'No, no more thought,' I said. 'More leaving. Let's go.'

'One second,' said Margot. 'There's just one more thing.' She moved her hand slowly towards Rachel's bedroom door. 'I just have to see for myself, to confirm it's real.'

'Don't, Margot!' I pleaded. 'Don't do it. I already took one for the team – you don't need to be scarred for life too!'

Josie pressed call and held her phone to her ear. 'I warned you, Margot.'

'Josie, wait!'

Guess what? Josie did not wait. 'Police, please.' She stared at Margot. 'Hello, our neighbour has died. Yes. Three Copsey Close . . .'

'I have to do it!' Margot opened the door, put her head into Rachel's room and gasped. She quickly slammed the door shut and ran down the stairs, behind that sweet-sour scent. 'I shouldn't have done that, Wes!' she screamed from the hallway. 'I should *not* have done that!'

3

Back in the doughnut, Josie had her arm round Margot's shoulder. Margot wiped her eyes with her sleeve. 'Like, I knew that you said Rachel was dead, Wes.' She sniffed. 'I *did* believe you, I swear. But . . . I also kind of didn't.'

'Like you said, you had to see her yourself,' I said. 'And now look . . .'

Margot nodded. 'I know. I'm sorry. I think a little part of me thought it was a game, like we were at one of those murder-mystery parties.'

'Wes wouldn't joke about something like this,' said Josie.

'I know,' said Margot. 'And I promise I'll never, ever make my Corpsey Close joke again either.' She took a deep breath and looked over at Rachel's house. 'We're going to have to work so quickly.'

'Wait. You're serious, aren't you? You think it's really murder,' Josie whispered.

'I do,' she said. 'And someone from last night did it. We planned this party, now we have to put someone in jail. We have to do right by Rachel. It's the Copsey way.'

'I never, ever thought we'd earn murder-investigating badges.' Josie sighed. 'This was not part of the strategy.'

I gulped. 'We're doing this? For real?'

'We have to,' Margot whispered. 'I'm in.' She looked at Josie, who nodded.

They both looked at me. I closed my eyes and sighed, knowing we were about to walk down a dark path, wishing I never made promises . . . or did favours. 'Where do we start?'

'With the guests, I think,' Josie replied.

Margot nodded and exhaled. 'OK, so we were there, then we went home. I didn't come back to kill Rachel. I'm assuming you two didn't either?'

'I swear on the Copsey Code that I was at home,' said Josie. 'Ask my parents.' She looked at me. 'Wes? Where were you?'

I wrinkled my nose. 'You being serious?'

Josie nodded. 'We have to rule suspects out. For the record.'

I sighed. These two are so stupid sometimes. 'Look, I was at home. You know I share a room with my brothers – ask them.'

'All right,' said Margot. 'Three guests down, five to go.' She paused and looked at Josie.

Josie closed her eyes and shook her head the tiniest bit. They were communicating without words, without me.

'What?' I said. 'What's the problem?'

'Nothing. Nothing . . . yet. Let's start with Whisper,' Josie said. She looked at Margot, who quickly nodded.

'Yep, Whisper. Good place,' she replied. 'Good person.'

Ah, I knew what this was about. This was about Mum. I spoke up immediately – they were not going to try me like this. 'Mum was at home all night too, OK? I know what you're thinking and, well, don't!'

They looked at each other. Josie held her phone out and began typing. 'How do you know she was there?' she asked gently. 'Just for the record.'

I stared at her hand and felt my temperature begin to rise. 'I was in her room before she went to sleep, innit – she was home all night because I heard her. She was awake. Giggling.'

Why did I have to add that detail, man? Instant regret.

There I went, making them think Mum was sus – more sus than they already did.

Well played, Wes. Slow clap for you.

Margot bit her lip. 'Giggling at what?'

'When? What time?' asked Josie.

My hands balled into fists. 'Look, I dunno, all right? I went to the loo, and I thought I heard her talking with someone –'

Margot tried to disguise her gasp as a cough. Fail. 'We need to know who that was.' She tried to wave her hand, all casual.

'Just for the record,' added Josie, sounding sorry. Good, she should be sorry. 'We need to know that, and why Rachel was being a bit funny with her when she arrived – plus the ingredients of the potato skins that only Rachel could eat –'

Nah. Too much, too far, too soon. I lost it. 'That was vegan cheese and it wasn't Mum, all right! Why would she send me, first thing, to the house of her friend she'd flipping killed hours before?! What kind of mum would do that? *Especially* when Mum knows how I feel about ghosts?' I jabbed at my forehead. 'Are you dumb? Think about what you're saying!'

Margot and Josie glanced at each other.

'Stop giving each other signals too!' I snapped. 'I can see you!' My heart thumped in my chest. 'Talk about someone else, yeah. Whisper came next. What about him?'

Josie touched my arm. 'Listen,' she said quietly, 'we have to establish the facts if we're going to solve this.'

'We're going to have to think terrible things and ask tough questions,' added Margot. 'Especially if we want Rachel to rest.'

I stared straight ahead. She was right, but well wrong to use my weakness as a weapon. So I told her so. 'Don't do that. Don't play me, Margot. I know you don't believe in ghosts. What about Whisper?'

I could feel them trying their hardest not to look at each other. Margot cleared her throat. 'Right, well, as we said last night, he didn't seem to believe Rachel was sick.'

'He brought over that tea,' I said, trying to calm down. 'It's all over her bed. Who knows what's actually in it? *That* could be the murder weapon.'

'Hazel drank some, didn't she?' added Josie. 'We need to find out how she's doing.'

'See if she's still alive, you mean?' I said.

'Honestly . . . yes,' said Josie quietly.

'Please no,' said Margot. She rubbed her temples. 'Not a serial killer. Not today, Satan.'

'And what about Hazel?' I asked. 'She's Rachel's landlord – what if Rachel hadn't paid the rent? Spent it all on that Amazon tat?'

'It's a motive,' said Josie. 'Money's always a motive.'

'And so is jealousy,' Margot added.

'Lauren,' they whispered in unison.

'Exactly,' I said. 'Lauren's got a stronger reason to do it than Mum. She thinks Rachel was cheating on her, didn't like it when Mum was trying to set Rachel up with Auntie Molly, kept going upstairs – maybe it was her who did something with the lock on the bedroom? What if her oils were poison, hmmm? And Apollo. What about *that* fraud? No one changes their name for no reason.'

'There are loads of reasons, though,' said Josie.

I put my hand up to stop her. I didn't need her list. 'He called her out for saying she's famous.'

'And he told her to go back to London,' said Margot.

'But she didn't want to.' Josie tapped her lips. 'Also, she had a super-weird reaction to his book, right?'

'You saw that too?' said Margot.

'I clocked it, yeah. Her face fell; something about it was sour. Apollo Fortune . . . new name . . . running from his old days maybe?' I took a breath and thought for a moment. Yeah. Those other people were way more sus than Mum.

Weren't they?

'We need Apollo's book.' Margot looked over at Rachel's house. 'But I can't go back in there. Not yet.'

The sound of sirens grew louder and louder as they approached the close. Margot was right. She wasn't going back in that room or anywhere near the house for a while. The cops were here.

A police car screeched to a halt in front of us. An ambulance rolled to a stop outside Rachel's house.

There came that sick feeling of doom – the feeling you get when you are trapped in a nightmare and can't shake yourself awake.

'Wesley?' Mum called from our front door, her voice all wavy. She tightened her dressing-gown cord round her waist and padded towards us in her slippers. She wobbled, shaking with every scared step. 'What's going on? What's happened?'

I knew I had to tell her at some point, but not like this.

'Mum.' I could feel the tears welling in my eyes. I looked back at my friends for support.

Margot gripped my hand but began to step away. 'Tell her,' she whispered. 'She has to know.'

My stomach fell. 'Mum . . . we have bad news.'

'What, Wes? What?' She stared into my eyes, searching for answers to her desperate questions.

The left-hand door of the police car opened and an officer stepped out. He adjusted his hat and walked towards us.

Mum began to cry. 'Is it your sibs, Wes?' She death-gripped my arm, her voice frantic. 'Tell me it's not my kids. Please! Not my babies.'

'It's not, Mum. It's Rachel. She's gone.'

'Gone where, Wes? What do you mean?'

I put my hand over hers. 'Rachel passed away, Mum. She died.'

Mum's face fell, and so did her body.

4

The policeman took his hat off and held it in front of him solemnly, revealing the smoothest white head I've ever seen. He took a sharp breath before he spoke. 'I'm PC Stevens,' he said gently. 'We're here about your friend, Rachel?' He looked round our group. 'Josephine Williams?'

Josie raised her hand. 'Here,' she said, like the cop was taking the register.

He smiled. 'Thank you for calling – I'm sorry about what's happened. Since you made the call, and discovered Rachel –'

Josie shook her head. 'No, I didn't.' She pointed at me. 'He did. Wesley Evans.'

I gulped. I hadn't done a thing, but it felt like Josie was stitching me up somehow, saying my full name like that.

'You found her, Wes?' Mum's face crumpled. 'Oh, my son. My baby.' She squeezed my arm, in real danger of snapping it, but a broken arm was the least of our worries.

'All right,' said PC Stevens, 'first things first – can we easily access the house? It's number three?'

Margot nodded. 'Yes. We left the front door open.'

'OK, good, great.' He turned towards his colleagues – another cop and two paramedics leaning against their vehicles. He nodded and pointed towards Rachel's house; they acknowledged him wordlessly and went in. He took out a small notebook from a pocket on his padded vest and kneeled down next to us. He looked up at us with kind eyes. 'You've been very brave – I know that this is very scary. Now, if you feel up to it, I'd like to ask a few questions – just to help us understand what might have happened to Rachel.'

We looked at each other nervously.

'Go on, Wes,' Mum croaked. 'Tell the officer what you know.'

My mouth flapped opened, but no words came out. I didn't know what to say. I didn't want to say anything.

Margot looked at me from the corner of her eye, watching me flounder like a fish out of water. 'I'll start. Last night we helped Ella –' she nodded over at Mum – 'throw a surprise party for Rachel.'

'She was forty,' added Josie. 'We found a few of her friends.'

PC Stevens nodded. 'That's very kind! Which friends?'

'Well, there was –' Josie began.

'A few of them, yes,' said Margot, cutting her off, waving her hand. 'I'm not sure I remember all their names,' she lied, protecting our own investigation. 'I'll find the guest list and let you know.'

The policeman nodded again. 'Thank you.'

'She didn't feel too good,' Mum said. 'Rachel had an IBS flare-up and needed to rest, so the party was over quickly. I made special food just for her.'

Flashback to Mum's potato skin next to Rachel on her deathbed.

Mum, say less. You'll be in the frame if you keep flapping your gums.

'Oh?' said PC Stevens. 'That's nice.'

'Yes,' said Mum. 'Including potato skins, her favourite. We hadn't been so close recently – I've had a lot on my plate – so I wanted to do something nice for her.'

Mum wouldn't shut it, so I had to do something to stop her. 'I painted Rachel a banner!' I shouted. I pointed to the paintbrush behind my ear. 'She liked it and wanted me to paint something. I said I'd go and see her, in the morning. So I went in –'

'How?' he asked.

'I have a key – like I said, she's my friend,' Mum said. She blinked. '*Was* my friend.' Her breath caught in her throat and she turned away.

I continued. 'I went in. I called her name again and again – no answer. So I went to her room and . . . and I saw that something was very wrong, then I found my friends.' I pointed at Margot and Josie.

'And that's when you called?' PC Stevens said, looking at Josie. 'Straight away?'

Josie paused for a moment.

'Yep.' Margot nodded. 'Immediately.'

'Did you try to move her or anything?'

As if. I shook my head vigorously. 'No way.'

'And did you touch or take anything from around her or from the house?'

'No, we didn't.'

PC Stevens put his hand on my shoulder. At first I thought how nice he was, comforting me, but, no, he was using me to steady himself, and trying to style it out. 'OK, thank you. Very useful.' He looked at Mum. 'Do you have contact details for her family, any known next of kin?'

'I . . . I don't, I don't know – I d-don't think so?' she stuttered. 'But I met her landlady yesterday – I can get in touch with her. She might know?'

'Yes, please – or pass any contact information on to us,' he said. 'We can make the difficult calls.'

Mum nodded, then suddenly said, 'C-can I see her?' Like she had just realized her time with Rachel was over. 'Can I go in the house, be with her?'

PC Stevens shook his head. 'I'm sorry. Now we've been called, we have to treat this as an investigation. If it's not clear how she died, we have to rule out foul play –'

Margot took a loud, deep breath.

'– and that depends on our findings.' He reached into another pocket and pulled out a card. He handed it to me and tried to look directly into my eyes. I'm not one for eye contact, not like that, with a stranger, so I stared down at the concrete.

'I have to go and help my colleagues help Rachel now,' he said. 'But if you need anything, remember anything, or need to . . . tell me something, just give me a call. Any time, OK?'

'OK.' I took off my phone's case and popped his card between it and my phone. 'We will.'

5

The TV wasn't on in our living room: that's how you knew something super serious was happening. In that rare silence, Mum folded herself, origami-like, into the corner of our green sofa. She dabbed her eyes with a crumpled tissue, then stared out of the living-room window. She breathed out slowly.

'Here.' I handed her a fresh mint tea in her favourite mug, her giant 'World's Best Mum' one.

She nodded her thanks and breathed the scent in. 'I just,' she started, 'I just don't know how this happened.'

Josie and Margot, sitting close together on the floor, nudged each other on what they thought was the sly, but they're not slick. I saw them. I stared at them until they noticed.

Mum, unaware of all the silent communication, continued. 'You don't just . . . die. That's not real. This isn't real. Not my friend.' She looked down at Josie and Margot and smiled weakly. 'You know, you three are really lucky.'

I leaned on the door frame. 'Yeah, right. It's the worst day of my life.'

'Yeah, yeah, of course, baby. I'm sorry.'

'How are we lucky?' asked Margot, her voice soft.

Mum rolled her eyes – not at Margot – but to keep her tears from falling. 'It's just that . . . you three have each other. It's hard to make friends when you're older –'

'You are *not* old,' said Margot. Normally I'd call her a buttkiss for this, but not today. Today wasn't normal. I needed her on Mum's side.

'Well, older than you lot. Plus, throw being a mum, on my own, into the mix. It's hard to get a break and even harder to meet people you like, who get you. It's funny, when she first moved here, I wanted us to be like you three – the Copseys but oldies. A distraction from the drudge of it all.' Mum sighed. 'Friendships are so important as you age, but they're so . . . underrated. Don't do what I did –' she started to cry – 'and take it for granted, pull away when it got too much. Because, as quickly as it starts, it can be over in an instant.'

I ran to hug her. My poor, not-guilty Mum.

'I understand,' said Josie. 'I read it's important to maintain friendships for your health and well-being.'

'Yeah,' said Mum. 'It is.'

'Did you get a chance to see Rachel again last night?' asked Margot. 'Wes thought he heard you laughing, I think.'

She didn't dare look at me. If she had, she would have seen the actual steam streaming out of my ears.

'Margot . . .' I growled.

Mum suddenly had a case of the blinks. Rapid eye movement. She broke out of her hug and looked at me. 'No? W-what? I . . . I was watching television, Wes. Alone. Yeah, a film. *Clueless.*'

Margot bit her lip and looked over at Josie.

They weren't buying it, and you know what's worse? Neither was I.

Mum, what's going on? What have you done?

She kept going. '*Clueless* is a classic – one of Rachel's favourites.' She exhaled. 'God, I miss her already.'

'Us too,' said Margot. 'It's a shame she never got to act in her play . . .'

Mum nodded. 'I wish I had known about it, but like Lauren said last night, people *do* have a right to privacy. Especially while they're . . . working things out.' She glanced at me as she said that. Maybe it was a call for help?

'Maybe she was protecting herself?' I offered. 'You know, like, if something went wrong with the play, she wouldn't have to explain herself.'

Mum murmured her agreement. 'I understand that feeling. One hundred per cent.'

'But she told Hazel and Lauren,' said Margot.

Mum rested her fingers on her chin. 'Hmmm. Yeah. Why did she tell *them* and not *me*?' She laughed slightly bitterly and her eyes narrowed. 'I was a bit hurt by that, actually.'

Margot turned to look at me. Mum! Stop talking! Stop giving motives!

Mum sipped her tea and furrowed her brow. 'I don't know about those two – well, Hazel seems nice. Lauren? She was . . . interesting, and those oils she brought? When I put them in Rachel's burner last night, they smelled off to me.'

'They did?' asked Margot. She bounced her knee against Josie's, who was already typing.

Mum nodded. 'A bit rancid.' She paused and thought for a moment. 'But what do I know?'

That's the spirit, Mum – shift that blame. I came in with an assist. 'Yeah, the room smelled bitter when I was in there and, also, what if they thought Rachel was gonna get rich from the play and they wanted her money, hmmm? Think about that!' I said in Margot and Josie's direction.

Josie sighed and shook her head.

Margot mouthed, 'No! Stop!'

'I don't think Rachel was struggling, though – not judging by her deliveries.' Mum sighed, unaware of the investigation happening around her ankles. Her eyes returned to the window. 'None of that matters now anyway.' She smiled to herself then gently sang, 'Enjoy yourself, it's later than you think.' Mum looked at me. 'Words to live by. Me and your dad used to love that song, Wes. I know Whisper likes it too.' She rested her mug on the floor. 'And, speaking of the devil, I need to call him.' She exhaled deeply. 'Margot, can I use your Fakebook to message the other guests? I don't have their numbers.'

Margot waved her away. 'Don't worry. I can do that. I've got it.'

Mum shook her head. 'Come on, that's too much to ask. That's adult work.'

'It's absolutely fine. I'd be happy to,' Margot said. 'I have all their details; you call Whisper and I'll get in touch with the others.'

Mum smiled at her. 'That's so kind of you, thank you. You're a good one.'

'So what, me and Josie aren't?' I pouted, pretending to be hurt.

Mum tutted sarcastically before she left the room. When she reached the top of the stairs, she burst into sobs.

6

'Before you start, Wes,' Margot whispered, 'don't be mad with us for investigating, all right? If we're going to solve Rachel's murder –'

'And have her not haunt Copsey Close,' added Josie in a low voice, 'we're going to have to ask tough questions – and be subtle. We did warn you.'

I nearly bit my bottom lip off, trying to stop myself cussing them out.

'You know I love Ella,' said Margot.

'Love is putting her in prison and making me and my sibs orphans, is it? That's love to you?' I snapped. I couldn't hold it.

Margot blinked. 'Wes, no. What? If we know who she was really with last night, if they were clinking glasses – something you do when you're celebrating – and really watching *Clueless* –'

'And if we know what's actually in those potato skins –' Josie added.

'We can rule her out.' Margot slapped her hands together. 'She'll be clean.'

'Rule her out,' I demanded. 'Now.'

Margot looked at me and slowly shook her head. 'Wes, you know we can't. Not yet – the food, the late-night talking, watching the film. It's not clear. What if the police knew this? It wouldn't look . . . great.'

She was right. My heart sank.

Josie put her hand on my arm. 'I know this is heavy,' she said. She paused. 'I have an idea.'

'What is it? I don't like your ideas. They're trash mostly.' Yeah, that was a lie. I was just being snappy.

'Well, speaking of ruling people out, why don't you take a step back from this case? We can do all the work, and . . . when your mum checks out, you can check back in?'

'*A step back from this case?*' I spat. 'Listen to yourself! You've been a detective for what? An hour? And you're already giving it the big one.' My chest burned. I gulped down breaths to cool it. 'I can't quit, can I? *I'm* the one whose mum's hurting. *I'm* the one whose family might get more broken because of this. *I'm* the one who found Rachel – *I'm* the one she's haunting.' I went toe to toe with my tears. 'Plus, I can't trust you to do it properly either. You lot are lost without me.'

Margot and Josie looked at me. While my breathing slowed, my lips quivered.

'You finished?' Margot asked gently.

'Never,' I said quietly. I looked up at them, sniffed and wiped my eyes.

'We've got you, OK?' said Margot. 'I get how you feel. Inside I'm *freaking*. None of this is an easy-breezy joke to me.'

'Me neither,' said Josie. 'But we're the Copseys. We celebrate the good times and get through bad times together. We also help everyone, including ourselves. So, what do you want to do? Can you handle this, Wes?'

Man. I cuss these girls sometimes – arguing is my love language – but they really, truly had my back. Always. I looked up at the ceiling, half expecting to see Rachel floating around up there. I knew what I had to do. I looked down and nodded. 'I'll try. I'm gonna try – but you're gonna have to be easy with me. This is a lot. I might get snappy.'

'Snappy?' Margot smiled. 'That would be new for you. However will we cope?'

Above us, Mum paced around her room.

'Shut up, you.' I exhaled. 'OK, what else do we have?'

'Look, maybe your mum does have a boyfriend?' Josie said. 'That would be nice.'

I sighed. 'Would it? Dunno about that. But let me see what I can find out.'

'That's the spirit,' said Margot. 'Wait! Drat, not spirit. Sorry, Wes. That would be excellent. You also raised an excellent point about Rachel owing money. Hazel is her landlord and maybe she hasn't been paid – that's a motive right there.'

'And Lauren is jealous – maybe there was something poisonous in those oils she brought. You and your mum both said they smelled off, Wes,' said Josie. 'Plus, it could have been her in the hoodie standing outside last night.'

'Right,' I said. 'We could look into that as well as Whisper's tea and –' my voice lowered – 'Mum's potato skins, but I'm telling you it's vegan cheese.' I took a breath and thought for a moment. 'What about this play she was supposed to be in? Why didn't she tell Mum about it, but told Hazel and lock-toucher Lauren? I know it was her fiddling with it. I can tell.'

Josie shook her head. 'No, we can't tell. We need facts.'

'The whole play thing is strange,' said Margot. 'OK, take Hazel, if Rachel owed her rent, the play could get her off her back for a while – incoming income.'

'And she told Lauren because they're friends,' said Josie.

'Hmmm,' said Margot. 'Two things on that. The first one is Lauren and Rachel were more than friends possibly – like Wes suggested.'

'Maybe Mum knows about it? I could ask?'

'You could, but everyone was talking about privacy, so I doubt it,' Josie replied. 'Plus, they weren't speaking as much recently, remember?'

Mum's footsteps sounded on the stairs.

'Your second thing, Margot?' I hissed. 'Quick!'

Margot shrugged. 'There is no play. Rachel just made it up.'

'Why, though?' I asked.

'Why not?' said Margot. 'We know she likes to change her mind and is not always clear. Plus, I mean, Apollo made up his new name. Maybe Rachel is like him. Or, maybe, she just liked lying for fun. Or – what if she was living a double life? Split personality? Alter ego, even?'

'OK, Margot, calm your conspiracies,' said Josie.

Mum appeared in the doorway. She smiled at Margot. 'You get in touch with the guests yet?'

'No, not yet. We, we're –' Margot glanced at Josie and me – 'grieving. Sorry. I'm on it now.' She reached for her phone.

'What you so happy about, Mum?'

'I just got off the phone with Whisper – we're giving Rachel a nine night, starting this evening!'

'What the heck is a "nine night" when it's at home?' I asked, looking at my friends.

THE COPSEYS' INVESTIGATION INTO THE
MURDER OF RACHEL KOHL

VICTIM: Rachel Kohl

AGE: 40

OCCUPATION: actress

CAUSE OF DEATH: TBC. Something she ingested or inhaled?
Potato skin, sorrel tea, oils?

DATE OF DEATH: between 10:00 p.m. on 9 April and 9:00 a.m.
on 10 April

FACTS (?) AND EVIDENCE:
- Lived at 3 Copsey Close – opposite Wesley
- Liked shopping – lots of deliveries, a spare room full
  of empty boxes (but her house was pretty bare??)
- Has a locked front bedroom (code set to 0000) –
  mentioned something about cars behind it??
- Had IBS? Whisper not sure?
- Cast for a role in a new play? Only Hazel and
  Lauren aware

INVESTIGATION QUESTIONS:
- Who killed Rachel?
- How?

- What time?
- What's the lock's code?
- Who was Rachel on the phone with when she arrived at the party?
- Who was outside Rachel's house?
- Who is Rachel's next of kin?

INVITED GUESTS AKA SUSPECTS	RELATIONSHIP	MOTIVE	BIRTHDAY GIFT	QUESTIONS
APOLLO FORTUNE	Old friend – lived together in London	Selfishness? Wanted her to return to London . . . or else?	A collection of his plays	• Why did Rachel have a negative reaction to her present? • What was Rachel like in London? Apart from not famous?
CAROLINE NICHOLLS	Unknown	?? Did not attend the party Believed to be in Canada	Did not send one	• Who are you? • What is your relationship to Rachel?
ELLA EVANS – WESLEY'S MUM	Neighbour and close friend	Elimination? Rachel was being a bit much recently Ella needed a break . . .	Throwing the party with us and trying to set her up with Auntie Molly	• Why did Rachel not tell you about the play? Privacy and distance • What's in your potato skins? • Who were you really with on the night of the murder?

FITZROY 'WHISPER' JENKINS	Knows Rachel from their IBS support group	Elimination? Doesn't trust her; thinks she's faking her IBS?	Home-made sorrel tea	• What exactly is in your tea?
HAZEL WILSON	Landlord	Gain? Did Rachel owe her money?	A riding helmet	• Did Rachel owe you money? • Why the horse-riding helmet?
LAUREN ROBERTS	Masseuse – and maybe in a relationship?	Jealousy? Was Rachel cheating on her? Upset that Ella was trying to introduce her to Molly?	Aromatherapy oils	• Why were you so upset at the party? • Were you dating Rachel? • What's in the oils you gave her? What do they do?

NIGHT ONE

RACHEL DOESN'T REALIZE
SHE'S DEAD

1

'You don't know what a nine night is?' Whisper leaned forward until his face was close to ours. His eyes narrowed and his nostrils flared.

I gulped. Margot clawed the carpet behind us and began to scoot backwards like a dog with an itchy butt. We'd goofed – questioning him was a big mistake.

'You had to ask your devices and talk to robots for answers?' He shook his head and tutted. 'Young people these days.' He tapped his temple. 'Empty-headed. No sense of tradition.'

Josie looked at Margot and me before talking. 'Well . . . what we can gather is that it's like a party –'

'A celebration of the dead,' said Margot. 'Right?'

'*A celebration of the dead?*' Whisper snorted. 'Wrong. It's more than that. It's got meaning!'

Mum came in from the kitchen with a mug and handed it to Whisper. The tea sloshed around inside it, threatening to leap out and spill on his legs any second. She held out a packet of biscuits; he took three and clutched them in his free hand.

'Gluten free?' he asked.

'Of course,' she said. 'I'm not trying to hurt you, am I?'

I snuck a quick look at my friends when she said that. They were staring down at their hands, trying desperately not to look in my direction, or at each other.

Whisper raised an eyebrow before taking a cautious bite of his biscuit. Back in the kitchen, Mum was cooking, banging pots and pans together. 'So what do you know about nine night?' he said between mouthfuls of crumbs. 'Inform me.'

'Well, every night after someone dies, there's a . . . gathering?' said Margot.

Whisper nodded. 'Set-ups.'

'And at these . . . set-ups people pray, play games, eat and drink, yeah?' I offered.

'And tell stories about the person who passed,' added Whisper. 'That's right.'

'The ninth night is the most important,' said Josie. She looked sideways at me. 'Because that's when the spirit –'

'The duppy, please,' said Whisper. 'Be specific.'

'The duppy,' Josie corrected herself, 'goes to the spirit realm. For its final rest.'

I shuddered. 'Phantoms are literally floating around us. I hate it, but I know it. Like, go rest in peace, please.' I scratched at my neck. 'It is like when Grandad Alan was haunting me.' I itched harder.

'Stop that,' Josie said gently, pulling my hand away. 'You'll bleed.'

'And remember when Bobby from class had a ghost in his wardrobe? His brother co-signed that, so I know that was legit,' I said. 'That's two independent sources, to put it in words you like, Josie.'

'I wouldn't say brothers are independent sources, but OK,' said Josie.

'Afraid of duppies, Westley?' asked Whisper.

Being a chicken isn't a good look, but being a liar isn't either. 'I'm . . . just nervous about things I don't understand. But –' I pointed at Josie and Margot – 'they don't believe at all.'

'They should.'

'Hold on!' said Josie. 'We just needed to really research it –'

'I didn't believe,' said Margot, cutting in, 'but I'm starting to.'

'You're right to be cautious, son, because duppies are very real. They exist.'

'Told you!' I smiled smugly at Margot and Josie.

Whisper continued. 'And if you've wronged them, they right it by hurting you, making you sick –'

I groaned and buried my face in my hands.

'But not yet. The duppy is still with Rachel. For now. It won't rise until night three.'

I looked up. 'Oh God, what?'

'Oh yes,' said Whisper. 'Between night one and three Rachel doesn't even know she's dead yet. Everyone is confused; no one wants to believe she's gone.'

I sat forward. 'And then?'

'Then the next three days are about acceptance – Rachel and us coming to terms with her death. The duppy wakes up. On night six she begins to really leave, whether she likes it or not. If she doesn't want to go and she's restless, that's when the duppy makes the most trouble, those last three days.' Whisper shook his head and took a long swig of his tea. 'Like I said, nine night is not *just* a party.' He pursed his lips and shook his head. 'Not *just* a celebration of the dead. Over here, the tradition is not strong – all the young people have become so English – but back home, in Saint Vincent, we believe everyone's got a little bit of evilness inside them.'

Margot nodded. 'Totally agree with that.'

'And when we are alive, we – most law-abiding citizens anyway, not all of us – don't listen to the badness; we listen to our hearts, and the good things our minds tell us. But . . . when our hearts stop beating, and our minds stop talking and the evilness is unleashed . . . well. It can be a disaster.'

'So that's why you have the nine night?' asked Josie. 'To make sure the duppy goes away forever.'

'Exactly!' said Whisper, his eyes bright and wide. 'They have nine days and nights after death to do as they please, finish up their earthly business, tie up their mortal loose ends, and then they must rest. Forever.'

'How . . . how do you get them to go away for good, for real?' I asked. I liked the sound of forever, but I needed to be sure.

'Well, we make the ninth night very special, to make them happy. The other eight nights and days they go back and forth between their bodies and the places they liked to be —'

Dislike. I leaned over. 'I'm gonna be sick.'

'But on the last night we know for sure they're coming back; they go to the place they last lived, to the room they loved most. We make it nice — exactly how they want it to be, so they leave happy, fulfilled, waving goodbye to their family and friends.'

'And then they're gone gone?' I asked.

'They are gone gone,' he replied with a nod. He swallowed hard, and looked behind him, out of the living-room window across to Rachel's house. A lone cop stood beside their blue-and-white POLICE DO NOT CROSS tape.

'Rachel,' Whisper actually whispered.

2

Mum tidied round Whisper while he tapped his foot to a Spice Girls song. Josie, Margot and I huddled in my kitchen.

'Yeah,' I said in a low voice, crossing my arms. 'That's settled – I ain't playing about with no duppy.'

Margot shuddered. 'It just got even more real.'

'Real paranormal,' said Josie. She tutted, drumming her fingers against the kitchen counter. Her fingers inched towards a plate of sausage rolls. She took one and looked at it cautiously before bringing it to her mouth.

'What, you *still* don't believe? You don't think it's legit?' I shook my head. 'Look, I know Whisper's a suspect, but you've googled "nine night" – everything he said is true. There's a Wikipedia and everything.'

Josie shrugged and swallowed her snack. 'I'm ... persuaded, but since I can't prove it either way, what I think doesn't matter. What *does* matter is that we keep the

Copsey Code and help Rachel. Now we have a deadline – nine days.'

'You're right,' said Margot. 'We've got to get organized.' She brought her hand to her mouth. 'Gosh, I'm starting to sound just like you, Josie.'

'That's normal,' she replied. 'That happens with good friends. They take on each other's traits and habits – they merge sometimes.'

I stuck my tongue out. 'Gross. I'm not doing no merging, not with either of you. I'm just investigating and sorting this out so I can live.' I shuddered. 'I can feel her, I swear. Let's crack on – what are we asking? What's the plan?'

Josie grabbed her phone and pulled up our notes. 'We go guest by guest and ask at least one question. So, with Whisper, we need to find out what exactly's in his tea.'

'Right,' said Margot. 'We know the tea seems OK because, when I messaged Hazel, she was, well, well –'

'But,' said Josie, 'there might be something in it that Rachel was allergic to, or it might have reacted badly with any medication. So let's confirm the ingredients and take it from there.'

'Let's ask Lauren what was in those oils too and what they're supposed to do,' I said. 'Same reasons.'

The smell of baking potato skins wafted from the oven. Margot sniffed the air. 'We need to know what's cooking,' she whispered. 'Ask Ella what she put in Rachel's special skins.'

'She said vegan cheese! How many times!' I huffed.
'But fine.'

'With Hazel, any debt,' said Josie.

'I asked Apollo for a copy of his book,' said Margot.

'Let's ask him what he thought Rachel made of his
plays,' I said. 'Because we know she wasn't impressed.' I
took a deep breath. 'Come on then, let's go.' I straightened
up and began to walk to the living room.

Margot pulled me back. 'Wait a sec!' she said. 'Two
things first.'

'Go on.'

'One. We need to be brave – we'll be sitting with a
potential murderer or murderers, plural. Poisoners by the
look of it.' Her eyes narrowed.

'I am being brave!' I lowered my voice. 'I'm ready to
send you to the realm, Rachel.'

'Two. We have to be slick, smooth and shady – we can't
just accuse people of murder.'

'She's right. That's very important,' said Josie. 'We have
to act natural. We can't get caught out because we're
being too bold and brash.'

I nodded and flicked my fingers in the direction of the
living room and began moving towards it.

'One other thing!' said Margot.

My shoulders slumped. 'You said two things! What
else?'

'We *have* to stick together, OK? We're a team, right?'

'Definitely,' said Josie.

'Yeah,' I said. 'We will.' I backed out of the room slowly. 'Into the poison pit I go.'

I walked into the living room, all casual-like, with my hands in my joggers, Josie and Margot behind me. Mum was standing on the arm of our sofa, reaching up, fixing the edge of the curtain that had slipped off the pole.

Whisper watched while she fiddled. 'You do all these things yourself?' He grimaced. 'You need your husband back. Get him to help.'

Mum laughed. 'You know what? I just might.'

'Nah, she doesn't need to do that,' I said, stepping into the room. 'I help.' I pulled at the hem of her skirt, to tell her to get down. I took her place. I looked down at Whisper; he looked up at me.

'You don't miss your dad?'

This question again? I shrugged. 'Nah.'

'You don't want to kick a ball around with him or something?'

'I'd like to kick him in the –'

'Wes, enough,' Mum warned. 'Besides, who knows what the future holds.'

'The future holds nothing but my hands round his neck.' I took a deep breath. 'So, Whisper, remind me, what was in that tea you brought for Rachel?' I glanced over at my friends. They nodded back. Green light.

Whisper twisted his body towards me. 'The sorrel?'

'Yeah. That one.'

'Hibiscus, lime and cloves, I think. I'll ask Thelma.'

That's not what he said last night, I swear. I looked over at Josie and Margot – their eyes were wide. It wasn't. I held on to the curtain and tried not to fall.

'Why, you want to try some? Hazel liked it.'

I wasn't going anywhere near it. 'Erm . . . maybe?'

'Well, Thelma made a big batch. We drank it last night and this morning. Still good. I'll bring some tomorrow.'

'OK, great,' I said. 'Thanks.' I thought for a quick second of a follow-up question. 'Did you watch Thelma make it?'

Whisper looked up at me. '. . . No?'

'Ah, I was just wondering if there was anything else in it?'

Whisper sat back and kissed his teeth. 'Nothing else is in it. Boy, what you getting at?'

I looked at Josie and Margot for support. They shook their heads. Red light. I'd gone too far.

'Nah, nothing. I'm getting at nothing. I was just asking. Thought I'd make some for Mum.'

'Ah, son, that's kind,' Mum said. 'Always thinking about me.'

'He's not thinking about you,' Whisper muttered.

Whisper was wising up. He was on to me.

'I was!'

Through the window I saw Apollo approaching our door, head to toe in sleek black. I dropped the curtain.

'Someone's here.' I squinted as if I was only just recognizing them. 'Ah, it's Apollo.' I jumped down. 'I'll let him in.'

Whisper's eyes burned holes in my back as I walked to the hallway. Margot and Josie quickly followed behind.

'Well, that was bad,' Josie said, folding her arms.

'But you did good,' whispered Margot. 'Those weren't last night's ingredients. They're completely different, actually. We've learned something.'

'Whisper did say his memory's not that good, though,' I said, thinking back to last night. 'Remember he thought he knew Rachel from somewhere else?'

Apollo knocked on the door. 'Hello? Am I in the right place?'

'OK, we'll park that and keep it pushing,' I said. 'I'll be slicker. Rachel, pack your bags – you're going on a trip. Your final destination.'

I opened the door to Apollo, his lips and chin quivering. The white booklet under his arm stuck out in sharp contrast to his inky black outfit and shiny leather shoes. His red, sympathetic eyes looked at me, then at Josie. When they landed on Margot, he spoke. 'Morgana, is it really true? My Rachel is gone?'

Margot nodded. 'I'm so sorry.'

Apollo's hand flew to his mouth and tears sprang from his eyes. 'I told her to get out of here, but she wouldn't listen. Rachel *never* listened.'

3

Apollo stood in the middle of my living room. It was his stage now, and, man, did he love the spotlight. He held his glass up, but let his head hang down. 'To Rachel,' he said. 'Darling, darling Rachel.' He took a sharp breath, threw his head back and stared at the ceiling. 'If you only knew how much you'd be missed. I loved you dearly. So very much. Whatever happened to you –' he waved his hand around the room – 'whoever did this to you –' he glanced at Whisper and Mum and Whisper leaned back, his nose wrinkling – 'I vow to fight them, God help me. Hold me back.' His voice broke. 'Hold. Me. Back.' He sighed, then looked at me. 'You can turn the music back up now.'

Mum dabbed at her eyes. 'That was lovely.'

Terrible taste, Mother.

Apollo smiled and mouthed 'thank you' at her and gulped his drink. He winced. 'Strong,' he said, coughing, beating his chest with his fist.

Whisper eyed Apollo coolly, looking at him from his head to his heels. 'Nice words,' he said. 'Lots of "I"s and "me"s, though. Remember nine night is for and about *Rachel*, not *you*.'

Apollo took a step back and glared at Whisper. 'Hmmm,' he huffed. 'Your . . . ritual, your rules, I suppose.'

Above us, the light flickered a bit.

'See,' said Whisper, pointing to the ceiling, 'Rachel agrees.'

The room suddenly felt freezing cold. 'You think she's here?'

Whisper chuckled. 'Who else would it be?'

I shook my head at my friends. This was real. Real serious.

Apollo looked over at Margot and rolled his eyes in Whisper's direction.

She smiled at him, and patted the white book next to her on the floor. 'Thanks for this,' she said. 'It's so kind of you to gift me a copy.'

Whisper shook his head and tutted.

Margot noticed. 'I thought it would be nice to read it, to bring us closer to Rachel,' she said. She took a deep breath. 'Writer to writer, did she ever inspire your work?'

Oh, Margot was going in.

Apollo blinked quickly and smiled. 'Of course.' He waved his hands. 'Everything is inspiration. Stories are all around us – you just need to look and listen.'

'When did you meet Rachel?' asked Josie.

'Ah, it must have been six or so years ago – 2017? Yes, right around Christmas.'

Mum winced. 'Oof, that was a bad Christmas.' She chuckled.

'Why, w'happen?' asked Whisper.

Mum shook her head and began to struggle with an answer. I stepped up. I knew what happened. I was there.

'That's when Craig —'

'Your dad, Wes,' she said quietly.

'He ain't my dad. December 2017 is when he left. He's a cheater – Auntie Molly caught him in town holding hands with a homewrecker. Merry Christmas.'

Apollo coughed awkwardly.

'Wesley,' Mum hissed. 'Enough. That's the past.'

'Well, I'm sorry to hear that,' said Whisper. 'I understand you now.'

I leaned over Margot to grab Apollo's book and flicked through its pages. One of the stories towards the middle, called *Close*, had three characters: Rachel, Rocky and Naomi. I put the book in Margot's lap. She, in turn, nudged Josie. *This* was the play we needed to read.

I spoke up. 'What did Rachel think of your work? She like it?'

Apollo pursed his lips. 'She, erm, she loved it. Yes, she was a big supporter of my work.'

The ceiling lights twinkled. I gasped, and swung my head in Whisper's direction. He nodded slowly. Rachel was trying to tell us something. But what? I reckoned she thought his plays were pony; she didn't like what she saw when she took a look.

'Was she ever in any of your plays?' asked Josie.

Apollo snorted. 'God, no!'

'Why not?' said Margot. 'Didn't you want to work together?'

'Or was it because she never listened?' I asked. 'That's what you said when you came here today.'

Apollo grimaced and sucked in air between his teeth. 'You know what? She didn't really listen. That's true. Not to stage directions, not in life.' He sighed. 'I'm really not one to speak ill of the dead, darling, but –' he put his hands out, pressing the air in front of him, to soften the incoming blow – 'she just wasn't. Very. Good?' He laughed to himself. 'Terrible, in fact, which is why I was *very* surprised to hear about this . . . this . . .' He wriggled his fingers in the air, as if he was casting a spell to conjure up the words. 'This starring role of hers.' He shook his head. 'Where? With which company? It's just . . .'

'It's just what?' Margot asked, breath bated, waiting for his answer.

'It's just that she was always . . . forcing the acting thing. Always. Performance wasn't her forte; she had other strengths, but she was so dead set – sorry, sorry, *excruciatingly* bad turn of phrase there – on pursuing it. Just absolutely driven.'

'She *was* dramatic, though,' said Whisper. 'Right, Ella? Always prancing and strutting around at our group?'

Mum smiled and sighed at the memory. 'She was, but yeah, she didn't say much about . . . actually acting or working as an actor. Not to me anyway.'

'Nor me,' said Whisper. 'But, like I said, I saw that face before.'

There was a knock at the front door and when I opened it my heart stopped for a second.

Lauren, her grey hood over her head, glared down at me with burning red eyes.

Looking just like the person I saw last night.

Hazel stepped out from behind her, holding a platter of sandwiches. 'Hello, Wesley.' A smile crept over her face. 'Let us in?'

4

I let Hazel and Lauren into the hallway and hung back to catch my breath.

Lauren.

Lauren?

Lauren still had her hood up when she entered the living room. I stared at Margot and Josie until they noticed. I narrowed my eyes, and slowly turned my head in Lauren's direction.

Margot got it. She gasped.

'What?' Lauren snapped.

'N-nothing.' Margot spun round, searching for something to say. 'Erm, I'm just . . . surprised to see you and Hazel arriving together. Just like last night.'

'Why?' said Lauren. 'We come from the same direction, leave about the same time.'

'Oh,' said Margot. 'I guess that makes sense.'

It didn't make sense, not really.

Hazel and Lauren offered sombre hellos and cheek kisses to the adults. 'When I got your message about Twelfth Night –' Hazel began, handing her sandwiches to Mum.

Whisper tutted. 'Nine night.'

'– I just thought what a lovely thing to do at such a tragic time.'

'Sure you did,' Lauren muttered.

'And how kind of you, Ella, to offer your home.' Hazel walked to the window and stared at the policeman standing outside Rachel's. 'They're not letting me into my own house,' she said. I clocked a tangy bitterness in her voice.

'*Your* house?' said Lauren. 'Ain't really yours, is it?'

Hazel raised her shoulders.

Lauren shrugged hers. 'It's Rachel's.'

'When did they say?' asked Whisper. 'Because nine night is supposed to be at the house of the deceased.' He looked at me and my friends. 'Another name for nine night is dead yard because it's held at the yard of the dead.'

'Obviously,' scoffed Lauren.

'If this was back home, lots of people would come,' said Whisper. 'Whole villages.'

'Interesting,' said Hazel.

'Because there were so many people, not everyone would come every night. No space to hold them. But, since there's only us, you all have to come to all nine.' A smile crept over his face.

'We do?' Apollo muttered. 'Gosh, that's a commitment and a half.'

'That's what we do where I'm from.'

Hazel's brow furrowed. 'Well . . . I'll see. I'll see about that. Yes, I understand that this process is . . . important in your culture, so I'll do my best to make it work.'

'It depends on the investigation, doesn't it?' said Josie. 'It might have to be here if the police suspect Rachel was murdered.'

By mentioning murder, Josie sucked all the air out of the room, out of the adults' bodies too. They gasped in unison, like the idea had just entered their minds for the first time. Liars. Forty-year-olds don't just die, do they?

The light above us dimmed. Rachel agreed. They don't.

'She wasn't murdered,' Lauren said sternly.

'No?' asked Josie. 'How do you know?'

Apollo clutched his chest before Lauren could answer. 'Murdered, darling?' He looked at everyone in turn and began backing up. He laughed unconvincingly. 'You don't believe that, do you?' He stared at his glass, then scrambled into a seat on the sofa.

Josie opened her mouth to speak, but Margot tugged on her arm and shook her head, silently begging her to button it.

'Oh, they believe it all right,' said Whisper. 'They think one of us is the culprit.'

Lauren let out a loud, bitter, incredulous laugh.

'They don't think that, Whisper!' Mum said. She looked at us. 'Do you?'

'Not at all,' Margot said, the friendliness in her voice sounding so fake. '*The police* might think that is all Josie said. *We* don't think anything – we just want to remember Rachel in the right way, in the right place. At her house.' She looked at Hazel. 'What will happen to her house?'

Hazel's jaw tightened. 'Well, no one can go in until the police have finished.'

'And her stuff?' I asked. 'Where's it going?'

'Nothing can be touched or moved until they find her next of kin. That's the law.'

'She has sisters,' said Mum, tapping her lip. 'I'm sure of it. I don't remember their names, though – I'm not sure if she told me.'

'Sisters?' Apollo wrinkled his nose. 'She never mentioned them to me.' He cradled his head. 'Darling, why these secrets?'

'Well, there's a woman's name on her lease: her guarantor, and in case of emergency. I know that,' said Hazel.

'Is it Mum?' I asked.

Hazel shook her head. 'It definitely doesn't say Ella. Something with a "K", I think. Katie maybe? I'll check this evening. I haven't been in my office today.'

'You haven't called her yet?' I could tell Josie was shocked by Hazel's lack of action.

'No, not today – but I've tried that number many times,' said Hazel.

'And?' I asked.

'And the person hasn't a clue who Rachel is – wrong number.'

The three of us sighed in frustrated unison. 'Who answers then?' I tutted.

'A man – he says he doesn't know a Rachel and ends the call.'

'That's odd,' said Margot. 'But why did you call him so often?'

Hazel squirmed in her seat. 'Rachel could be . . . quite unreliable,' she said. 'Late on her payments.'

I swear the light above us got a bit brighter.

Rachel was telling us she did owe money? But why spend it all on Amazon?

'She's got all that stuff, though . . .' I wondered out loud.

Mum shook her head. 'That can wait – what's going to happen next? Her funeral?'

'The council will arrange one,' said Hazel.

'They'll just chuck her in the ground,' said Whisper sadly. 'Cruel and cheap.'

'They won't,' said Hazel. 'It's happened before; they don't do that.'

Before? I looked at Margot and Josie. Josie was on it – already taking notes on her phone.

A knock at the door.

'Wes, would you get it?' Mum took a deep breath. 'That be your sibs. Jaden left his keys at home, I think.'

There weren't three children behind the door, though. There were two adults, and one was PC Stevens.

He clutched his hat to his chest. The woman held out her hand. 'I'm DCI Lawrence,' she said, 'the senior investigating officer looking into the death of your neighbour Rachel Kohl.'

5

I gawped at the cops.

'It's all right,' DCI Lawrence said gently. I shook her tanned hand. 'Nothing to worry about. We're going door-to-door and just want to chat.'

A chat? Yeah, right. PC Stevens already had his notebook in his hand.

'Can we come in?'

I nodded and stood aside.

'Wow.' PC Stevens chuckled as he entered the living room. 'A full house.' He nodded at Mum. 'Hello again.' He looked around the room. 'I'm PC Stevens and this is my colleague DCI Lawrence.'

Colleague? That was his boss. I could tell – more letters in her title.

'We wanted to catch up with you.' He flipped through his small notebook, then looked up at Mum. 'Ella. To find out about Rachel's party.'

'Well, that's rather convenient – everyone that was there is here now,' said Apollo. He pointed, then waved his hand in a circle. 'You can do all your enquires in one hit.'

'That *is* convenient, isn't it?' said DCI Lawrence quietly.

Apollo gulped and now no one wanted to be the first to talk.

Whisper grumped and looked out of the window. Hazel smiled and sat forward, keen to catch the coppers' eyes. Lauren folded her arms defiantly. Apollo tucked his hand under his chin and looked on. And Mum? Well, Mum tried to make them feel welcome.

'Drink? Something to eat?' she said nervously. She fiddled with the end of one of her locs. 'We have sandwiches, sausage rolls, oh, and I have potato skins in the oven if you want some?'

Margot's back straightened. 'What's on those skins, Ella? They're so tasty.'

Mum smiled. 'You like them? It's the vegan cheese I bought for Rachel.'

Margot and Josie nodded at each other.

'Told you,' I mouthed in their direction.

DCI Lawrence put her hand up. 'No, no, thank you – we're not staying.' She slowly scanned everyone in the room, then smiled. 'Did you all know each other before the party?'

Hazel and Lauren glanced at each other, and then stared at the floor.

'I'd never met any of these people before yesterday,' said Apollo, solemnly swearing by putting his hands on his chest, distancing himself. He pointed at Margot. 'That little girl catfished me into coming.'

Whisper tutted to himself and laughed.

Margot's eyes doubled in size. 'I didn't!' She turned to PC Stevens. 'As I said earlier, it was a surprise party, and these were the only people we found online so we invited them, OK?' She took a deep breath. 'The only way I knew how.'

'And now, tonight, we are holding the first of nine nights to honour Rachel,' said Whisper, coming in with an assist. 'You'll have plenty of time for questions. You know where we'll be.' He huffed and folded his arms.

'I understand,' said DCI Lawrence, staring into his eyes. She broke her gaze with a smile. 'I will, of course, be reaching out to you individually, pending Rachel's post-mortem.'

The vibe in the room changed when she said that. I looked up to the lights, but Rachel had nothing to say. Lauren didn't use words either but began to take deep breaths. She started crying and shrank herself small in her hoodie.

'In the meantime, I just have a couple of questions for the group.' DCI Lawrence looked at Whisper, pretending she was asking permission, but was actually putting him in his place. He looked back at her with pursed lips. 'How was Rachel acting at the party? How was she feeling?'

'Not very well,' said Hazel. 'The party wrapped up early and, speaking of which, do you know if it'll be possible to get in the house tonight? I'm the owner.'

DCI Lawrence shook her head. 'But we will let you know. What time did you all leave?'

'Around nine thirty,' said Josie. 'We were the last to go; we had some tidying to do.'

'And I left just before them.' Apollo dug into his trouser pockets. 'I might have my train ticket here – evidence, if you want.'

'That won't be necessary at this stage,' said DCI Lawrence. She looked round the group. 'And you all went home? If we need confirmation, we'd get corroboration?'

Everyone nodded.

'Final question, before we leave you to your wake,' she said, 'for those of you who live on Copsey Close. Did you hear or see anything out of the ordinary last night?'

Margot shook her head. 'I didn't.'

Josie agreed. 'Me neither. My bedroom's at the back of my house.'

DCI Lawrence turned her gaze to me and Mum.

Mum fiddled with her hair. 'No,' she said nervously. 'I stayed up and watched a film downstairs. *Clueless*.'

PC Stevens leaned forward. 'Classic. Love that film.'

DCI Lawrence narrowed her eyes at him, then turned to me. 'Anything?'

I gulped. I wanted to tell them about Lauren, but not with her right there. Bruh, I needed witness protection first.

'There's something, isn't there?' said DCI Lawrence, leaning forward. 'Or someone?'

'If you know something, boy, say it!' said Whisper, encouraging me, his eyes egg-sized.

I had to check with my friends.

I looked over at Margot and Josie.

Josie nodded, but Margot was shaking her head. She thought our detective days were dunzo.

'Well?' asked PC Stevens.

I closed my eyes. 'Last night I was in my mum's room before she went to . . . watch her film.'

Mum smiled nervously at me.

'When I looked out of the window, there was someone, a tall person in a grey hood, looking up at Rachel's house.' I glanced at Lauren and shrugged. 'They seemed familiar, that's all.'

DCI Lawrence followed my gaze, and so did everyone else in the room.

'What?' Lauren snapped. She stood up and walked to the doorway. She put a hand on her head.

'Familiar how?' asked PC Stevens. 'The grey hood and anything else?'

'It was the way they were standing – one hand on the hip, the other on their head. I just recognized it.'

Lauren quickly shifted her position. 'I wasn't there!' she said.

'Well, well, well.' Apollo was enjoying his turn out of the spotlight. 'Maybe there was something in those oils,' he muttered.

Lauren glared at him.

'Sorry?' said DCI Lawrence. 'I didn't catch that.'

'Nothing,' said Apollo. 'Nothing at all.'

Mum spoke up. 'At the party, when Rachel came in, she was shouting at someone on her phone. She told us it was someone called Lauren –'

Lauren put both hands on her head. 'Wow, great. Thanks!'

'– but *this* Lauren was upstairs,' said Hazel, jumping in, 'just before the surprise.'

'That was *not* me!' Lauren shouted. 'I'm not the person on the phone or the person in the street.'

Hazel nodded. 'Lauren went home. I saw her leave, and she wouldn't have been on the phone – the house was silent; we would have all heard her.'

A key turned in the front door. 'It's my other kids,' said Mum.

Jayden poked his head round the doorway and stumbled back in shock at the amount of people in his living room. He leaned into the hall and signalled to Jordan and Kayla to stay where they were. 'Cops and more,' he said in a low voice. He looked round at everyone, then at Mum. 'Another party? Yesterday's at Rachel's, then whoever was here last night –'

So there *was* someone here last night. God, we'd just got through the vegan cheese thing, and now this? I didn't dare look at Josie or Margot, but I know their minds were whirling, like hamsters on their wheels.

'Maybe brothers *are* independent sources,' Josie whispered.

'And now this?' Jayden continued. 'So sociable these days, Mumma Bear.'

Mum walked slowly over to my sibs, the weight of all the eyes in the room on her back. 'Kids,' she said, sighing, 'come upstairs. There's something I need to tell you.'

DCI Lawrence nudged PC Stevens. 'Get everyone's details, then meet me at the scene.'

6

'You know what?' I said. 'We're gonna go too.' I looked at Josie and Margot, who stood up immediately.

'Yes –' Margot eyed me – 'we're . . . going to mine?'

I nodded.

'To have a break,' she continued. She crouched and picked up Apollo's book. 'Thanks again for this,' she said. 'And for calling me a catfish to the cops,' she muttered.

'Enjoy,' Apollo said.

Lauren glared at us as we left. In the hallway we looked at each other, knowing not to speak, not to say a word until we were safe, far away from this house.

Outside, we ran past Rachel's, past the policeman guarding it, and into Margot's house.

We were silent on her stairs. Margot's bedroom door was open. Her walls were covered with colourful Post-it notes filled with quotes – words she likes, things she's overheard, conversations from dreams she's had. First, she threw Apollo's script on the bed, then herself. Josie lay next to her, and I sat on the floor, looking up at them.

'Where to even start?' Margot said breathlessly.

'With Lauren,' said Josie. 'She's looking like the prime suspect now, Wes.'

'Don't,' I groaned. 'I had to tell the police what I saw, didn't I? She's gonna kill me next, right?'

'Maybe,' said Margot. She sat up and smiled.

'She might, though,' said Josie quietly. 'How are we going to get through eight more nights with these potentially dangerous people?'

'By doing our best,' I said. 'We tried hard tonight – we learned some things. Rachel was pointing us in the right direction through the lights.'

Margot looked at Josie sideways. 'Well, I don't know about that,' she said. 'But I *do* know our interrogation skills are not sharp enough yet, and the police are way ahead. We know Rachel was a bad actress now, though, according to Apollo –'

'Who completely threw you under the bus,' I added. 'How did those wheels feel?'

'I hate him now,' Margot spat with pure venom.

'It's why she wasn't famous in London. We also know Rachel didn't always pay her rent *and* has at least one sister, who no one seems to know,' said Josie.

'A possible sister with a phone number that goes to a random man,' I added.

'Whisper's ingredients list is completely different today –'

'But Mum's wasn't! Vegan cheese!' I gloated. 'She wouldn't make those again if she was using it as a weapon, would she? Told you!'

'Right, that's true, but . . .' Margot paused. She strained her neck to look over at Josie, then down at me.

'But . . . ?' I asked.

'There *was* someone in your house last night.'

'Jayden confirmed it,' said Josie. 'And, before you get mad, you said we'd stick together. We promised.'

I bit my tongue. I'd made a promise and I shouldn't have. Again. 'OK.' I breathed heavily through my nose. 'So what now?'

Josie looked at her phone. 'You have to work on your mum. Get her phone, ask her slyly, talk to your sibs. Do something – any one of those things.'

'Fine,' I lied. It wasn't fine at all.

'We also need Rachel's sister's name. To do that we must get close to Hazel,' said Margot. 'She's our focus tomorrow night.'

'We need Lauren back onside too,' said Josie.

'I don't want to be on any side of that girl,' I said.

'Do you actually think she did it?' Margot asked. 'Like, really, really?'

I shrugged. 'I dunno – but if it's between her and Mum, then, yeah, she's the guilty one.'

Josie shook her head. 'That's not how justice should work, Wes.'

'I know! Look, Lauren and the person I saw had the

same shape, same stance and the same hoodie, though. I'm just saying.'

'It could fit,' said Josie.

'Hazel was vouching for her,' said Margot. She played her stomach like a drum. 'Something's odd about them two. I swear they know each other.'

I put my elbows on the bed. 'Right?! They also looked at each other when DCI Lawrence asked who knew who.'

'But why hide it?' said Margot. 'It's not like we knew them before the party.'

'Or give a fig,' I added.

'Privacy,' said Josie. 'They all love privacy. Right, so we need a plan.'

'You have one already?' I asked.

She shrugged. 'Basically, yes. We have some to-dos. I'll research Whisper's tea recipe –'

'Lauren's oils first, though, yeah? She's the priority, don't forget.'

Josie nodded and looked over at Margot. 'Read some of Apollo's plays, but especially the one with Rachel, Naomi and Rocky?'

Margot sighed. 'I feel like my anger towards Apollo is going to taint my reading, but of course I'll do it.'

'Wesley –'

I put my hands up before she said it. I knew what was coming. 'I'll talk to Mum.'

DAY TWO
TUESDAY 11 APRIL

1

I ain't a wimp, but yeah, I made sure I stayed at Margot's until everyone left mine. I told her and Josie that I needed to pace myself, but if I'm being real, I didn't want to run into anyone. Especially not Lauren, not by myself.

I needed a minute just to, like, think and make sure I did my part of the investigation properly. I only had one chance to get this right, one chance to get Rachel to the other realm.

When I got back, I didn't sleep in my room. I chose the sofa. I didn't want to answer any questions my brothers had – what Rachel looked like when I found her, how I felt about it all and exactly who the people in our house were or might be. I didn't want to ask them questions about Mum either, because if I did, and it went left, she would know the terrible, dark-sided things I was thinking about her.

Those shady thoughts spun around my head all night. Mum being over Rachel. Rachel being funky with Mum. Mum grinning at her phone and her late-night guest . . .

I was being silly, surely? There was no way she was really involved, right?

So, yeah, I didn't speak to her. I drove myself insane instead. Mum was in bed when I got in and, when she popped down in the middle of the night to throw a blanket on me, I squeezed my eyes shut and pretended I was asleep.

I really dozed off once she left for work and my sibs went to holiday club. I didn't remember any dreams; the waking nightmare was enough.

It was raining when I really woke up. I kneeled on the sofa and stared at Rachel's house from the front window. The cop standing guard had gone, but their blue-and-white tape remained, joined by a few bunches of plastic-wrapped flowers. I gazed at them, wondering who left them, until a white van pulled up and fully blocked my view. After what seemed like forever, a driver, pencil behind his ear, got out with a large thin brown box in his left hand. He looked down at the flowers, over the police tape, then around the close in confusion.

Another delivery for Rachel. They were still coming after she'd gone. It was still our duty to receive them.

I tiptoed barefoot across the close in the shorts I slept in, with my phone in my pocket. I nodded at the driver. 'That for Rachel Kohl?'

'Yeah,' he said. 'Yo, what happened here? Someone get stabbed or something?'

I shook my head. 'No, but Rachel died.'

He put his hand to his mouth. 'Nah, you serious?'

'Yeah. It's crazy. Did you know her? Sorry if you did – I just blurted that out.'

'Nah, nah, you're good. I *feel* like I know her a bit, you know? I was always coming here, dropping her stuff off.' He rubbed his chin. 'Like, you always wonder what people are about, don't you?'

I nodded yes, but I didn't know what he was on about really.

'You know, you read these names on these parcels, see their houses, and when you're on the road all day you make up lives for them. You wonder if they've got kids, support the Hatters, or like, I don't know, pineapple on their pizza –'

Gross, no.

'Little things like that.' He looked down at his parcel. 'Rachel Kohl. Like what kind of a name is "Kohl"? Was she German or something?'

'Nope,' I said. 'She was Black.'

The driver raised an eyebrow. 'There are Black people in Germany, bro.' He tutted and looked up at her house. 'What happened? Do you know?'

I took a deep breath. 'I saw her the day before. She was OK – a little bit sick, had a stomach ache. The next time I saw her, she was dead.'

The driver took a couple of steps back. 'You found her? Oh, that's heavy. You good?'

'I've been better, but yeah, I'm working it out. We'll figure it out.'

'We? What's to work out?'

I looked at him and tried to shrug casually. 'Nothing. I dunno.'

'Hmmm,' he said. '"Nothing" and "I dunno" is right. Don't get mixed up in grown people business. Nothing good comes of it.' He handed me Rachel's package. 'Guess you can keep this one; she's won't miss it, will she?'

'I ain't no thief,' I said. 'It still belongs to someone, doesn't it?'

I stared at the driver and he stared right back. A Copsey Close stand-off. My phone beeped inside my shorts.

'You take care of yourself, yeah?' he said as he opened his van door. Instead of watching the road, he maintained eye contact as he reversed his way down the close and on to Copsey Avenue.

I tucked the package under my arm and checked my phone. Josie.

It's time to investigate. Meet at Margot's.

2

Margot opened her front door. 'That was quick.' She looked at my shorts, laughing. 'Pyjamas? We're not having a sleepover; we're working. Leave the door open for Josie.'

'Leave it out – I was collecting a delivery, then I kinda got into it with the driver.'

'Oh yeah?' she said, walking up the stairs. 'What did they say?' She stopped on the landing. 'Wait, you didn't tell them about our investigation, did you?'

'Nah, course not! I just said we had things to work out and he was like, "No, you don't."'

'Sounds riveting, truly.'

I sat on the edge of her bed while she lay down. 'Funny. It was more of Rachel's stuff,' I said with a sigh.

'Yet none of it in plain sight. 'Tis a mystery indeed.'

'Well, it's behind that bedroom door, innit? We know that.'

'Has to be,' said Margot. She looked at her window and let out a massive yawn. 'Sorry, sorry.' She put a hand to her mouth. 'I didn't really sleep.'

'Yeah, me neither. I kipped on the sofa.'

'Why?'

I shrugged. 'Yesterday was a lot. Honestly, I didn't have the energy to get into it with my brothers –'

'Or Ella?'

'Or Mum, yeah,' I said.

We sat in silence for a moment, then she turned to look at me. 'I really hope she's going to be OK,' she said gently.

'I'll tell you who's doing OK,' said Josie, pushing Margot's bedroom door open. 'Me.'

I jumped straight out of my skin and on to the bed next to Margot. 'Jesus Christ, Josie, where did you spring up from?!' I said, holding my chest.

Josie gestured behind her. 'The front door was open. I assumed for me?'

'It was,' said Margot. 'But you could have given us some warning! Thought I was going to have a heart attack.'

'Why?' She squinted. 'Have you two got secrets?'

'Don't be stupid,' I said. 'We were just talking about Mum.'

'Oh?' Josie sat down at Margot's desk. 'Did you talk to her?'

I shook my head.

'But you will later, won't you?' she asked. 'You know you have to.'

I sighed. 'I know. I know. So, tell us, why are you so good? You burst in here, shouting about being OK . . .'

'I got somewhere with my research last night, somewhere good.' She laced her fingers together and put her hands on her head. 'Sorrel tea. At Rachel's party Whisper said it had –' she sat up to pull her phone out of her back pocket – 'sorrel buds, some orange zest, fresh ginger, right?'

'I think so,' I said.

'And last night he said hibiscus, lime and cloves.'

'Which one's the right recipe then?' asked Margot.

'Both!' said Josie. She threw her hands in the air. 'Both are right! Sorrel and hibiscus are the same plant. So, either way, it's the truth. Also, none of those ingredients are poisonous – unless they're ingested whole or drunk in massive quantities, which obviously didn't happen. He brought a small flask, and, of course, Hazel drank it first. You know what else?'

'What?' said Margot.

'Sorrel tea really is good for the gut. It literally improves digestion! Google says so.'

'So what's your verdict then?' I asked.

'My verdict is we can rule Whisper out – for now. It makes it easier for us to concentrate on the others.' She looked at me. 'See how that works? This is why we need answers.'

'Great work, Josie, well done,' said Margot. 'Progress!'

'Thanks. I also checked out Lauren's oils –'

'And?' I asked.

'The first one, marjoram. Great for stomach aches and cramps, so that's fine. The other one, Roman chamomile –'

I sat forward. 'What about it?'

'So it soothes body aches and cramps, but it also makes you sleepy.'

'How deep a sleep are we talking?' said Margot, her eyes growing large. 'Not like . . . eternal sleep?'

'No,' said Josie, shaking her head. 'But if you use too much, it can make you drowsy.'

'Wait,' I said, standing up, 'OK, say the bottles are legit, no tampering happening. Lauren gave them to Rachel and . . . waited for her to go to sleep? That's why she was hanging about outside? Waiting for her to nod off and then . . .' I ran my finger across my throat. 'Ooh, I like that! That makes sense!'

'Except . . . it doesn't,' said Josie quietly.

'Why not?'

Josie sighed. 'Lauren told Rachel to put a few drops of each oil in her burner and bath. She didn't touch the bottles again after that.'

'Wait, who did then?' As soon as I asked, I knew the answer. Theory instantly debunked.

'Your mum,' Josie said. 'She was the last person in Rachel's bedroom. Before . . .'

'Before what?' I said, feeling the fear creep in.

'Before you went home. Before you heard the giggling and the clink-clinking of glasses,' said Margot with a sigh.

3

This was bad.

'So what now?' I snapped. 'You're ruling Lauren out?'

'No way.' Josie shook her head. 'She's still super suspicious.'

'Right!' I said. 'She was weepy and creepy and walking around the house a lot, don't forget. That counts – even if it wasn't her in the close. Also, there was something off about those oils.' I shook my head. 'They didn't smell right; I don't care what you say.'

'Look, I'm just saying we have to use the facts and evidence we have to make a decent deduction,' said Josie. 'That's why Whisper checks out for now.' She shrugged. 'It's what we have to do – that's how you investigate.'

I put my hands over my face and screamed – and swore – into them. My mind was making perfect circles again. I pulled my palms down my face. 'You think they teamed up? Mum and Lauren in it together and celebrating after? In my house?'

Josie looked at Margot, confused. 'No . . . ? I literally just said we need evidence. We have none for that scenario. This is why you have to talk to your mum, OK?' She reached up from her seat to touch my arm.

I managed to croak out an 'OK'. My throat was beyond dry. I took a deep breath. 'Can we look into those oils a bit more? Like get a second opinion?'

Josie nodded. 'Yeah, and I know just the place.' She looked down at my shorts. 'If you put on some proper clothes, we can go.'

'Fine, I will. Can we move on from Mum now?' I asked. 'Just for a bit?'

'Sure,' said Josie. She turned to Margot. 'Did you read Apollo's plays?'

Margot leaned over the side of her bed. She picked up Apollo's work and waved it in Josie's direction. 'I did indeed.'

'Find anything?' I asked, hoping there'd be something to put Apollo in the frame.

'OK, so there were lots of different scenes, mostly of male characters with some variation of his name.' She laughed. 'A man talking about his life – his upbringing, family, hopes and dreams, his struggles and triumphs. So far so boring, but there was one part called *Close* –'

'The one with Rachel in it, right?' I asked.

Margot nodded. 'Plus a Naomi and a Rocky.'

'Is it "Close", like "Copsey Close", or "Close" as in "I'm gonna close the case"?' I asked. 'Or like "close friends"?'

Margot shrugged. 'I'm not sure yet.'

'Well, what happens?' asked Josie.

'So it's set in the afternoon, after school, in a shop.'

'Like a corner shop?' I wondered aloud.

'Exactly,' said Margot. 'Rachel and Naomi are in this newsagent's and they're looking at all the sweets and crisps and whispering about Rocky – a boy Rachel likes, who's in the shop with his friends. Rachel is *obsessed*, but doesn't have the confidence to talk to him, so she's asking Naomi what to do and what to say.'

'What does Naomi think?' asked Josie.

'Naomi's vibe is like, he's not that great, girl, but if you like it, I love it. I'll support you.'

'A good friend then,' I said.

'Yeah,' said Margot. 'I can't work out if they're best friends or they're sisters or whether Naomi has a crush on Rachel –'

'Does it matter?' said Josie.

'Maybe not.' Margot shrugged. 'But I like to read between the lines; it gives me a sense of character, I guess.'

I rolled my eyes. This girl. 'What happens in the end? Does Rachel talk to Rocky?'

'She does. He's paying for a Mars bar, and she says, "I like your accent," and he's like, eyebrow raise, "Thanks," and leaves.'

'That's it?' I said.

'Yep, that's all he says – but Rachel's all giddy, light-headed and in the middle of saying something about him when –' she clapped her hands together – 'the play ends mid-sentence.'

'It's not finished?' said Josie. 'Why would Apollo put an unfinished play in his book?'

Margot sat up straight. 'Well, two reasons. One, drama and artistry – it's *supposed* to end like that.'

Josie's nose wrinkled. 'If you say so.'

'Or?' I asked.

'Or, two, Apollo didn't write this. It's so different from the rest. This felt . . . so real and interesting. Alive.'

'And that's why Apollo wanted Rachel dead,' I said.

Josie raised her hand. 'Hang on a moment.'

'Because she wrote this; she was a better writer and he didn't like it!' I shouted.

'And she didn't like him taking her work either, judging by her reaction,' said Margot. 'We'll ask him tonight – after you get dressed, Wes.'

4

I looked up at the shop's sign.

'Holland and Barrett? They know about oils here?'

Josie nodded. 'It's the only place in town I could think of where we could look at the bottles, get some advice –'

'And smell them too? Do you think Holland and/or Barrett will let us do that?' I asked.

'They'll have testers for sure,' said Margot. 'And if not, I have money; we'll buy some.'

I shook my head. 'Nuh-uh, Margot. I don't want murder weapons near us.'

'Well, everything has the potential to be a murder weapon,' she replied. She took her house key out of her pocket and put it between her knuckles. 'See?'

I stared at her. 'Margot, there is something seriously wrong with you.'

She laughed. 'You know I'm right.'

I'd never been inside a Holland & Barrett before, no reason to. The shelves were attached to wood-panelled walls, and there were rows of pills, powders and potions.

'Yo,' I hissed at my friends as they walked down the aisle in front of me. 'Is this a shop for witches or what?' I stopped and picked up a packet. 'Whey power? As in curds and whey?' I shook my head. 'What in the Miss Muffet is this for?'

Margot flexed her arm. 'It's good for you! Makes you strong.'

A tall, thin man wearing a dark grey apron stood between Margot and me. His name tag said JONATHAN, but he looked like that Lurch out of *Wednesday*. He pushed his black glasses up his nose. 'Can I help you?' he asked in a tone that told us he didn't want to help at all.

Josie tapped him on the back. 'Yes, please. We're looking for two oils. Roman chamomile and marjoram. Do you have them in stock?'

Jonathan narrowed his eyes. 'What do you want them for?'

'We're just interested.' I shrugged. 'What do they do exactly?'

He sighed. 'Well, do you need calming down or soothing? They both work for that.'

'Is there anything in either of them that's poisonous?' asked Margot.

'Everything's a poison in the wrong hands,' he replied.

Margot grinned like she had won a prize.

'But, no, these are fine – we wouldn't sell them if they were harmful. Just go by the instructions.'

'And if you didn't?' I asked. 'What if you, like, ate them?'

Jonathan raised an eyebrow. 'We don't recommend that.'

'I know, I know – but what if someone did?' I asked. 'What would happen?'

'Well, they might be sick and get drowsy –'

'Would they die?' asked Margot.

Jonathan stepped backwards and stared at us. 'Not unless they drank litres of it.'

I looked at Josie, who smiled back. She was right. Again. 'Can you show us where they are, please?' she asked.

'Oh no.' Jonathan shook his head. 'I'm not selling them to you. Not after this conversation.'

'Can we just smell them then?' Margot asked, smiling sweetly.

He began walking backwards. 'I'll bring them to you,' he said without blinking or looking behind him.

'God, he's weird,' Margot muttered.

'Because you two made it weird with your questions!' Josie groaned through gritted teeth. 'Right, he's incoming.'

Jonathan brought over the tiny bottles, one in each hand. 'Chamomile,' he said, wafting it quickly under our noses. 'And the marjoram.'

Yeah, that's what Rachel's room kind of smelled like. 'What would happen if you mixed them together?' I asked.

'And burned them?' asked Margot. 'In one of those things with water and a little candle – not just set them on fire.'

Jonathan put a dab of both oils on his palms and rubbed them together. 'It would smell a bit like this.' He put his hands out.

Yeah, I know, it's weird to sniff a rando's hand, but needs must. Mixed together, they no longer smelled so nice. They were slightly sour, just like Rachel's room. I looked at Margot and Josie. 'Yeah, that's it. That's the smell.'

He looked at the three of us in turn. 'Anything else?'

I sighed. 'Nah. I think we're good here.'

As we walked through Wardown Park to catch our bus, I kicked at the gravel and the weeds on the path. 'That felt pointless,' I grumped.

'It wasn't,' said Josie. 'You got your second opinion on the oils – we know they're not toxic, not in the amounts Rachel had, so we can rule them out as a weapon.'

'Plus, we're off the close for a little bit, taking a walk where Rachel used to go,' said Margot. 'Can you feel her spirit here, Wes?'

I shook my head. 'Nah, not really. The only spirits here are in those bottles under that bench.' I peered down to look. 'No Rachel, just rum.'

There was a dirty and dull brass plate screwed into the bench's back. When I read what was etched on it, my heart stopped. 'OK, wait, this is beyond weird,' I said to my friends, who had started to walk ahead. 'Come look at this plaque thing!'

'*In memory of Rachel Cole, 1983 to 1998,*' Josie read. 'Oh, wow. That's so sad – and strange how people can have similar names but live completely different lives, isn't it?'

'Truly. Her Mothership gets emails for other Verity Andersons all the time,' said Margot, waving her hand. 'She sees their credit-card statements, wedding-planning arrangements, gets job-interview requests – all because the senders have just got her email slightly wrong. She even arranged to meet up with one of them for a drink once.' She sighed. 'She would. Any excuse.'

'It's got to be a sign, right?' I said.

'A sign our bus is coming, yes,' said Josie, pointing to the other side of the road towards a parade of shops. The bus was about to turn the corner.

We waited for the traffic to stop before crossing. When it cleared, I grabbed Josie's arm. 'That ain't who I think it is, is it?'

Margot and Josie followed my gaze. Whisper was standing outside a betting shop, looking down at some slips of paper. He stuffed them into his blazer pocket and patted the saddle of a bike leaning against the wall. He walked past it and peered into the windows of the vacant shop next door. Whisper shook his head and returned to his bike. As he swung a leg over the frame, he turned towards us and clocked us dead on. We gasped.

He gasped too, and, without a second glance, he quickly pedalled away.

NIGHT TWO

NIGHT TWO

1

Margot closed her front door behind her. 'I know you ruled him out, Josie, and I agree with you –'

'But?' said Josie. 'I hear a "but" coming.'

'But –' Margot smiled – '*if* you weren't doing anything that suspicious, you wouldn't do this, would you?' She stopped in the doughnut, looked behind her, clutched her chest and gasped, then mimed cycling away. 'Surely you'd be just like, oh, that's Ella's boy and his friends, no? Let me see how they are? Let me buy them some sweets.'

'Right?' I agreed. 'It just wasn't that deep, was it?'

'Not at all,' said Josie. 'It's lower down our list, but let's ask him about it.'

Margot nodded. 'The priority is asking Apollo about *Close*.'

'And seeing if Hazel knows anything else about Rachel's family,' I said.

Josie nodded and put her hand on my shoulder. 'We'll also stick together and make sure Lauren doesn't kill you for giving her description to the police last night.'

I pursed my lips at her. 'Don't even start . . .'

Josie glanced over at Rachel's house. The police tape was still wrapped round her gate and the light was on in her living room. Her locked front bedroom was dark. She turned back to Margot and me. 'I wonder if they've spoken to Lauren – or anyone else, for that matter?'

We walked up the path. 'We'll find out soon enough.' I fished in my pocket for my key. I'd just kissed the lock with it when the front door slowly opened. I pasted a fake smile on my face, expecting to see Mum on the other side. Tonight, we'd talk.

But it wasn't Mum behind the door. It was Whisper.

'Children,' he said, leaning towards us, 'welcome, welcome.' He opened the door wider.

I glanced back at my friends and chuckled in nervous confusion. 'Bit weird to welcome me to my own house,' I said, my forced smile fixed. We stepped in and I poked my head into the living room. Empty. This wasn't good. I dropped my smile and light tone instantly. 'Where's Mum?'

Whisper pointed up the stairs. 'Giggling on the phone like a teenager.'

I felt a hand on my back. I don't know if it was Margot or Josie, but one of them was telling me to be calm, to go easy.

'When I looked through the window and saw it was you, I thought I'd just let you in.'

I looked up the stairs. I could hear Mum moving in her bedroom.

She was safe – but maybe we weren't.

The three of us huddled in the hallway. Whisper loomed over us – even though he had never seemed tall before.

'Do you know who she's talking to?' asked Margot, looking up. She slowly backed herself against the wall and bumped off the radiator. A single sock drying on it fell to the floor.

'Molly.'

I relaxed. My auntie.

Whisper tutted, shaking his head in Margot's direction. 'You three are *very* nosy.'

Margot gulped. 'I'm interested in people, what they do, who they talk to, where they go . . .'

Whisper narrowed his eyes. 'Is that so?'

'Yeah,' she said, her bottom lip quivering a little bit. 'It is so.'

My eyes jumped between Whisper and Margot; like I was watching a tense tennis match.

'W-well, we thought we saw you earlier, in the park,' Josie blurted.

Margot sighed. The tennis ball hit the net. We'd lost the point.

Whisper laughed, baring all his teeth and some gum. 'I *thought* I saw you too, but I can't see so good that far.'

'What were you up to?' asked Josie, trying to act casual. 'Anything nice?'

'Ah,' he said. 'Placing bets and minding my old business. Any further questions?' Whisper pursed his lips. 'You know, I used to know a lot of children –'

'You did?' I wondered out loud.

'Yeah – and you three aren't normal ones.'

'Well, we're not normal,' said Josie, standing up straight, bringing herself up to Whisper's height. 'We're Copseys.'

'Oh my God, Josie.' I buried my head in my hands and shrank against the front door. 'Stop. Cringe.'

Josie's shoulders slumped. She looked gutted. 'I'm sorry, it just felt right.'

Whisper chuckled. 'Now *that's* normal.'

Mum came down the stairs, gripping her phone. 'Wes!' She put her arms out for a hug, and I hugged her back. It was comforting, but I was cautious. Cautious to cuddle my own mother! How sad is that? 'Haven't seen you all day!'

'They were in the park,' said Whisper confidently. 'It *was* them.'

Mum smiled. 'Oh, that's nice. That's nice, yeah,' she said, seeming distant.

'You good, Mum?'

She blinked and looked at me. 'Yeah,' she said with a sigh.

'Nice phone call?' I took a deep breath. My interrogation was about to begin. 'Whisper said you were giggling?'

'Boy . . .' he warned.

Mum shot him an icy look, then quickly softened her face. 'N-no. I was just talking to Molly. She's at the airport now, and will be round tomorrow. I had to tell her what happened.' She shook her head. 'It just . . . brought it all back again. I thought I was getting used to it.'

'It only happened yesterday,' said Josie.

'It will come in waves,' said Whisper, nodding knowingly. 'When the tide's out, you feel all right – you almost forget the sadness. But when that tide comes crashing back in –' he pushed his finger forward, close to Mum's face – 'it feels violent. Fresh. Overwhelming. Makes you feel . . . guilty for thinking you were getting on with it.'

Mum wiped her eyes. 'Yeah. That's exactly it.'

Whisper patted her on the shoulder. 'You'll be all right.'

There was a knock at the door and, since my back was on it, I turned to open it.

Apollo.

'I say, darling, is the gathering in the hallway tonight? Is this part of your ritual, Whisper?' He laughed.

Whisper didn't.

2

Mum handed Apollo a glass of red wine and sat next to him. 'Thanks,' he said, sinking into the sofa, crossing his legs with a sigh. 'You know, the past few days, since this happened –'

'It was literally yesterday,' I said. These people, and I'm including Mum in this, were very keen to move on from Rachel's death.

Too keen.

'– I've just had this thought going round and round in my mind.'

'There are thoughts in there?' said Whisper from the armchair, holding a cup of tea. Mum had moved the coffee table next to him, and he'd laid out his dominoes on the top. Margot sat on the floor on the other side, attempting to play. As if she knew the rules. 'That's news to me.'

Apollo closed his eyes and ignored him. 'The thought just keeps saying death is certain; it's coming for us all.'

I leaned in the doorway and looked down at my friends. Margot sighed and shook her head. Josie typed notes on her phone. I looked up at the light for a sign from Rachel, but she had somewhere better to be tonight, it seemed.

'So why not . . . why not *live*?'

'Hmmm,' Mum murmured. 'That's a good point. Me too. I'm going to work harder on my relationships –'

Margot's head shot up. 'Really? How?'

'Concentrate on the game!' Whisper shouted, slamming down a white-spotted domino.

Mum smiled. 'I don't have many friends, so I'm going to appreciate the ones I have. Anyway –' she gently touched Apollo's knee – 'sorry, I interrupted you. What does living – really living – mean to you? What's your plan?'

Apollo took a breath in through his teeth. 'Well, I'm throwing myself into my work.' He raised his glass in front of him. 'I won't be held back any more.'

'What's holding you back?' I asked.

'Fear of failure, the usual,' Apollo said. 'Thinking I'm not good enough.'

Margot stared at the dominoes. 'I think you're a good writer,' she lied. I could tell. No eye contact. 'I read some of your work last night. I . . . enjoyed it.'

She was going in.

Without looking at Mum, Apollo thrust his wine glass into her hand. He sat forward, almost falling off the edge of the sofa. 'You read some, darling? What did you think?'

He put his hands out. 'Now, be honest – I like critique. I can take it.'

'Bet you can't,' said Whisper. He sipped tea and winked at Margot.

'Well, I liked *Apollo's Agony*. That one grabbed me.'

'It did, darling?' He turned to Mum. 'That one's about the time I got my first spot.'

'Right . . .' Mum replied.

Apollo waved his hand. 'Go on, what else? What else did you like?'

'*Titus Apollocus* was a lot.' Margot shuddered. 'Visceral.'

Apollo clapped his hands together. 'Your taste.' He chef-kissed his fingers. 'Impeccable.'

Margot glanced at Josie, then me, then over at Apollo. 'But my favourite piece –'

'Yes, tell me!' he said, his begging eyes wide and eager to know.

'Was *Close*,' said Margot. She stared at Apollo, waiting for his reaction, as did everyone in the room.

'The only one that didn't have your name in the title,' I added, a nice little jab to make it worse.

Apollo's eyes flashed, and he snatched his wine glass from Mum's hand. He took a gulp and sat back. 'It's very different from . . . my other work,' he said quietly.

'Yep,' Margot agreed. 'I could feel that. I really liked the characters.' She shifted slightly on the floor to include Mum and Whisper in the conversation. '*Close* has three – the others mostly have just one.'

Yeah, one person called Apollo. This psycho.

'In this one someone's called Rachel –'

'It's *not* about her,' Apollo blurted out, looking around the room, begging for people to believe him.

'Then you have Naomi, Rachel's best friend –'

'They're more like sisters, I'd say,' said Apollo, drumming his lip. 'I wrote them to be like sisters, yes.'

Sure you did, liar.

'And a cute boy with a funny accent that Rachel has a crush on.'

Mum grinned. 'Oh yes? What's his name?'

'Rocky,' said Margot.

'Oh.' Mum sat still. She stared at Margot for a moment. I looked at her. 'What?'

Mum shook her head and smiled. 'Nothing.' She waved her hand. 'I'm being silly. Nothing.'

'Rocky like the boxer,' said Whisper. He set his tea down next to his dominoes and sparred with the air in front of him. 'That's a good film.'

'Yeah,' said Mum quietly. 'I like that one too.'

Apollo nodded. 'It moved me.' He looked down at Margot and raised his glass in her direction. 'Thank you for reading them. I do appreciate it. And, you know, in the spirit of living and throwing myself into work, I've booked a little theatre space near home for some intimate performances. Come!' He looked at Josie and me, then at Mum – but definitely not at Whisper, who chuckled. 'All of you. See how you feel about *Apollo's*

Agony when you experience it live – you might change your mind.'

Whisper smiled. 'No thanks, this is painful enough.'

I looked at my friends, then spoke up. 'You know, that might actually be cool. Can I go, Mum?'

'I'll think about it,' said Mum, glancing sideways at Apollo. 'You'll need to go with an adult.'

'We could go up with my dad?' said Margot. 'He goes to London every day; we can just tag along.'

No eye contact. Well played, Margot.

'OK,' said Mum.

'Great! Come to rehearsal, early in the day.' Apollo tapped his feet excitedly. 'I'll get you all standing under the spotlight.'

'Yeah, sure,' I said. 'Where is it?'

'Hammersmith,' said Apollo. 'West London. Have you been there?'

Margot nodded. 'Been there? I'm *from* there. My mum lives there.'

'Oh, well, that's just perfect – you can visit her, then me – or, better yet, bring her along.'

Margot shook her head. 'She's on holiday – and she's put the house on Airbnb so it's a no-go zone at the mo.'

Josie held her phone out. 'Can we come tomorrow? We've got time.'

'Tomorrow I'm booked solid. Thursday?' said Apollo. 'Day after?'

'Fine!' we answered in unison.

There were three short knocks on the door. Tap, tap, tap. I leaned into the hallway to see if it was Lauren or Hazel. Through the glass I could see it was both. The two of them, together again.

I was closest to the door so I had to get it.

And get into it with Lauren.

3

I steadied myself before I opened the door. I gulped down a deep breath and quickly ran through ideas on how to handle my main opp, Lauren. I was like WWJD – What Would Josie Do?

I decided to be charming, Wes-style. It was the only way. I faked a smile and opened the door. 'Hi!' I said, making sure I nodded and looked at Lauren to show her I wasn't a threat, not right now anyway. 'Everyone's here.' I put on a confused laugh. 'How come you two *always* come together? Crazy coincidence, am I right?'

Lauren opened her mouth to respond, but Hazel jumped in first. 'Oh,' she said, waving her hand, 'I've been giving her a lift since I dented her car. We live close and it saves the environment – I don't mind the company either.'

'Ah,' I said, still looking at a silent Lauren. 'How are you both anyway? You good?'

'Not bad, Wesley,' Hazel said. She looked over to Rachel's house. 'Still can't get back in,' she said, shaking her head. 'I just hope they're being . . .'

'Thorough?' said Lauren, staring at me.

This woman hated me.

'Of course,' said Hazel. 'And careful.'

'Right,' I said nervously. 'That's important.'

I leaned out of the door to look. Same as earlier: police tape but no police people.

'You wondering why they haven't arrested me yet?' said Lauren, her eyes burning holes through my body. 'That why you're not letting us in? Waiting for the cops to scoop me up?'

I gulped and gripped the edge of the door. 'Lauren, listen. I just told them what I saw – I wasn't saying it was *you*, was I?' I looked at her. 'Plus, you're not wearing your hoodie today, so they can't get you – you look too different.' I tried to laugh at my oh-so-witty joke, but she didn't, of course. 'But, yeah, I'm sorry if it made you look or feel bad.'

Lies. I wasn't sorry.

'Whatever,' she replied. 'It doesn't matter anyway. It's pointless.'

'Pointless how? How can an investigation be pointless?'

Lauren looked around the close and shrugged. 'This one just is.' She glanced sideways at me and sighed. 'You know what? I don't need this.'

'Lauren . . .' said Hazel slowly.

Lauren surveyed the darkening sky. 'I just need a moment. I'll be back.'

I peeked at Hazel, who watched Lauren stomp down the close towards Copsey Avenue. Hazel shrugged and stepped into the house. 'Oh, dominoes!' she said to Whisper. She looked down at Margot. 'I'll play you next.'

'No Lauren?' said Apollo, drumming his chin. 'Arrested?'

Josie gasped. 'No way!'

Hazel narrowed her eyes at Apollo, her normally soft face hardening. 'No.' She looked at me. 'She's gone for a walk, hasn't she?'

I nodded. 'Yeah.'

'Hmmm, on a perp walk to jail,' Apollo whispered.

Mum stood up to give Hazel a seat on the sofa. 'You heard anything?' She wrapped her arms round herself. 'They called you yet?'

Hazel shook her head. 'Nothing from the police,' she said. 'Lauren hasn't heard from them either.'

Margot looked confused at that.

'I've tried calling, but they don't have any information, not yet. What about all of you?'

Mum, Whisper and Apollo shook their heads. Hazel sighed. 'It's the waiting that's getting to me,' she said. 'Feels like I'm not doing anything constructive or useful. Apart from tending to the horses, of course.'

'You have horses?' said Margot, sitting up.

Hazel nodded.

'Wow,' said Whisper. 'You race them?' He leaned forward, turning a domino over in his hand. 'You got any tips? I'm always ready to place a bet on the gee-gees.'

Hazel laughed gently and shook her head. 'No, no, I don't race. I just teach people to ride. That's how I met Rachel.'

I looked at Margot and Josie. Interesting.

'Rachel wanted to ride horses?' Apollo sat up. 'That doesn't . . . track,' he said, laughing at his joke.

'Yeah,' said Mum. 'I'm sure I remember her telling me she didn't like them.'

'It's more than that – she was allergic,' said Apollo. 'We went to a friend's – a real horse girl's – country house one summer day and she was sneezing up a storm!'

Hazel rubbed her chin. 'Hmmm, she did have a cold on the day.'

'What happened?' I asked.

'Well,' said Hazel, 'Rachel reached out because she wanted to learn – it was something she'd always wanted to do, had to do, in fact –'

Apollo shook his confused head.

'So we arranged a time, and when she arrived at mine – the riding school is attached to my house – she said she had a bit of a cold. By the time we got to the horses she wasn't doing so well.'

'Did she actually ride?' asked Margot.

'Rachel got on Bellamy, but she was sneezing so much – and was so very nervous – that we ended the lesson. She was disappointed, to the point of tears. It was very sweet.'

'Oh,' said Josie, looking at her phone. 'Is that why you gave her a horse-riding helmet for her birthday?'

Hazel nodded. 'Yes, I was hoping she'd find the courage – and be well enough – to get back in the saddle. It wasn't to be, but at least I was able to give her a home for a while.'

The living-room light flickered. Rachel was back!

Mum looked up and tutted. 'Need to change that bulb. They're supposed to be long-life. What a scam.'

'I *love* horse riding,' said Margot with a sigh. 'Miss it.'

'You'd be very welcome at my school,' said Hazel. 'I'd love to have you.'

'How about tomorrow?' said Margot quickly.

Hazel blinked quickly. 'Tomorrow I'm booked, but Friday's more free.'

Margot looked at Josie and me and we nodded. 'Great,' she said. 'Can't wait!'

Apollo chuckled. 'Look at you lot – the theatre *and* horse riding this week? Really getting around.'

'It's good for them to get out, learn things, take their mind off this,' said Mum. 'It's what Rachel would have wanted, I think.'

The overhead light above us flashed brightly just once. Rachel agreed. The plan was planning.

Mum's phone beeped. 'Oh!' she said. 'Molly is about to get on her flight.' She closed her eyes and made the sign of the cross on her chest. 'Safe travel, sis,' she said as she tapped out her message.

'Oh! That reminds me. Speaking of sisters,' Hazel said, sitting straighter and addressing the room. 'I called Rachel's next-of-kin number on her lease again, but it was disconnected –'

'Or you've been blocked,' said Margot.

'Did you look at the name?' I said, suddenly nervous.

This could be the big breakthrough our investigation needed. I held my breath.

'Yes,' said Hazel. 'Her name is Caroline Nicholls.'

Caroline Nicholls.

The only guest who hadn't come to Rachel's party.

4

Margot handed her dominoes to Hazel. The three of us tiptoed out of the living room, but stormed up the stairs. The sibs were still at holiday club, so we had the privacy of my room for now. Downstairs, someone turned on some music and the adults laughed at something together.

Guess what? Whisper laughed the loudest. Surprise.

'Caroline Nicholls,' said Josie breathlessly. 'The sixth invitee.'

'But she's in Canada, innit?' I said.

Margot nodded and put her phone in front of her so we could all see the screen. We looked at Caroline's lightly tanned face and long blonde hair.

I wrinkled my nose. 'They don't look like sisters. I mean, this lady looks fully white. So what's this? Rachel was adopted?'

'Maybe, or they might have been really close and called each other sisters?' said Margot.

'Possibly,' said Josie. 'My mum calls quite a few older women "auntie" and they aren't real relatives.'

'OK, that's cool and all, but, like, none of that explains why Caroline wouldn't know who Rachel was when Hazel called her,' I said. 'What kind of next of kin is that?'

'And why would a man be answering her phone?' asked Margot.

'Maybe she's just got a deep voice?' said Josie. 'Don't judge.'

'So what now?' I asked. 'Message Caroline?'

Josie took a sharp breath. 'We'd have to be *really* sensitive – Hazel doesn't have her number, so she probably doesn't know that her sister's dead. You didn't message her about it, did you, Margot?'

Margot shook her head. 'I only told the people who came to the party.' Her hand trembled slightly and her phone wobbled. 'Gah, I'm nervous, but I think we should do it. She needs to know. Agreed?'

I nodded. 'It's the best lead we've got.'

Margot took a deep breath and began to type. *Hello Caroline, we have some sad news about your sister, Rachel. Please let me know when you get this.* She looked up. 'How's that?'

Josie nodded, but I shrugged. I'd just tell her if I was doing it. Just give her the bad news in one hit.

Margot winced as she pressed send on the message. 'OK, done. Hopefully we'll hear something soon.'

'You know what? I want to call that number,' I said. 'The one that Hazel has.' I sat on my bed. 'Something smells like salt fish. I want to see if it's really, actually disconnected or whoever just blocked her like you said, Margot. I mean, I would block Hazel if she was blowing up my phone constantly.'

'We could try to find it when we go to Hazel's?' said Margot. 'She said her home and stables are at the same place – maybe her office is too?'

'Trespassing . . .' said Josie through her teeth.

'Don't care,' I said. 'The only passing I care about is Rachel's, to the other side. You saw the lights go wonky, right?'

They nodded.

'You know that was Rachel, don't you? Telling us we have to go to Apollo's and Hazel's.'

Josie didn't know or believe. She changed the subject.

'Nice lie about your dad, Margot,' she said.

Margot took a little bow 'Thanks. Yeah, he's not coming with us. And, yep, to your point, Wes, I felt Rachel tonight too.'

'Can you feel this?' said Josie, punching her playfully on the leg.

'I tell you what I'm not feeling – Hazel's horses.' I shuddered. 'Too big. They can end you in an instant if they feel like it, with their giant heads and hooves. They're not to be trusted.'

Margot smiled and went to the window to gaze over my concrete yard. 'They're amazing, Wes. You'll see.'

'I'm good being blind, thanks.'

Josie looked down at her phone. 'It's interesting, don't you think, that Rachel was really trying to ride, even though she was allergic and afraid?'

'Another one of her contradictions,' said Margot.

'Hmmm,' said Josie.

The smell of cigarettes wafted up from the yard. 'Gross,' I spat. 'Who in the hell is smoking in this era and economy?' I ran to the window.

'I bet it's Apollo,' said Josie.

We looked down. It was Hazel, and she wasn't alone. Lauren was back. Her arms were folded tightly across her body.

'Together again,' Margot whispered.

'Right!?' I opened the window wider. 'I said that to them when they arrived.'

Hazel chuckled in a low voice, putting the cigarette to her lips. 'So your money's on Ella? Mine is. She has keys – who knows what happened later? I told the police that.'

I could feel my blood start to simmer and my heart hop. Not only was she talking about Mum, but she said she wasn't one for betting too. Josie grabbed my shaking hand.

'Stop it, Hazel,' said Lauren.

Inside the house, Whisper laughed.

'Eurgh, his voice,' Hazel spat. 'Seven more nights of him slamming down those dominoes?'

'It's a nice thing to do,' said Lauren with a sigh.

'Nice? Nice would be finding that Caroline Nicholls. You have to help me.'

'I don't have to do anything for you, Hazel. Not again. Not any more.' Lauren threw open the kitchen door and walked back into the house.

Hazel threw her still-smoking cigarette on the ground. 'Coming, Whisper!' she trilled.

I closed the window and stared at my friends. 'Those fake, sneaky snakes!' I grabbed at my chest. 'They think Mum did it too? They're talking to the police about her.'

'Only Hazel said that, not Lauren,' said Josie.

'Why are you defending them?!' I shouted, pacing around the room.

'I'm not,' Josie muttered. 'I'm just giving you the facts.'

Margot put her hands on my shoulders, but looked at Josie. 'Let's talk about some other facts, OK? It looks like Lauren and Hazel do know each other . . .'

'But are hiding their connection,' said Josie.

'Maybe they did do this together?' suggested Margot.

'Not if Hazel thinks Mum killed Rachel!' I snapped. 'That was a private conversation!'

Margot and Josie stood in silence with that truth. The truth that only made Mum the chief suspect.

'Well, that could be their cover story,' said Margot desperately. 'Pinning it on Ella is their alibi.'

'That could be true,' said Josie slowly, keeping her eyes on Margot. 'What if Lauren hurt Rachel to get her out of Hazel's house? A favour? That's why Hazel's so keen to get hold of Caroline.'

'And you did think you saw Lauren that night,' said Margot, squeezing my shoulders. 'Remember?'

'And they have to come to nine night because otherwise they'll look guilty,' I muttered, not believing any of the words that left my lips.

'Right,' said Margot, nervously glancing back at Josie. 'Right.'

They were trying their best, but I knew what I had to do.

I had to speak to Mum. For real this time. No messing.

DAY THREE
WEDNESDAY 12 APRIL

1

So last night was fun. Instead of sleeping or thinking about how everyone thought Mum was guilty, I had this dream where Mum and Rachel swapped places.

Yeah.

Mum was in the morgue and Rachel was all up in my house, cooking dinner, sleeping in Mum's bed, trying to give me advice. She straight up took over. Whisper was there too, sipping his sorrel tea. He was laughing, shouting, saying, 'I told you so.'

I woke up thinking him and Rachel's duppy were in cahoots to cause chaos and, honestly, I wouldn't put it past them.

Weird dreams are the worst, but real life wasn't much better. I had to face Mum this morning. It couldn't wait.

The sibs were gone when I got out of bed. The smell of bacon wafted up as I walked down the stairs. Music was on in the kitchen. Mum was singing, badly.

She had her back to me, loading the washing machine. In went pants, socks, my jeans and a large grey hoodie.

Wait.

A grey hoodie?

'Mum!' I shouted over the music. 'Mum!' I rushed over and grabbed her back. She gasped, jumping in shock. When she recognized me, instead of calming down, she slammed the washing machine's door shut and quickly turned it on.

'Nah, Mum.' I shook my head. 'What's going on?'

'What?' she shouted over the music, pretending not to understand.

I pointed to the machine now gurgling, filling with water. 'Whose hoodie was that?'

'I can't hear you,' she said, pointing to her ears. 'Turn the music down.'

I stared at her as I felt behind me on the counter for her phone. When I found it, I looked at it, ready to shut down Spotify.

But I didn't like two things I saw.

The first was her new background photo. A smiling selfie of her and Rachel.

The second was a message. I couldn't tell who it was from. Instead of a name there was an emoji of a boulder. The message said, *Yeah? He said that? Me too. I feel the same.* There were four red heart emojis after it.

He?

Four? Red? Hearts?

My heart pounded. *Who was this?*

Why were they messaging her like this?

Did she have a boyfriend? A girlfriend? Lauren? Is that why she wasn't wearing her hoodie last night? She left it here by mistake?

My mind and stomach churned like they were in that washing machine.

I looked up at her and saw her gulp. We stared at each other until I turned the music down.

I took a deep breath. 'Mum, don't play me, OK?'

Her eyes grew large. 'I-I don't know what you mean, Wes.' She hurried over to the cooker and shook the frying pan. 'Ready for a bacon sarnie?' she said lightly, avoiding eye contact.

A sure sign of guilt.

'Whose hoodie was that?' I asked quietly.

'Oh,' she said, waving her hand, 'that's yours, isn't it?'

I shook my head. 'We both know it's not.'

'Ah, well, it must be mine – you know I have loads of old ones lying around for when I'm cleaning and tidying.'

I have never seen this woman in a hoodie. Not once, in my whole eleven years.

'Is it Lauren's?' I asked. 'The one she was wearing after Rachel's party? I saw someone like her in the close. You know that.'

Mum laughed. 'Now why would I have her clothes, Wes? I barely know the girl.'

'You tell me.'

Mum drummed her lip. 'You know, she may have left it here after one of the nine nights – and that's how it ended up in the washing basket.' She slapped her forehead with the palm of her hand. 'Ah, that makes sense now!'

'It doesn't.' My lip wobbled. 'You're not being real with me, Mum, and I'm worried.'

'Worried about what?' she said, intently flipping the bacon in the pan. The fat spat at her and sprayed all over the hob.

'That you've done something!' I shouted and began counting on my fingers. 'You're supposed best friend's dead. Her flipping ghost is floating around. You're acting weird, clinking glasses in the middle of the night, washing random clothes, getting messages from people with no names – just emojis – and people think you're moving mad!'

She tightened her dressing-gown cord round her waist. 'Which people?'

'Oh, that's the important thing, is it?' I said, snorting hot air out on to my lip. 'What's going on?!'

Behind me, on the counter, her phone beeped again. I looked over at her and she gasped and bounded over, but I got there first.

This message wasn't from Boulder Bae or whoever that chump who sent four red hearts was. It was from Auntie Molly.

Mum peered over my shoulder to see the screen.

Are you telling them? You need to. What will Wes say?

'*What's Wes going to say?*' My hand trembled. 'About what?'

Mum bit her lip and looked down. 'Nothing, nothing yet,' she said quietly.

'*Nothing?*' I shouted. 'Oh, it's just *nothing* that you – and now maybe with an assist from Lauren by the looks of that jumper in the wash – have something to do with what happened to Rachel?!'

Mum wrinkled her nose and stood back. 'What?'

My heart raced. 'Yeah! Well, that's what it looks like!' I raised my voice. 'You're either dating her, or, like . . . I dunno – doing death with her!'

My bottom lip was trembling out of control and I . . . I just screamed in frustration in her direction. I hit the counter with a closed fist and stomped out of the kitchen.

'Wes, wait!' Mum called behind me, but I was already halfway up the stairs.

In my room, I reached under the pillow for my phone. A message from Josie in Copsey Chat was waiting for me, but I swiped it away, along with angry tears.

Instead of calling the Copseys, I messaged Auntie Molly.

2

I'd stopped crying but I was still fuming when I stomped over to Margot's. My mum was beyond sus now – she was straight up lying to my face. My face! Her own son's! Murderer or not, this was still an offence. I could not believe she was doing me like this. How could I defend her – against Margot and Josie or, worse, Hazel – if she didn't tell me the whole truth? How could I, her top boy, believe in her?

I couldn't. I'd never been more scared. My world as I knew it was shifting under my feet and evaporating behind me.

I banged on Margot's door, then checked my phone to see if there was any word from Auntie Molly.

Nothing.

What a pair of snaky sisters those two were. Hissing and hiding secrets together.

I looked over to Rachel's house and nodded, basically letting her know I was still sending her to the other realm. The plan was still on. The police tape that had been wrapped round it had gone.

Margot opened the door. 'All right?' She leaned forward and peered at my scowling face. 'I'll take that as a no.'

I stomped up the stairs behind her. Josie was sitting at Margot's desk. 'Morning, Wes.' She looked at Margot, who lay down on her bed. 'Go on then, what happened?' She drummed her fingers on the desk. 'Did you speak to your mum?'

I rubbed my face and didn't answer. My phone danced in my pocket. Auntie Molly.

Stay out of grown people's business, Wesley.

When I tell you I threw that phone, I mean I properly launched it at Margot's bed in frustration. It narrowly missed her legs and bounced off the mattress, landing face down on the floor.

'She's guilty,' I said flatly. 'Mum did it.'

'What?' Margot hissed, sitting up. 'No.' She shook her head. 'No, it's impossible.'

'Let's hear him first,' said Josie quietly. 'We need the evidence. Wes, go on.'

'She's a liar for a start,' I said, my hands in my hair, massaging my head, working out all the whirling thoughts and feelings in there. 'I went downstairs, right, into the kitchen. She's doing a load of laundry and guess what was in there?'

'Your sleep shorts that you tried wearing on the street yesterday?' said Margot.

'Not funny and no. She was washing –' I balled my hands – 'a grey hoodie.'

Margot clutched her chest; she didn't move or say a word. I looked over at Josie, whose eyes were on stalks at this point. 'Was it one of yours?' she asked, pulling her phone towards her on the desk.

'I would know if it was mine, wouldn't I? Stupid!' I said. 'It wasn't!' I took a breath. 'Sorry for calling you stupid. I'm just mad.'

'Yeah, not cool, but carry on,' said Josie. 'Was it the same one the person you saw in the close was wearing?' She looked over at Margot, who was still frozen solid. 'Margot!' she shouted, clicking her fingers. 'We haven't got time to play statues or whatever it is you're doing! Three, two, one – get back into the room!'

Margot blinked. 'Is it Lauren's?' she whispered.

'It blinking looks like it!' I said. 'Even if there's the tiniest chance it's not, it still doesn't belong to anyone in our house, so, yeah, there's someone on the scene. I also saw her phone – twice! – and there were two bad messages on there. Not one. Two!'

Margot buried her head in her hands. 'I almost don't want to know,' she said. She looked up and flopped her arms beside her on the bed. 'Ella, why?' she shouted to the day-glo stars on her ceiling.

'Margot, please!' said Josie. 'Who were they from? We need details.'

'She had a message from Boulder Bae –'

'Boulder Bae?' whispered Margot. 'This is who we think she's been seeing? Clinking glasses with? Do you think it's Lauren? Ella and Lauren?' Margot shook her head. 'Not a match.'

'Well, it's someone she's clearly loving on – I'm not stupid. No name saved in the phone, just like this rock emoji instead. Plus, get this, there were hearts at the end of the message. Red ones – not normal friendly ones, in like white, yellow or green. Love ones.'

'How many hearts?' asked Josie.

'Four. Flipping four!'

'Oh, snap,' said Margot under her breath. 'You might be right.'

'*Might be?* I know I am! Ask me how I know.'

'Go on,' said Josie. 'How?'

'Because, while we were getting into it and I was interrogating her, her phone went off again –'

'Boulder Bae?' asked Margot, drumming her fingertips together.

I shook my head. 'Auntie Molly.'

'Oh,' said Josie, disappointed.

'Wait until you near what she said. She said, "*Are you telling them? You need to. What will Wes say?*"'

'No. Way,' said Margot. She tutted and sighed. 'Well, well, w-Ella.'

'Right!' I said. 'So I did what needed to be done and I texted Auntie Molly immediately and was like, yo, I saw that message you sent Mum, what's going on? What do I need to know?'

'And?' said Josie.

'And she just told me to stay out of adult business.' I sighed and lay on Margot's bed next to her. 'I can't believe it,' I whimpered, covering my eyes with my arms. 'I can't believe this is happening to me.'

I heard Josie set her phone down on the desk. 'OK, first of all, well done for speaking to her.'

'Oh yeah, it went great. I'm so proud of myself.'

'There are some scenarios we can develop from this information,' she said.

'The best, most positive one being she's not connected to Rachel's death at all, but she's got a secret boyfriend,' said Margot. 'Could it be Craig?'

'Better not be!' I snapped. 'But Mum did bring him up the other night. Asked me if I miss him.'

'So did Whisper,' said Margot. 'Maybe there's something in that.'

'Hope not,' I said.

'Or,' said Josie, 'the alternative is that your mum and this person –' she paused to find her words – 'got rid of Rachel together when you went to bed and then they celebrated later.'

'And that person is Lauren,' I said. 'To think I had a dream last night where Mum and Rachel swapped places, and I felt all sick and sad about it. Now I'm, like, maybe –'

Margot leaned over and covered my mouth with her hands. 'No, no! Don't say that! *Never* say anything like that.'

'Not out loud at least,' added Josie.

'Lauren and Ella working together just doesn't fit,' said Margot. 'They didn't know each other before; your mum was talking about setting Molly and Rachel up. It doesn't work.' She shook her head. 'We're missing something.'

'Yeah, we are,' I said. 'The truth. I hate secrets; they make my stomach hurt, so me and Mum promised to always tell each other the truth. Like . . . this is so crazy. She was just lying to my face, Margot. Doing up Pinocchio.'

Margot nodded. 'Yep, yeah, I hear you and I'm really sorry, Wes. On the other hand, though –'

'There is no other hand! This is limbless.'

She started again. 'On the other hand, if this is the best-case scenario and Ella is now seeing someone, that is her right. She's an adult with the right to privacy. Remember, she's more than just your mum, you know – murder suspect aside – outside our investigation.'

All I could do was grunt at her honestly fair point.

Josie broke our few seconds of silence with one of her polite fake coughs. 'Ahem, speaking of the investigation, where's the police tape? It's the reason I called this meeting.'

'You didn't call diddly, Jo,' I said. 'But, yeah, I clocked that too.'

'Do you think they've solved the case? Before us?' said Margot, disappointment dripping off every word. 'They can't have.'

'I mean, they might have,' I said. 'They are professionals.'

Margot leaped off the bed. 'I'm not having that,' she said. She paced around her room, biting at her nails. 'I'll do something. Find out what they know.' She looked down at my phone, still face down on the floor. Margot squealed when she picked it up and showed us the case.

Inside was the business card PC Stevens gave me on Monday. A smile slowly crawled towards Margot's shining eyes.

3

Margot looked between her phone and the back of mine as she punched in the numbers. She cleared her throat in preparation. 'I'll just act natural,' she said. 'I'll ask for an update and, whatever the outcome, I won't scream or do anything silly. I'll stay in character, OK?' She took a deep breath. 'I'll channel Her Mothership.'

'The cops aren't just gonna tell us who the murderer is, Margot,' I said. 'He ain't gonna announce it like it's the BAFTAs or something.'

'He's right,' added Josie. 'Put us on loudspeaker, so we can hear?' She took deep breaths. 'I'm nervous. More than I thought I would be.'

My heart was pounding too. Too fast for my health and sanity. I had to be put out of my misery. I leaned over and tapped the green button on Margot's phone. She shook her head as the ringtone reverberated around her room.

'PC Stevens,' the voice said on pick-up.

Margot closed her eyes. 'Ah, hello? PC Stevens? This is . . . Morgana Foxley calling,' she said in the coldest, sharpest, poshest voice I'd ever heard. I looked at her, floored, truly stunned at her tone. Best actress in a mystery goes to Margot. I stared at her face. *This* is what her mum sounds like? Like an evil headmistress at a boarding school? No wonder she's obsessed with mine.

Josie rolled her eyes; she'd heard this voice before.

'This is he. Hello there, how can I help?'

'I'm calling in regard to the death Rachel Kohl, of three Copsey Close? My daughter and her friends have been . . . involved in the case.'

'Oh?' said PC Stevens, sounding unsure. 'Oh yes! That's funny timing.' We heard him flicking through his notebook. 'Sorry, who is your daughter? Are you Margot's mother?'

'I am she, yes,' said Margot, trying to fight back a smile. 'Using my maiden name. A long story for another time.'

'Ah,' said PC Stevens. 'Margot is using your Facebook profile, just so you know. You might want to change your passwords.'

Margot winced. 'I . . . I will speak to her. PC Stevens, you said funny timing – funny timing how? My daughter and her friends are *sick* with worry – absolutely consumed by it. I'm told there is no longer a police presence on the close and I'd like to be updated on the murder investigation and get the children into counselling as soon as possible –'

'Wait, Ms Foxley – Morgana, if I may. Murder? The children told you this was a murder case?'

Margot paused. 'Well, of course, PC Stevens. What are they to think? What do I tell them?'

There was silence on his end.

'You can tell them their friend wasn't murdered. You can start there.'

The three of us stared at each other in complete shock. Time slowed around us.

Margot steadied herself against her bedframe. 'I'm sorry, what?' she said, her mother's voice starting to slip away.

Josie put a steadying hand on her back to help her keep up her act.

'Their friend was not murdered – she died of natural causes. I hope that brings them some comfort in this terrible time.'

It did. The weight of a forty-year-old woman lifted off my shoulders. Mum *hadn't* done dark-sided stuff after all. Sure, she was still a toxic liar, but not a murderer. I could work with that. I sighed and smiled, but, as soon as I did, I regretted it.

The weight was back, but now floating around me. Rachel's duppy.

Margot looked disappointed somehow. 'Well, that is indeed good news – they have nothing to fear now, except ghosts,' she said, staring at me. 'But, PC Stevens, if I may, what happened? It's rare for forty-year-olds to die suddenly, surely?'

'Well, funny timing –'

There he went again.

'We had confirmation. Her autopsy report was emailed over this morning.'

We waited for him to continue, but he didn't. We looked at each other.

'And the verdict was . . . ?' Margot asked.

'Ah,' he said. 'Complications from cancer, Morgana. An internal bleed, I'm very sorry to say.'

We stared at each other in the saddest shock. My eyes stung with incoming tears. Cancer? And *nobody* knew?

'I plan on calling Rachel's close friends, those who I've met in person. I've only spoken to one of them so far this morning.'

'Who was the first?' asked Margot, trying to stop her voice from wobbling.

PC Stevens paused. 'It's OK to cry, Morgana,' he said quietly. 'It's terrible. A colleague returned Rachel's belongings to her house,' he continued, ignoring her question. 'We'll issue the paperwork and look after her until we can find her next of kin. They'll need to register her for a death certificate.' He paused. 'We, erm, can't find details for Rachel, but, rest assured, I'm on it.'

Margot swallowed. 'And what if you don't find anyone? What then?'

PC Stevens took a deep breath. 'Well, we can make the arrangements,' he said. 'But it is better for family – and friends if need be – to be involved. It's better for the deceased.'

I gulped. Rachel's duppy brushed past my ear as if to tell me 'I told you so'.

'We'll be involved,' said Margot. 'We'll make sure of it. Thank you for your update. I will pass it on to . . . the children.'

She quickly ended the call and sat on her bed. 'Cancer,' she said softly. Josie put an arm round her shoulder. 'Rachel died of cancer.' Margot put her head in her hands and began to cry.

'It's terrible,' I said gently. 'The *only* positive is that we haven't been hanging around with killers – or will be hanging around killers for another week.'

'That's true,' said Josie, wiping her eyes. 'We can feel better, safer, about going to nine night now. We can bring this investigation to a close.'

'No, we can't!' Margot and I shouted in unison.

'Why not?' said Josie. 'Oh, you're not serious, are you?'

I pointed to my shoulders. 'Her duppy,' I whispered, 'is right here. I can't live like this forever. Do you want to be haunted until you die because you thought you were too cool to believe in ghosts, Josie? Because when Rachel's tugging your toes in the night, hiding behind your desk and rocking up in your dreams like she did mine, do *not* come crying to us. You know why?'

'Why?'

'Because it will be your fault. And you know what I'll say?'

'What?'

'I told you so,' I hissed. 'I know how much you hate that.'

Josie shuddered. I got her where it hurt.

'And, to make sure we get her to the other side, we have to tie up loose ends and help her finish her business here on earth – that's what Whisper said, right?' said Margot, looking at me. 'We have to find her next of kin – PC Stevens said he was struggling, but why? Because, as we know, so much is unclear – her friends don't know her whole truth, do they? Whisper has his suspicions about her. Apollo's play *Close* is totally about her, whatever he says –'

'Lauren and Hazel are hiding something that might tell us more,' I added. 'Plus, we haven't told her sister Caroline yet either – or found out facts about Rachel from her.'

'Don't forget Ella and Boulder Bae,' said Margot, looking at me.

I hadn't. I wish I'd never given them that name either. 'They ain't got nothing to do with this.'

'I'm not so sure,' said Margot. 'Remember your mum said she wasn't close to Rachel recently – is that person the reason?'

'Hmmm,' said Josie. 'Plus the Amazon boxes, Rachel's locked bedroom door –'

'Exactly. *That's* where we have to do the final nine night. *That's* where she has to pass through to go to the other realm,' I said. 'Whisper said they go through their favourite places, and that's gotta be it.'

Margot nodded. 'So we get to the bottom of everyone's . . . weirdness. Through that we find her family and send Rachel off properly. We can't leave it to the police and to Hazel.' She shuddered. 'Are we all still in?'

'Girl, I never left. I'm not leaving until Rachel does,' I said.

Josie paused, then nodded. 'Me neither.' She looked down at her notes. 'These aren't fit for purpose now . . . What next?'

Margot's eyes flashed. 'PC Stevens said that we were the second people he told, right?'

Josie nodded again. 'And they'd returned her things.'

They both looked at me.

'You still have the key to Rachel's, right?' asked Margot. 'Because we don't have much time.'

4

When I went back for Rachel's key, Mum had gone to work. Good job and all, because we'd have to get into it, do sorries and cuddles – maybe she'd throw a light grounding my way for popping off like that. There was no time for that.

Rachel would not wait. I refused to let her wait.

Margot and Josie stood outside my front door, keeping an eye on the close. Looking out for Lauren or Hazel or both together, knowing them. I bet one of them – I was leaning towards Hazel, since she had form for it – called PC Stevens. Rachel's key was on my mantelpiece. I snatched it, stuck it in my pocket and pulled my hood over my head.

'Got it,' I whispered to my friends.

I shut the door behind me and we ran across the road. As I put the key into Rachel's door, the two of them covered me. It unlocked, I pushed it and we jumped inside, shutting the door quietly behind us.

We were back and oh yeah, Rachel was still here, for sure. I could feel her, all around us.

Margot and Josie felt her too; they put their backs against the hallway wall and reached for each other's hands.

Josie nodded. 'I get it now,' she whispered.

I never said I told you so, but oooh, I wanted to, I tell you.

Margot glanced at the front door, then looked up the stairs. 'Right, we don't have much time – if PC Stevens has spoken to Hazel, I have a feeling she'll be here soon. I get the vibe she wants her house back. So I think we do two things – check Rachel's bedroom because we haven't had a good look at it and we might find something out about Caroline.'

'We should try that locked door again,' I said. 'Or at least see if someone has touched the numbers.'

'Exactly right,' said Margot.

'It probably would have been the police, but it's definitely worth a look,' said Josie. She took a deep breath. 'Ready?'

Margot and I nodded and followed her up the stairs. The door to Rachel's room was open and a clear plastic package lay on her bed. Inside was the Spice Girls T-shirt she was wearing on Sunday night and on Monday morning when I found her. Something shiny shimmered in the light as I leaned forward to take a closer look. 'It's her necklace,' I said, turning away to blink back tears. I didn't want them two seeing me this sad.

Margot patted her chest. 'Yeah,' she croaked. 'She said that she, Rachel, had the other half, didn't she?'

I nodded. 'Maybe it's here?'

'Hopefully,' said Margot softly. 'OK, I'm investigating.'

I hung back for a bit, looking at Rachel's necklace, feeling her in the room, remembering the last time I saw her lying on the bed. I glanced under it, half expecting to see the paintbrush I'd dropped. I felt empty and hollow, like my stomach had been scooped out.

'I think I've found something!' said Margot. 'Come look.'

We huddled round Rachel's dressing table. There was a photograph attached to the mirror – one of those ones taken in a booth. You know, if you need one for a passport or something. It looked old, and it was. The Rachel in the picture was much younger. She looked only a bit older than us, fourteen maybe. Rachel had long black braids and she looked straight into the camera. She wasn't alone, though. Another girl, around the same age, sat statue-still next to her. Her long wavy blonde hair flowed out beneath a bucket hat. I squinted at the picture. 'Yo, is that Caroline?'

Margot reached into her pocket for her phone and pulled up Caroline's profile. She put the images side by side. 'I mean, it kind of looks like her, but I'm not sure.'

'Different angles,' said Josie. 'So it's hard to compare. They've both got long blonde hair; that's all we can get from this.'

'But it's something,' I said. 'It's some kind of a lead, right?'

'Sure. It's Caroline or someone Caroline-connected,' said Josie, nodding.

I took a picture of the picture, then zoomed into it on my phone. 'Rachel's wearing her necklace,' I said. 'But I can't tell if the other girl is.'

'Wrong angle.' Josie sighed. 'It's not much help.'

'I don't know – it must be a significant photo if she kept it for so long and put it in her bedroom where she could see it,' said Margot. 'It's not nothing. Right, next location.'

Rachel's front bedroom. The combination lock was still there, but this time the numbers weren't four zeros. There was one zero, but also three sixes. The Devil's number. If not him, then his evil minions. Welp.

'Why would someone do that?' I shuddered.

'Someone . . . or *something*,' said Margot with a gulp.

Josie bit her lip. 'It's just a coincidence. Surely.'

Margot shook her head. 'I doubt it. Look at what we're dealing with here with this case. This isn't coincidence – this is a message.'

'Don't, Margot,' I said, feeling the hairs rise on my neck. 'Don't even joke.'

'I'm not.' She inched her fingers forward. 'I don't know if I want to touch it. It might burn a hole in my hand.'

I didn't want to either, same reasons, but I closed my eyes and reached forward. It was comfortably cold. I twisted the numbers round and pulled with no plan. It made no difference.

'We'll have to try again later. Keep hold of that key, Wes.' Josie turned to us. 'Wait. Nine night will be here from now, won't it?'

'According to Whisper, yeah,' I said. 'But Hazel's not gonna be into it, since she can't stand the sound of his voice.'

'I mean, he's loud sure, but that was so rude!' said Margot. 'She's definitely not as nice as she pretends to be.'

'I'll never forgive her for trying to stitch Mum up,' I said, walking down the stairs. I shut the front door, and we stood outside Rachel's, looking up at the front bedroom, silently wondering what was behind the window.

Margot wagged her finger up at it. 'I will get inside you. You *will* give up your secrets.'

A small blue van drove up the close and pulled up beside us, AAA LOCKSMITH in sticky silver letters on its side.

A short woman carrying a toolbox whistled as she got out. 'Excuse me!' she said cheerfully, squeezing past us and walking up Rachel's path. She inspected Rachel's front door and began tapping away at the lock.

I looked down at the key in my hand, then up at Josie and Margot.

Margot shook her head. 'I told you time was tight, didn't I?'

NIGHT THREE
RACHEL'S DUPPY RISES

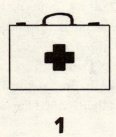

1

Margot looked over to Rachel's house, at the lights on in the living room and the figures moving around inside it. 'Whisper got his way – nine night has moved to its rightful place.'

'Thank God,' I said. 'Easier to get Rachel into that room and the other realm now.'

'Wonder how he did it?' Josie wondered as we walked there.

'The duppy, duh,' I said. 'Told him – and Hazel – through the lights, obvs.' At Rachel's door I took a pause before knocking. Not only did we have to investigate, but I also had to face Mum after this morning's kitchen kick-off. I kissed my teeth and sighed.

'Are you going to tell them we're here?' asked Josie. 'Or does the duppy know that already?' Why she was chuckling when it wasn't funny was a question for her silly self.

'Josie, stop playing. I'm just thinking. I have to make nice with Mum, or avoid her –'

'Also, they,' said Margot, pointing at the house, 'don't know that *we* know what happened to Rachel, so they might want to break the news.'

'So we act natural?' I said.

'You say that like acting natural is natural to us.' Margot laughed and then leaned forward and knocked on the door.

Mum opened the door and smiled nervously at me. The smell of fried food rushed towards us. Oh, it smelled good, but I had to deal with the bad first. Mum being the bad.

'All right, you three?' she said. 'You got the messages about the change in location then?'

I shook my head. 'Nah, I haven't looked at my phone. We've been busy.'

'I mean, we could tell,' said Margot, pointing to the window. 'Whatever you're cooking smells awesome, by the way.'

Mum smiled. 'Thanks, and, yeah, of course you noticed. Come in, eat.' Mum and I hung back to let Josie and Margot in first. 'You want to talk about this morning, Wes?' she asked with concerned eyes.

I did, but not with everyone here, not yet. 'When we get home, yeah?' I said.

I was still mad; I could tell by that familiar prickly feeling on my neck. I walked in front of her into the hallway. The package I'd taken in for Rachel leaned rain-warped and wrinkled against the wall. I turned to Mum. 'Thanks for bringing that over.' She nodded and tight-lipped smiled.

When I spun round to walk into the living room, I crashed right into Lauren. A small box she was carrying fell from her hands on to the floor in front of me.

'Watch where you're going,' she snapped, leaning down to reach the box, but I got there first.

I turned the box over in my hands. '*Buprenorphine*.' I sounded it out slowly under my breath. It was a big word, don't judge. I looked at the sticker on it. It was a prescription for Rachel Kohl. I looked up at Lauren, who gulped.

'Lauren,' I said, way louder than necessary to get the attention of my friends who were now sitting on the living-room floor, 'why do you have Rachel's medicine? Her smoking patches?'

The lights in the living room flashed, just as they had on the night of her party.

'Well, hello, Miss Rachel,' said Whisper, putting down his fork. 'Welcome home.'

I looked in Lauren's eyes. She needed my attention right now. 'Why you got these?'

'Wes,' Mum said behind me, putting her hand on my shoulder, 'there's something we need to tell you about Rachel – we all got some news this morning.'

'OK . . . ?' I said, knowing exactly what was coming.

'Rachel had cancer,' Mum said quietly. 'That's how she died. It wasn't . . . anything else you might have been thinking.'

'Or investigating,' Whisper added.

I looked at my friends.

'Act natural,' Margot mouthed.

'Oh,' I said, pretending this was news. 'That's so . . . sad.' I narrowed my eyes at Lauren. 'But why do you have her smoking patches, though? Can't afford your own?'

Lauren lunged forward as she tried to snatch the box from my hands. 'These aren't smoking patches – Rachel never smoked, no matter what she said at her party. I know that for a fact.'

'I knew it!' said Apollo and Whisper in unison. Whisper's fork fell to the floor, taking rice and peas along with it.

'These are for serious pain relief, for her cancer,' said Lauren, tears starting to form in her eyes. 'Cancer I knew she had this whole time.'

2

'What?!' said Hazel, spilling her sparkling water. 'You knew Rachel had cancer, and you didn't tell me?' She looked around the room and quickly corrected herself. 'Us, I mean. Why didn't you tell anyone?'

'She didn't tell me . . .' Mum whispered. Her eyes darted around the hallway. She blinked back tears, which she hastily wiped away with her sleeve.

'I *knew* something wasn't right,' said Whisper, pointing a finger. 'But I never thought cancer. Poor, poor Rachel.' He stared down at his plate. 'My appetite's just gone.'

Lauren stared at the ceiling and bit her lip to stop it from quivering. 'I wanted to tell people – of course I did!' She looked at me. 'You especially – I knew where your mind was going.'

'No, you didn't,' I spat.

'It wasn't me outside her house that night – you get that now?'

I looked back at Mum, who stared down at her feet.

'Darling, why didn't you tell us?!' Apollo shouted from the living room.

'Yeah,' I said. 'Were you in love with her?'

Lauren looked shocked. 'What? No! She was my client. I can't share the things they tell me.' She shook Rachel's patches near me. 'I needed to double-check to make sure I wasn't crazy, that these weren't anything to do with smoking.'

'How did you know she was sick?' Margot asked gently from the living-room floor. 'Through your massages?'

'No,' said Lauren, shaking her head. 'Massage doesn't work like that, not really . . . but . . .' She sighed. 'One day she came in, and she was just crying, silently crying as she lay on the table.'

'Oh gosh,' Mum whispered behind me.

'Rachel told me that day. She said she didn't want anyone else to know. What could I do?' She dug into her pocket for her phone and waved it in front of me. I leaned over to look. 'I tried. I messaged her over and over – to get more treatment, serious treatment, anything, but she said she didn't want it. She wasn't interested at all.'

'Why not, though?' I said, completely confused. 'Why not fight? Keep going?'

'Some of those treatments are very hard on the body,' said Whisper solemnly. 'I've seen it with my own dad, rest his soul. It was no life.' He pursed his lips and shook his head.

'Really sorry to hear that,' said Apollo quietly. He put his hand on Whisper's shoulder. 'I saw the same with my dad too.'

Whisper looked up at Apollo and patted his hand. 'Sorry to you too.'

'Exactly,' said Lauren. 'It can be very tough. Rachel said she didn't want to go out like that – her exact words. She needed her energy, she said, to do things, to live the life Rachel wanted.' Lauren laughed sadly. 'Doing her "Rachel" thing again.'

'Do you think she was hanging on for her role?' asked Apollo. 'In that play?'

'Honestly?' said Lauren. 'I'm not sure that play's even real. She said she was on the phone with me when she came into the party and we were running lines. Not true. How many massage therapists called Lauren can you have at once?'

Apollo rubbed his chin. 'Hmmm, you're right.'

'So she *didn't* have a job on the way,' Hazel huffed. She crossed her arms and furrowed her brow. Everyone looked at her. 'I mean . . . it would have been nice for her, wouldn't it?'

'It would've,' said Lauren. She sighed and threw her head back. 'I just . . . it's just all so sad. I haven't been right since she told me, and worse since she died. I've just been gutted. I just want to give her a good send-off –'

'Hear, hear,' said Whisper. He reached for his fork on the floor and raised it in Lauren's direction.

'And find her family,' I said.

'Yes, and get all her things to them,' said Hazel. 'It would be really nice for them.'

'And nice for you too,' said Lauren. She burst into tears, her cheeks bright red.

'Lauren,' Hazel said in a tone that sat somewhere between sympathetic and sinister.

'Let it out, Lauren, let it out,' said Whisper. 'We need to start letting Rachel go. This is normal. Typical for night three – everyone confused and shocked. It's hard for everyone, including Rachel, to accept. Her duppy rises tonight.'

I gasped as the lights above glimmered. Rachel had risen for real.

'See?' said Whisper, sitting back with a self-satisfied smile on his face. He used his floor fork to eat some rice. Gross.

I looked at Josie with the same smug expression. She stared at the carpet.

'I really must fix the electrics,' said Hazel.

There was a knock at the door and most of the others jumped, then laughed at how ridiculous they were being.

Everyone apart from me and Whisper. We shared a knowing nod.

Mum smiled at the front door. 'Molly's here.'

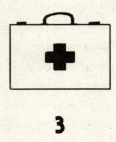

3

See, I would normally rush to hug Auntie Molly. I loved her and I liked her – that's how you know you are really about someone in your family: you'd *want* to be friends with them even though you don't *have* to be. But today? Nah. I felt no connection – not after that text message she'd sent me. Keep me out of what's happening, and I'll keep you out of cuddles. Simples.

Molly – just Molly now, no Auntie, because that's what she gets – walked into the room. She was wearing all black and her straight black bobbed hair swung around and she looked at everyone in the room. When she got to me, she narrowed her eyes, then smiled.

I didn't smile back. I rolled my eyes instead.

'Hello, hi,' she said to everyone else in turn.

'Well, hello!' said Whisper, his eyes shining. He put

down his plate on the floor and took off his hat. 'Nice to meet you, miss.'

'Auntie Molly!' said Josie, as she got up off the floor to hug her. They knew each other; they'd met loads of times. Margot hadn't, and she just stared at her, then jumped in front of Josie to introduce herself. Hazel stood up to let Molly have her seat next to Mum.

'Thanks,' she said. 'I am so sorry for your loss. For all your losses. I know my sister really loved her.'

I snorted at that. Mum didn't, not that much.

'I was hoping to meet her.' Molly looked at Mum. 'Sorry, sis,' she mouthed.

Mum nodded and looked down into her lap.

'We just found out how she passed,' said Whisper. He took a sip of his tea.

Molly looked at him, waiting for him to tell her.

'Cancer,' I said, doing Whisper's job.

'Oh?' said Molly. She looked around the room. 'You didn't know she was sick?'

'Only Lauren did,' I said, pointing to her.

Molly nodded in her direction. 'You all thought it was something else?'

Whisper chuckled into his tea, while looking at me.

'There were some theories flying around,' said Apollo, waving his hand. 'But that's in the past now. We're here to focus on celebrating her life. For six more nights.' He looked into his glass, pulled a face and swallowed his drink.

'Indeed,' said Hazel. 'Let me get you a drink or a plate of food?' She looked at Whisper. 'Whisper's wife made some rice and peas – and we have fried chicken. It's lovely.'

'Oh, just some water, please,' said Molly. 'I've already eaten.'

'OK,' said Hazel, and she left the room.

Molly looked around. 'So . . . tell me about her?' she said. 'What was she like? Who was Rachel?'

'Now *that's* a good question,' said Whisper.

'It is?' Molly seemed surprised. 'Why?'

'She was well confusing,' I said. 'That's why.'

'Nice, though,' added Margot.

'Rachel could be really fun and silly.' Mum laughed to herself, probably at some memory.

'Very creative,' added Apollo.

'She was keen to try new things!' Hazel shouted from the kitchen.

'She didn't have IBS and I knew it,' said Whisper. 'I told you.'

Molly looked at Mum, confused. Mum shook her head, letting her know she'd fill her in later.

Mum's phone beeped and lit up in her lap. Molly nudged Mum and raised her eyebrows. 'Oh yeah?' she whispered.

It had to be Boulder Bae. Look at them laughing, playing in my face.

Molly leaned over Mum to take a closer look at the phone. She gasped and quickly sat back, her eyes wide.

Mum laughed nervously. 'What?'

'Is that Rachel?' Molly whispered, staring at Mum.

'Yeah!' Mum smiled. 'We took that last month, when we –'

'Ella, that's . . . her. I'm sure of it.'

4

Mum's face fell through her feet, then the floor.

If she could have gone pale and white, she would've. She crumpled. She gulped. 'You sure?' she asked, her voice yo-yoing.

Molly nodded and stared at her. 'Positive.'

Mum looked around the room with a wide smile wobbling on her face. 'Excuse us a sec?'

'Of course,' said Hazel, as she leaned in the doorway with Molly's glass of water in her hand. She faked a yawn. 'Actually, why don't we call it a night?'

'But –' Whisper began.

'Yes, I think we'll leave it there for now. We can regroup tomorrow, yes?' She sighed, then slumped. 'It's been a heavy day, hasn't it? Lots to take in.' Hazel stood straight then began clearing the cups and plates dotted around the living room.

Descision made. The night was over.

Margot and Josie stood by me as everyone began to file out.

'Oh my gosh,' said Margot under her breath. 'What. Was. That?'

'Dunno,' I said through tight teeth. 'They ain't gonna tell me either – not easily anyhow.'

Apollo stood in front of us, his hands on his hips. 'We're still on for tomorrow?'

'You what?' I asked.

'London? Theatre? Me?' he said. 'Remember?'

'Oh yeah, yeah.' No, I'd completely forgotten.

'We remember,' said Margot. 'Josie booked the train tickets earlier. We're set.'

I leaned over. 'D'you get me one?'

They looked back at me as if I was stupid.

Hazel began to not shoo us out of the house exactly but directed us to the door using her body, sweeping us up, pushing us forward. 'See you tomorrow!' she said, beaming, then shutting the door behind her. We could see her leaning on it through the glass.

Lauren sighed and looked up at the house. She got in her car and drove away. Apollo glanced at his phone and quickly paced down the close. Whisper unlocked his bike and cycled into the night, his red rear light flashing back at us like a warning. I looked up at my house, at Mum's bedroom window. The light was on, and through the net curtain I could see Auntie Molly pacing back and forth.

When I looked back at Margot and Josie, they were already staring at me. 'Yo, like, I . . . I don't even know where to start with that.'

'I do,' said Josie. 'From the beginning. So, we now know Rachel had cancer and she wasn't murdered – the oils had nothing to do with it. We're off to London tomorrow to meet Apollo.' She took a breath. 'But new task, ranking number one on the top of our to-dos, is the connection between Molly, your mum and Rachel. Wes, what's going on there? What does Molly know about Rachel?'

'Ella looked so shocked,' said Margot, shaking her head. 'I'm worried.'

'Me too,' I said.

Margot tried it. 'Do you think we should go over to yours and –'

'Not a chance.' I shook my head. 'Please, they're not going to tell us a thing.' I shuffled my feet. 'I know I need to know, because this information might help Rachel pass through, but I don't even know if I want to know, you know? It ain't gonna be good. Whatever it is.'

'I kind of get that feeling,' said Josie with a shudder. 'I really do.'

THE COPSEYS' INVESTIGATION INTO THE
~~MURDER~~ LIFE OF RACHEL KOHL

VICTIM: Rachel Kohl

AGE: 40

OCCUPATION: actress?

CAUSE OF DEATH: ~~TBC. Something she ingested or inhaled?~~
~~Potato skin, sorrel tea, oils?~~ Complications from cancer

DATE OF DEATH: between 10:00 p.m. on 9 April and 9:00 a.m.
on 10 April

FACTS (?) AND EVIDENCE:
- Lived at 3 Copsey Close – opposite Wesley
- Liked shopping – lots of deliveries, a spare room full of
  empty boxes (but her house was pretty bare??)
- Has a locked front bedroom (code set to 0666) –
  mentioned something about cars behind it??
- ~~Had IBS?~~ Whisper not sure?
- Cast for a role in a new play? Only Hazel and Lauren aware

INVESTIGATION QUESTIONS:
- ~~Who killed Rachel?~~ No one
- ~~How?~~ Natural causes
- ~~What time?~~ That doesn't matter now

- What's the lock's code?
- Who was Rachel on the phone with when she arrived at the party?
- Who was outside Rachel's house? ~~Lauren?~~
- ~~Who is Rachel's next of kin? Her sister(s)?~~ Caroline Nicholls
- What does Molly know?

INVITED GUESTS AKA SUSPECTS	RELATIONSHIP	MOTIVE BEEF	BIRTHDAY GIFT	QUESTIONS
APOLLO FORTUNE	Old friend – lived together in London	Selfishness? Wanted her to return to London . . . or else?	A collection of his plays	• Why did Rachel have a negative reaction to her present? • Who really wrote Close? • What was Rachel like in London? Apart from not famous?
CAROLINE NICHOLLS	Unknown	?? Did not attend the party Believed to be in Canada	Did not send one	• Who are you? • What is your relationship to Rachel? Rachel's next of kin? Her sister??

ELLA EVANS – WESLEY'S MUM	Neighbour and close friend	Elimination? Rachel was being a bit much recently Ella needed a break . . .	Throwing the party with us and trying to set her up with Auntie Molly	• ~~Why did Rachel not tell you about the play?~~ Privacy and distance • ~~What's in your potato skins?~~ Vegan cheese • Who were you really with on the night of the murder party?
FITZROY 'WHISPER' JENKINS	Knows Rachel from their IBS support group	Elimination? Doesn't trust her; thinks she's faking her IBS?	Home-made sorrel tea	• ~~What exactly is in your tea?~~ Clove, orange, hibiscus. Hazel still alive. Not poisoned • Why are you so suspicious of Rachel?

INVITED GUESTS AKA SUSPECTS	RELATIONSHIP	MOTIVE BEEF	BIRTHDAY GIFT	QUESTIONS
HAZEL WILSON	Landlord	Gain? Did Rachel owe her money?	A riding helmet	• ~~Did Rachel owe you money?~~ Maybe – Rachel didn't pay her rent on time • ~~Why the horse-riding helmet?~~ Rachel tried to horse-ride • What is the deal with you and Lauren?

LAUREN ROBERTS CHIEF SUSPECT	Masseuse – and maybe in a relationship?	Jealousy? Was Rachel cheating on her? Upset that Ella was trying to introduce her to Molly?	Aromatherapy oils	• Why were you so upset at the party? Because she knew she was going to kill Rachel? • Were you dating Rachel? No. Massages only • What's in the oils you gave her? What do they do?: Oils were safe and legit. • What is the deal with you and Hazel?

DAY FOUR
THURSDAY 13 APRIL

1

My phone vibrated by my head. Josie in our Copsey Chat.

To make the train, we need to be in the doughnut in five minutes. I'm just saying . . .

Yeah, she was always just saying something.

I stretched and blinked to focus my eyes. I didn't sleep well, again. I had my eyes on the ceiling, waiting for Rachel, and one ear on the wall, listening into Mum's room.

What a waste of time that was.

Mum and Molly, the snaky sisters, shared their secrets in hisspers.

This morning there was nothing but silence.

I got up, showered quickly and got dressed – but not before doing some light cleaning. The bathroom was free, as the sibs had gone to their club, but they'd left it in a complete state. Wet towels and water everywhere, like a swimming-pool changing room. Like, I might be having a weird moment with Mum, but I wasn't gonna leave that mess for her. She didn't deserve that.

Her bedroom door was ajar and I peeked through the crack to see if she was still there. She was. She lay facing the window with her back to me.

'Mum? You awake?'

'Yeah,' she croaked.

I pushed the door open. 'I'm going out. I'll be gone the whole day, so I'm checking if you're good. And t-to say sorry for b-blowing up yesterday,' I stammered.

Mum rolled over. Her eyes were bright red, her face puffy.

'Yesterday's yesterday,' she said. 'Forget it. And, yeah, I'm fine, thanks.'

Lying again. Mum was hurting.

'You don't look fine.'

She tried to smile. 'It's my morning face, that's all.'

'Your mourning face? Oh, you had a weird dream about Rachel too? I had one yesterday.'

Mum barked out a bitter laugh. 'No. But I have been thinking about her, of course.'

My back stiffened; this was my chance to know her secret. 'Defo.' I paused, thinking of the right question. 'What kinds of things were you thinking?'

Mum chewed her lip before answering. 'Whether it was an accident or whether it was . . . intentional.' Her eyes began to water.

My phone buzzed in my pocket, but I didn't check it. I knew who it was and what they wanted. They could wait; there would be other trains.

'But, Mum,' I replied gently, 'we know it was cancer, don't we? It wasn't anything else . . .'

Mum looked at me, confused. 'Yeah. Yes, of course. Cancer.' Tears rolled down her face.

'You know what? I don't have to go out today. I can stay in; we can chat. Talk about Rachel . . .'

She wiped her eyes, then put her hand on her forehead. 'No, no. Go out. Have fun with the girls —'

'But I could —'

'I said no, Wesley. I'm good, I promise.' She softened. 'This is adult business, and you already take on too much. I'll figure it out, I promise.' She turned over in bed, away from me again. 'Have a good time, yeah?'

That wasn't a real question. It was a conversation ender.

I shut her bedroom door.

2

Josie and Margot's interrogation started as we took our first step towards the station.

'So?' Margot asked with what she *thought* was a casual sigh. 'How was last night? What happened when you got home?'

'You wanna know what went down with Mum?'

She nodded.

'Guess what? It was well intense!'

Her eyes widened with anticipation.

'Go on then,' Josie said breathlessly, eager for the 'exciting' update.

'Absolutely nothing. Her and Molly just whispered to each other in low frequencies that only fish or, like, whales or other reptiles would be able to understand.'

'Reptiles . . . ?' asked Margot. 'What?'

'Forget it.'

'So what did you learn?' asked Josie. 'Anything?'

'This morning she was being well weird. She said, "Oh, like, was it an accident or was it intentional?"'

'Strange,' said Josie. 'We know what happened to Rachel.'

'Innit,' I said. 'And no use asking Molly because she ain't gonna tell me jack. What's happening with you?' I looked at Margot. 'Did Caroline reply yet?'

She shook her head. 'Nope, and I don't want to push her too much, you know?'

'But pushing me to the edge is just fine?' I said dramatically, clutching my chest. 'Oh, I see how it is.'

Margot slapped me on the back. 'Stop it.' She laughed. 'Save the dramatics for Apollo.'

'It's here!' Josie shouted in front of us, holding her phone out, following the map. 'This is Apollo's place.'

I looked up at the building. It was a pub, a regular old pub with cigarette butts on the concrete round it and the smell of beer wafting from it.

'I thought we were going to a real theatre,' Margot grumped. 'The Lyric or somewhere decent. Where's the glam, the glitz, the bright lights?'

'I dunno that place – I know nothing about London – but if they had any sense, they probably told him *Apollo's Agony* wasn't gonna cut it. No seats would be sold for real.'

'We haven't been inside yet,' said Josie. 'It might be fine.'

'Doubt it.' I pulled the door handle.

A man with a bald head and big white beard stood behind the bar. He polished a pint glass with a white tea towel attached to his waist. Another man sat on a stool in front of the barman, flipping through the paper, a small glass of beer next to him. They both stared as the door slammed shut.

The barman pointed his chin at us. 'You lost?'

Josie stepped forward. 'Maybe? We're looking for Apollo. Apollo Fortune.'

The barman and his customer sighed knowingly in unison. 'He roping you into his dramas too, is he?' He pointed towards a set of stairs at the back of the bar. 'Tell him to keep it down; the customers don't like it.'

The man on the stool hacked out a tobacco-tinged cough-laugh.

We tiptoed apologetically past them and ran up the stairs and opened the door to a shadowy room. Like, everything was black in there – the chairs, the walls, the sticky floor. Apollo was wearing black too – a rollneck jumper and trousers – as he stood onstage. He had a hand on his chest and another out in front of him. He stared down at his feet.

'It was a different time. I was . . . a different person then.' His head shot up, he slapped at his chest and walked to the edge of the stage. 'But that boy, that *sad* little boy with that spot,' he spat, 'still lives within me.' He hung his head dramatically and the lights went out.

We were plunged into darkness. I didn't know whether to laugh or clap, so I did both – the second slightly louder than the first.

When the lights came back on, Apollo was right up in our faces.

He grinned. 'Thoughts?'

3

Apollo looked up at a small room above the stage. 'Peter, be a darling and pop the house lights on?' As the room brightened, Apollo sat next to us on a free folding chair.

'I'm delighted, so happy you've come, but it turns out I'm pushed for time.' He leaned forward, his forehead wrinkled. '*Apollo's Agony* is not quite working dramaturgically. I need to dig deeper – breach its emotional core, you know?'

'Totally,' said Margot. 'Sure.'

'But I've made space for you, of course. Wait there!' Apollo rushed to the back of the stage, grabbed some papers, then pushed a sheet in each of our hands. 'A quick scene for you all,' he said. 'You'll love this one. Wesley, you're Rocky. Morgana, my dear, you can be Rachel, and, Josephine, try Naomi on for size?'

'Wait! We're starting, just like that?' I asked

Apollo nodded. 'Trust your instincts – as you read, your characters will tell you what you need to do. I'll give you some context, though. In this scene, imagine you're at a school disco. Do you still have those?'

'Yes,' said Josie. 'I actually arranged the one before Easter.'

'Excellent. So you're there. You're dancing. Eating sweets. Rocky is talking with his friends in one corner. Rachel and Naomi are in the other, conspiring.' He clapped his hands together. 'Places! Peter, spotlights!'

The three of us looked at each other as the room dimmed. I walked to one corner of the stage then shut my eyes for a moment, imagining this was the hall at school. I could see the benches we sat on pushed against the wall and PE mats in a dark corner. The lights were purple and blue. I could see Mrs Herbert, our head teacher, trying to dance while I laughed at her with my mate Bobby. I was right there.

Margot spoke first. 'Naomi, he's here,' she said flatly. 'It's him.'

Josie looked down at her paper and then at me. 'I can see that,' she said in a sarcastic voice that didn't belong to her. 'I have eyes too.'

Margot and I shared an impressed look. Josie was really good.

'Do you, do you think I should say something?' said Margot as Rachel. 'Tell him how I feel? Tell him that one day we'll get married? That Rocky and I will have little pebbles.' Margot forced her laugh back into her mouth with her hand, then whispered, 'Sorry,' in my direction.

'You could,' said Josie with a shrug. 'But you could tell him other things – how well you can act, the horses you'll ride – how we'll travel the world one day. Real things.' She looked at Margot. 'Real things, about the real you. The things that matter.'

Margot gulped. Josie was taking this seriously and she realized she needed to too. Margot squinted at her sheet. 'But he won't care about that! Those are just our silly dreams.' As she waved her hand, she dropped her paper.

'They're not silly, not to me,' said Josie solemnly, channelling Naomi.

Margot scrabbled on the floor for her sheet. 'OK, I'm talking to him,' she said. She walked over to me and put her hand on my shoulder. 'Hi,' she said. 'I'm Rachel.'

I looked at the paper, at my one and only line. 'Rocky.' I put my hand out for her to shake.

Apollo clapped loudly and steadily as he walked from the back of the room towards us. I could see his eyes were damp. 'Brilliant,' he said. 'And you –' he pointed at Josie – 'you were . . . *triumphant*.' He clutched his heart. 'I could just feel it in here.' He beat his chest with his fist, then bit it.

'Thanks,' said Josie. 'I just read it really.'

'It was good writing too,' said Margot. 'Sort of. Same characters as *Close*, but it felt different.'

Apollo put his hand to his chin. 'Different how?'

'Just, I don't know. It felt a bit more . . . basic compared to *Close*.'

Apollo's jaw dropped. Like, unhinged.

'Wait, I didn't mean "basic",' said Margot, sensing she'd said something wrong. 'I meant . . . more essential, yeah.'

'Hmmm,' said Apollo.

'So, about Rachel –' I began, but didn't finish.

Apollo snatched the papers from our hands. 'Well, I need to crack on.'

'That's it?' I said. 'We just got here!'

'That's it,' said Apollo. 'Peter! Show our guests out, please.'

NIGHT FOUR

NIGHT FOUR

1

The train back to Luton was about to leave so we raced down the stairs to get it. The doors beeped.

'Wait, wait, wait!' Margot screamed, as if that would help. I squeezed through, then pulled Josie in, as she was closest. The doors closed on Margot's foot.

'Ow, oh my God, oh my God!' Her eyes widened in panic. Inside the carriage, a man in a suit leaned over to push the doors open, and she scrambled inside, breathless, hair all over her face.

'Thank you, thank you,' she said to the man. 'You saved my life!'

He rolled his eyes. 'This time.' He sighed and flicked his newspaper open.

Margot made a mocking face behind his back.

I caught my breath as the train rolled out of the station. Josie stared down at her phone. 'You know what, Jo? You could be an actress after that performance.'

'Yeah, yeah. It was four lines.'

'Four lines you smashed!' said Margot. 'Seriously, it was so good. I hereby award you your acting badge.'

'Yeah, you actually deserve it,' I said.

Josie smiled. 'Thanks, that's kind – and of course I accept it – but, really, acting's not for me. I'm doing something serious with my life, not playing pretend.'

'Mr One Line here enjoyed it too,' I said. 'Not the acting bit, but maybe making sets. When I closed my eyes, I really saw the hall. I reckon I could make a few props.'

'OK, idea,' said Margot. 'When we're older, I'll write the plays, you dress the stages and Josie can do something serious with them – like sell them.' She put her hands in the air. 'Copsey Productions. I can see it now.'

'I'm in – as long as I can live in your London house. Can't be getting on this train every day. Deal?'

'Deal!' said Margot, shaking my hand.

We put our hands out to Josie, who looked at them for a moment before smiling. 'OK, fine.' She playfully slapped them away and returned to her phone. 'Back to the important things,' she said. 'We didn't learn much about Rachel.'

'Learn much? We learned nothing – Apollo basically threw us out.' I looked at Margot. 'As soon as you called his writing basic.'

'Hmmm,' said Margot. She leaned against the doors, then quickly moved as they violently shook behind her. The man who saved her life tutted in her direction. 'I said what I said, and I stand in my truth. There was something about that writing today. Look, we know Rachel had a bad reaction to *Close*. We think it's because Apollo was borrowing from her life – it's not like any of his other plays.'

'There's no Apollo in it for a start,' I said.

'Right, or she wrote it herself. Last night Apollo said Rachel was creative –'

'But not a good actress,' added Josie. 'So that tracks.'

'Let's say Rachel wrote this, and she's Rachel in the story. This means Naomi's her friend. Could Naomi be the person in the photo? The one in Rachel's bedroom?'

'Hmmm,' I said. 'That makes sense. Close enough to write about her, close enough to keep her pic, close enough to be in *Close*, which we read on Copsey Close, as close friends.'

'All right, all right.' Margot laughed. 'It would be nice to meet more of Rachel's real friends. Wouldn't it?'

'Totally. Whoever or whatever helps her pass through gets a pass with me.'

Margot's phone beeped in her pocket. 'It's probably Dad.' She peered down the train. 'I hope he's not on this one, although it would be handy. The lie about him coming with us would come true.' She was shaken when she saw the screen. It wasn't her dad. 'Oh my God – it's Caroline Nicholls.'

'And?!' I gasped. 'What's she saying?'

Margot's forehead furrowed. 'I don't understand.' She put her phone under my nose. It said: *I know my sister is dead. Don't contact me again.*

2

We walked slowly up Copsey Close. 'Show me again?' Margot handed me her phone and I reread Caroline Nicholls's message. I shook my head and returned the phone. 'Nah, I can't actually believe that,' I said. 'That's next level.'

Listen, family can be annoying. I know this, it's my reality – Mum's moving mad, I'm on the outs with Molly, and my sibs sometimes push me to the edge, but this?

I know my sister is dead. Don't contact me again.

Colder than the Arctic Circle that is. I wouldn't even talk about Craig like that.

'Right?' said Josie. 'How . . . harsh.' She crossed her arms. 'I'm glad she didn't come to the party.'

'Same,' Margot muttered, holding her phone with one hand, drumming her lip with the other. 'Maybe they fell out –'

'You don't say,' I said. 'That ain't obvious?'

'I know, but really. What could ever be *that* serious? That you're like, "Yep, I know, bye," to the news that your sister died?'

'And even if it's *not* her sister, it's still harsh,' added Josie, rubbing her temples. 'I'm not sure what our next steps are.'

'Well, she said don't contact her again,' said Margot.

'And I don't want to, honestly.' I sighed. 'Not if she's gonna be like that. Not if she's not gonna help.' We approached Rachel's front door. 'But we should do a couple of things, I think.'

'Go on,' said Josie. 'What?'

'Well, firstly, Caroline said she knew Rachel died, but who told her? The party people are apparently the only people who knew her around here, so one of them must have told her. We know why – to share bad news. But how? When?'

'That's a really good point,' said Josie. 'Maybe Hazel's not telling the whole truth and they *do* know each other and her phone number works?'

'I mean, I don't trust Hazel, but why would she lie about that?' I murmured by Rachel's front door. 'It doesn't do anything for her. What does she get doing that?'

'Another good point,' said Josie, nodding.

'And, secondly, we've gotta find her real friends or family so she can cross over. Rachel needs her death certificate so her family can have her stuff too. We can only reach them through Hazel – she's the one with the phone number. We've gotta get it and call it ourselves. It's the only way.'

Margot grinned. 'This is very detective-y, coming from you.'

'Well, that message got me stressing. You can't treat family like that.'

'That is despicable!' Whisper shouted inside Rachel's house. 'You can't do those things like that! Not to the dead!'

'See, Whisper couldn't even hear us and he agrees.' I knocked on the door.

Lauren answered. 'Brace yourself.' She frowned. 'It's *a lot* tonight. A whole lot.'

3

Night four of nine night had truly gone off the rails or, more specifically, Whisper had. He stood in the middle of the room, his dark brown drink sloshing as he spoke. We sat on the floor, our front-row seats at the circus.

'But *why*, Hazel? Why did you do it?' he shouted. Hazel sat next to Mum, who had sunk into the sofa, arms crossed over her chest. When we came in, she offered us a solitary nod. That's it.

'What happened?' said Margot, keen to jump in the conversation. 'What did we miss?'

Hazel sat forward. 'I didn't mean to do it,' she said. 'Rachel's package was torn and open, and when I moved it out of the hallway, the canvas fell out. That's it – I'm not planning on using it.'

'But it didn't belong to *you*, Hazel!' Whisper sounded like he was gonna cry. 'You can't just open people's packages!'

Josie nodded. 'It's against the law.'

'I didn't open it!' Hazel snapped. She took a breath. 'I understand that you have your −' she waved her hand around − 'process. I do. I respect it. But this is *ridiculous*. There was barely any cardboard left on it!'

A thin white plastic-wrapped canvas lay against the wall under the mantelpiece. 'You're talking about this?'

'Yesh,' said Whisper, unsteady on his feet. 'Ready for a nice family portrait. A nice painting of Rachel and her family.'

'What family?' Hazel snorted. 'That's the big question, isn't it?'

'It is,' I began, but before I could finish there was a knock at the door. Apollo.

'I'll go,' said Lauren glumly. 'Anything to get away from this.'

A moment later, Apollo swept into the living room. 'We meet again!' he said to us kids. He then noticed the gloomy faces on the adults. 'You can cut the tension in here with a knife.' He laughed nervously, pretending to stab the air. 'What did I miss?'

'Nothing,' said Lauren, folding her arms, leaning in the doorway.

'Nah,' I said. 'We were just talking about families.'

'Oh, OK . . .' said Apollo. He removed his coat and laid it over the back of one of Rachel's chairs.

'Yesh,' slurred Whisper. 'I was saying family is important. All kinds of family. Blood relatives? Definitely. I miss mine back home − the ones who are lucky to be alive, and the ones who aren't. But also the family you find is *just* as important.' He raised his glass, as if waiting for a toast.

Apollo seemed touched and a little taken aback. 'You know, Whisper, that's absolutely right. I couldn't agree more.'

'Take the kids,' said Whisper. 'They're a family. You are a family, aren't you?'

We looked at each other. 'Well, I have enough sibs as it is – don't think I can handle two more sisters. Our house is full enough.'

'Tell me about it,' said Lauren. 'Sisters are stressful.'

Whisper stumbled in Apollo's direction, tripping over his feet. Margot put her hands up to protect herself.

'Steady, old boy,' said Apollo with a gentle laugh. He reached out for Whisper's elbow, but Whisper shrugged him off.

Whisper looked down at us in turn, then closed his eyes and tutted. 'You just remind me of my kids.' He choked back tears.

'Thanks?' said Margot. She looked over at us and made a surprised face.

'My son, the kids I used to keep an eye on –'

'What kids?' I asked.

Whisper shook his head, sighed and took a huge sip of his drink.

4

Mum stood up and reached for Whisper's glass. 'Slow down.' She smiled. 'It's not good for your stomach – and it'll be hard to get home. Eat something? You can't cycle if you drink much more.'

Whisper kissed his teeth and wrenched his arm away from Mum. 'I'm an old man; I know what I'm doing!'

'I beg to differ,' Hazel muttered under her breath.

'Wait, Whisper,' I said, pulling at the hem of his joggers, 'which kids did you look out for? Where?'

Whisper waved his hand. 'I used to have a little shop. Kids would come in for their breakfasts, lunches and dinner – prawn cocktail crisps and Lucozades.'

Apollo laughed. 'Three square meals then.'

'Where was your shop?' asked Margot.

I had an idea. 'Was it near the park? Where we saw you the other day?'

Whisper nodded. 'Next to the bookies, yes.'

I *knew* it. Right where we saw him on Tuesday. Minding his old business, exactly like he said.

'What happened to the shop?' asked Josie.

The light directly above her head twinkled.

Rachel returns! Was this a message? Actually, it didn't matter. I took it as a sign. A sign to keep going.

The three of us shared a look, while the adults turned to Hazel.

'The electrician's coming at the end of the week. It's booked; it'll be fixed,' she said.

That could wait, but our investigation couldn't.

'Whisper, did you retire?' I drummed my fingers on the carpet.

Whisper stepped backwards, bumped into the mantelpiece, then rested his glass on its edge. 'Yeah,' he said in such a low, quiet voice it was shocking coming out of his normally loud mouth. 'There was an accident. One of the kids got hurt outside. As hurt as you can get.' His eyes filled with tears. 'I was out the back when it happened, and I . . . I should've been there.' He reached for his drink and necked the last drop. He sighed. 'If you'll excuse me, I'm calling it a night.' He shook his head and smiled at Mum. 'You were right about taking it easy.'

Mum held his elbow to the door, while the rest of us did our best to avoid eye contact. When she returned to the room, it was silent.

Apollo spoke first. 'You know, I *did* like what he said about family. I don't speak to mine much any more.'

'Have you tried recently?' said Josie. 'I've wondered what you should do if you – and I'm not saying *you* did, Apollo – fall out with your family. How do you fix it?'

Mum snorted and folded her arms. 'You don't bother.'

I snapped my head round to look at her. When she caught my eye, she stared at the floor.

'I actually disagree,' said Hazel, settling into the sofa. 'It's worth trying your best.'

Lauren tutted. 'And if your best is bad? What then?'

'Well, Lauren,' Hazel replied, 'then I go to the stables. Horses never let me down.'

'Yep, I bet *they* never disappoint you,' said Lauren into her phone. 'Right, I've got a full day of clients tomorrow, and I need an early night. See you tomorrow. Again.' She left the house. Her car door slammed and she drove away.

Mum stood to leave too, but Hazel pulled on her arm. 'Stay a while? All of you? I have some vol-au-vents in the oven and no one to eat them with.'

'Vollo who now?' I said. 'You know what, nah, we're good.' Margot and Josie nodded. 'We've got things to do. We'll see you tomorrow afternoon at the stables? We're . . . keen to take a look.'

'I remember,' said Hazel. 'I'm looking forward to it.'

5

We huddled together in the doughnut. It was getting nippy outside.

'It's supposed to be spring,' said Margot, hugging herself and looking up to the sky.

'That's climate change for you,' replied Josie. 'It's a mess, this planet. I can't think about it too much, or else I won't be motivated to do anything.'

'What we have to do here with Rachel is plenty motivating, no?!' I asked. 'You saw her lights flashing, didn't you? *That's* motivation. Let's go over it.'

'OK,' said Margot, drawing a breath between her teeth. 'We're off to Hazel's, confirmed, so tomorrow morning's set. I have the address from her Facebook.'

'We'll need to get Caroline's number,' said Josie. 'Try to, at least.'

'Great.' I nodded. 'Now let's talk about Careless Whisper getting drunk like that.'

'Right!' Margot gasped, eyes wide and bright. 'A shopkeeper, eh?' She cocked her head to one side. 'I can see it – I can imagine him being fun and friendly with his flat cap in another context, you know? One where his friend hasn't just died.'

I nodded. I felt sorry for him. 'He looked well cut up when he talked about what had happened to that kid.'

'Yeah, it's really bad,' said Josie. 'That would really leave a mark on your life.'

'Defo,' Margot whispered.

'Right,' I said, stretching. 'We good here, happy with our progress?'

'Yes, boss,' said Josie, laughing. She did a little salute and stamped her foot.

'Hey now,' I said. 'No need to get in your feelings – I'm not stealing your top-dog spot.' I rubbed my forehead. 'Like I said, Caroline's message got me feeling some type of way – a bad, disappointed way. I was already invested. I mean sure, it got dicey with Mum, but that message made it clearer for me. You just can't treat people like that – dead or alive.'

'Hundred per cent,' said Margot. She looked down the close in the direction of Copsey Avenue. 'Hang on – who's that walking up our street? How *dare* they?' She laughed.

I turned to look. A tall figure with broad shoulders approached us. They wore a grey jumper and their hood was up.

I froze. I recognized them. It was *them*.

'Wait. That's . . . that's the person I saw outside Rachel's.'

I squinted to see better. Was it them? Was that the same jumper I saw in the wash? Was this . . . Mum's person?

Margot's smile dropped and she stepped to my side. 'Are you sure? You *have* to be sure now.'

I was. I felt it in my gut.

I peered at the person. 'Oi!'

They heard me, spun round and walked quickly away.

Nah, they couldn't do a U-turn and call it a day. Not on my watch.

'I said "oi"!'

'Wesley!' Margot hissed. 'Wait!'

'Don't call them over, Wes!' said Josie, backing up towards her house. 'Don't be insane!'

'Does that look like Lauren to you?' I asked them.

They ummed and aahed.

'Does it?!' I shouted.

They shook their heads. They were right. It wasn't her.

Before my brain, my friends, any fear or common sense could stop me, I flew down to the end of the close, running as fast as I could. When I reached the end of our road, opposite an old empty house called Beechwood, I looked left and right, up and down, both sides of Copsey Avenue, but the person was nowhere to be seen.

DAY FIVE
FRIDAY 14 APRIL

1

Loads of people think Luton is grey, bleak and dirty. I know – I've seen what haters have said online. And, OK, there are some bits like that, sure, but the *whole* town's not like that. You could say that about any place. We have grass and fields and parks here too. That's right, we do. I nodded to myself as I looked out of the bus on the way to Hazel's stables on the edge of town.

Margot leaned over, clicking her fingers in my face and stomping her riding boots. 'Are you hearing us? What you did was . . . not wise.'

'What?'

'Chasing that person?' said Josie, kicking my ankle. 'What if they'd hurt you, or us?'

'Hurt us how? They were going in the other direction. What were they gonna do? Teleport back to the doughnut and do me in? Be serious.'

'What if that was your mum's boyfriend and you scared him away?' Josie tutted. 'You didn't make a good first impression – you can't redo those.'

'If he was Mum's boyfriend and he ran away, what kind of wimp is that? Not one I want around her.' I shifted in my seat. 'I'm glad I ran him out of the close.'

Margot sighed. 'Listen, while this brave new you is cool – you used to be scared of your shadow –'

'And you couldn't keep a secret. Remember when you told Mr Kirklees everything?'

I rolled my eyes. 'That was the old me.'

'You just have to be careful,' said Margot. 'You don't know who that was, or what they could be capable of. OK?'

Josie nodded. 'She's right.'

'Fine.' I folded my arms. 'But that person knows something – and I want Rachel in the other realm pronto.' I whistled and jerked my thumb. 'Quick time.'

'Me too, and I agree,' said Margot. 'How could they be connected, though?'

I shuffled in my seat to face them. 'So I thought about this last night and this is what I've got. She might have owed him money and he's coming to collect.'

'Maybe,' said Josie. 'We know she didn't pay her rent on time.'

'And had a shopping addiction, possibly,' added Margot.

'Or she could have been seeing this person and they think she's gone AWOL, which, like, she has, but you know what I mean?'

'Yeah, literally ghosting,' said Margot. 'Duppy-ing.'

'And the last one is that maybe this person is into some dark things, criminal behaviours, and maybe Rachel knew something she wasn't supposed to. That one I'm still working out.' I locked my fingers together and wriggled my hands. 'That one's not quite fitting together.'

Josie thought for a moment and then wagged her finger. 'You could be on to something with that, though. Remember when she walked into the party? She was having that heated conversation.'

'Yep!' replied Margot. 'That could be shady business for sure.'

Josie reached up to ring the bell. She pointed out of the window as the bus passed by. 'There's Hazel's place right there.'

'And there are the horses,' said a giddy Margot, standing up. 'I can't wait to get back in the saddle.' She mimicked galloping and the noise of her boots vibrated around the bus.

'Enjoy it,' I said, walking down the stairs from the top deck. 'You lot give it the big one about danger, but there ain't no way I'm getting on a scary beast and trusting it with my life.'

The doors of the bus squeaked as they opened, and the wind rushed in. It was so gusty we walked along the smooth tarmac with our backs towards Hazel's place. It was a large detached house, wider than it was tall, with stables attached. The grass was green and lush and rolled away from us as far as the eye could see. There was a sign outside, driven into the gravelled ground: *Hazel's Horses and Spa*. I turned to my friends. 'Hazel didn't say anything about no spa, did she?'

'She didn't,' said Margot, brushing her hair away from her face. Her eyes grew big. 'But I bet –'

'Hang on,' I said. On the side of the porch was a bell. When I pressed it, we heard it chime inside the house, then a buzzer rang to let us know the door was unlocked.

When I pushed it open, Lauren was standing there, head to toe in angelic white. Her mouth hung open.

'I *knew* it!' said Margot.

'What are yous lot doing here?' she said, looking around nervously.

'We could ask you the same question, Lauren,' I said. 'Can we come in?'

2

'I've seen you lot every evening for five days – five days in a row now,' Lauren grumped, shaking her head. '*Now* you've come to work too?'

'We didn't know you worked here, did we?' I said.

'Well, I figured it out as soon as I saw "and spa" on the sign,' said Margot proudly. 'This is where Rachel came for massages, and now it makes sense why you and Hazel are always together.'

'What doesn't make sense is why you've never said you're connected.' I shook my head. 'What's the big deal?'

'There's no deal, and it's none of your business anyway,' said Lauren. 'I don't need to explain my life to no kids.'

She thought she had a point, but she didn't. I needed a reason to make her spill her guts. I thought for a moment.

'You kind of do,' I said. 'We can tell the police that you were creeping around the close. In fact, we saw you again last night.'

Josie nudged me. 'What are you doing?' she muttered under her breath.

Lauren folded her arms. 'That wasn't me and you know it,' she said. 'And what if I was? You think the police will arrest me for walking down the street? Doubt it.'

OK, that was a good point. That was a bust. I looked at the floor, racking my brains for something, anything. I thought back to her in our house, in Rachel's house. To her holding Rachel's patches. My head flipped up in her direction, narrowly missing her chin.

'Easy,' she said, putting her hands in front of her.

'You know what I *could* do? I could tell the cops you took Rachel's cancer medication.' I narrowed my eyes. 'And – and – and, like, you were going to do something bad with it.'

'Wesley, what?' said Margot. 'Stop!'

'In fact, I don't even need to tell the police – I could just tell the people at your spa that you steal from dead people.' I raised my eyebrows. 'How about that?' I cupped my hands round my mouth. 'Hello?' I shouted. 'Anyone here? I have something to tell you about Lauren!' I folded my arms. 'I could do that. Or leave you bad reviews online. Either or both.'

Lauren grabbed my shoulder. 'Stop it now!' she said in a low voice. 'I have a client in the relaxation room and another coming in a second. Don't do that – don't tell lies! You could ruin my business – and my life.'

'Then give us the score then,' I said.

Lauren sighed. 'Look, Hazel is my sister –'

'Your *sister*?' said Margot. 'I thought she was your boss somehow, and you were her, like, minion.'

'Kind of accurate,' Lauren scoffed.

'If you're sisters,' said Josie, staring at Lauren, 'why are you so weird around each other?'

'Wait.' I shrugged. 'Why is this a secret? No one cares about you and Hazel. Like, this is so low stakes it's almost embarrassing. What's the point?'

Lauren glared at me, breathing heavily through her nose. When I slowly moved my hands to my mouth, as if I was gonna shout again, she pulled them away. 'Look, when we were younger, she was a *nightmare*, like really – always telling me what to do, bullying me, thinking she was my mum. I didn't speak to her for years – when I left home, I was gone, gone for good. She wasn't my sister any more. I was done.'

'And then?' asked Josie.

'And then . . . life got tough. It was hard finding my feet. I started hanging out with . . . not good people and the trouble started. I knew I was walking down bad paths, but I didn't want to turn back for her to tell me I told you so, you know?'

Josie nodded sagely. 'I *do* know. That's literally one of the worst things you can say to someone.'

'Right,' said Lauren. 'But, you know, Hazel reached out. Offered me space to work here, and I appreciate it. I'm . . . just not ready to call her my sister again – you have to earn that title.' She shook her head. 'I don't agree with some of the things she does – things she wants me to do.'

Now this was interesting.

Margot leaned in. 'Like what?'

Lauren shrugged. 'She's likes money way too much, in my opinion. But what can I do or say when she's literally given me a free place to live and work? I have to put up and shut up.'

'Yeah,' said Margot, as she drew a sharp breath between her teeth, 'that's a tough spot to be in.'

My mind snapped back to the person in the grey hood.

'Do you have other sisters or brothers as tall as you who could . . . collect coins on her behalf?'

Lauren shook her head. 'I don't know who that person was. Sorry.' She thought for a moment. 'Maybe it was one of Rachel's old boyfriends?'

'Did she ever mention anyone?' asked Margot.

Lauren thought for a moment. 'Oh yeah, one Welsh guy.'

'Welsh?' I looked at my friends. 'Is that why she was doing that terrible accent at her party?'

'And is that person Rocky? From "Apollo's" play?' asked Josie.

The bell chimed in the hallway. 'I'm answering this door, and you're going to be cool, OK?' said Lauren, staring. 'I've told you enough, right?'

I nodded. 'Yeah, you have – and you know what? I'm sorry for coming in hot at you like that.' I rubbed my head. 'Things are a lot.'

'Tell me about it,' she said. 'I remember being young and snappy too. I'm not mad. I get it.'

'Where's Hazel?' asked Margot. 'We'd better go find her.'

'With the horses, waiting for you, I guess. This place used to be a doctor's surgery, so it's got lots of rooms. If you go through that door with a three on it, you'll get to the stables quicker than going the long way. It's through Hazel's office.'

Perfection. I pressed my lips together to stop smiling. 'Thank you,' I said.

'No snooping, though,' she said, wagging her finger as she walked to the front door.

When she raised an eyebrow, it felt like a dare.

3

Lauren walked her client up the stairs, speaking to him in a super-friendly calm voice – a voice I hadn't heard from her before. It was truly giving split personality.

We waited for her to disappear, then I reached for the handle of door three. As I did, Josie put her hand on my shoulder. 'What did we *just* tell you about being wild, Wes?'

'That could have been so bad,' said Margot, shaking her head. 'It was almost like blackmail.'

'Almost?!' Josie raised her voice. 'It was its literal definition!'

'Yeah, but it worked, didn't it? And now we know. We know Hazel and Lauren's whole deal and –'

'Now that weird conversation they had outside your bedroom window makes sense,' said Margot.

'Right, all of that's great, cool. But now we also have a stronger lead. A boyfriend. From Wales.' I brushed both shoulders. 'I smashed it – what's your problem?'

'You might have, but I don't like how you got there. Not at all,' said Josie. 'Wrong. Unethical. Against the Copsey Code. That's not how we do things.'

I shrugged. 'Sorry, not sorry.' I pulled the door open.

As I did, a gust of wind rushed through Hazel's corridor-like office, scattering the papers she had on her desk on to the floor. There was another open door at the other end of the office. Hazel was standing by it.

She was smoking again – foul, raggedy behaviour – and looking down at her phone. She glanced over at us once, twice, then jumped.

'Good God!' she shouted, quickly dropping her cigarette, taking out her earbuds, pushing her hair from her face. 'I was listening to a podcast while I waited for you.' She stamped the ground with her welly, then narrowed her eyes at us. 'Why did you come *this* way? Why not take the door in reception?'

'Lauren told us to come this way.' I shrugged.

'She said it was quicker,' added Josie.

'Oh, she did, did she?' Hazel paused for a moment, her words hanging in the air. She waved them away. 'Well, never mind that, let me introduce you to Bellamy. That's the horse Rachel tried to ride – come along!'

As we walked through her office, I loitered a little to

look around, trying to read the labels on her files, eyeing the sets of keys on her wall. Hazel wasn't having it, though. She glared over her shoulder at me. 'I said come along!'

Margot squinted in the sun once we were outside, walking over the field. 'I *love* the name Bellamy,' she said, shielding her eyes. 'Such a lovely name for a horse.'

'I love it too!' Hazel shouted over her shoulder. 'So did Rachel – she chose to ride her specifically. Her name has a lovely meaning in French –'

'"Beautiful friend", right?' said Josie.

'Exactly correct!' said Hazel. 'Hmm, the schools around Copsey Close are better than I thought. I'll put the rent up on my houses in that area.' She looked back and laughed.

None of us found that funny.

Hazel noticed. 'I'm joking. I don't rent houses for the money – I mean, Rachel never paid me past the deposit and first month.'

There! Confirmation from the horse's mouth.

'I do it to help people.'

'How many houses do you have then?' asked Josie. 'You know, to help people?'

Hazel looked down at the grass. 'A . . . few.'

'I bet you do,' Josie huffed.

We entered the stables and the stench immediately slammed into my face and punched its way up my nose. I gagged.

'Here she is. Meet the beautiful Bellamy,' said Hazel proudly. She stroked this giant brown horse with a matted black mane that needed a good shampoo, condition and comb.

Beautiful where? Bellamy wasn't cute to me, not even a little bit. She looked at me with her massive eyes and snorted, as if she was telling me to do one, so I did. I stepped all the way back. I wasn't about to be trampled or have my head swiped off by her huge swishing tail.

I covered my mouth and nose with one hand and swatted flies away with the other. There were piles of poo literally everywhere, so of course the flies fancied it and made themselves at home. Bliss if you were a bluebottle, I guess, but not for me.

Margot was loving it. 'Oh, she is lovely. You are lovely, aren't you, Bellamy?' she cooed with her mouth way too close to the horse's. Nasty. She looked up at Hazel. 'Can I tack her up?'

Hazel looked shocked. 'You know what that means?'

Josie answered for Margot. 'She's ridden horses before; she told you. I mean, look at her.' She pointed to Margot's riding boots.

Hazel chuckled. 'Well, yes, I suppose. Sometimes people come with all the equipment but without a clue. Yes, of course you can.'

Margot skipped to a bench with lots of straps, saddles and horsey bits I didn't give a fig about.

I nudged Josie and nodded in the direction of Hazel's office. 'I'm going in.'

'Be careful, OK? Not reckless,' she whispered.

'I will. Catch this acting.' I coughed twice. 'I'm so sorry, Hazel,' I said in my most polite voice. 'Where's the bathroom, please? I don't feel so good.'

4

I really did need the loo a bit, but I needed Caroline Nicholls's number – and to be away from those frowzy horses – way more. I speed-walked back to the glass door that led to Hazel's office. When I touched the handle, I looked back at the fields. Margot was leading Bellamy out of the stables and on to the paddock. Hazel was talking intensely to her, gesturing excitedly with her hands. Josie lagged behind them and was staring in my direction.

I chuckled to myself. I could tell she was bricking it from here.

But I knew what to do. I could handle it.

I opened the door and slipped inside Hazel's office, putting my back against the wall next to her desk. Her papers were still on the floor. I leaned forward, checking to see if they'd be able to see me moving about in here.

They would, so I had to be slick.

Upstairs, I could hear footsteps, so I had to be quick too.

I got on my hands and knees and crawled to Hazel's desk. I poked my head up, my eyes level with the scattered paper on its surface. I scanned what I saw – receipts and horse-riding permission forms – but no leases or anything that looked like that. I turned the pages on the floor, but nothing. I sighed and stood back up, hands on my hips, looking outside again to check the coast.

It was clear. For now.

I ducked back down and pulled open the set of drawers next to the desk. They rattled loudly, and I swore at the cabinet for being a potential snitch.

But bingo! Inside were lots of folders with little tabs on the top. Each one had an address written in bold black capital letters on it. I was in the right place. I read them aloud as I rifled through them. 'Eighteen Old Bedford Road, sixty-six Bute Street,' I muttered. I flicked and flicked, but I couldn't find the one I wanted. 'Come on,' I groaned. 'Three Copsey Close, please. Rachel! Some help, please?'

Upstairs, a door slammed and I could just make out a murmured conversation.

I got to my feet and stared at the desk again. I spoke to myself. 'It's here.' I tapped my head. 'It's got to be. Hazel got Rachel's file out because she needed the number, so it's not in the drawers.' I picked at the papers and shuffled them slightly. I moved a magazine, *Horse & Hound*, out of the way and beneath it was a folder with 3 COPSEY CLOSE on its tab.

Let's go, Rachel! I opened it and inside was her lease, three pieces of paper stapled together. I rummaged in my pocket for my phone as I flipped through the pages looking for a number. I found it on the last page. Caroline Nicholls's number. I snapped a picture of the prize and sent it straight to Copsey Chat.

As I congratulated myself on a job well done and began to leave, I caught sight of the key rack.

Hang on. Hazel changed the locks to Rachel's house, didn't she?

If a set of her new keys was here, I should take them. Right?

They might come in handy, I thought, especially if we wanted to crack Rachel's lock, and, besides, I already had Caroline's number, so getting the keys would be a nice little side mission, wouldn't it? Oh yes, it would.

I ran my eyes over the keys, reading their tags: 18OBR, 5FR. Hazel had not given them codes exactly, but she'd made their addresses as short as possible.

'Come on, three CC,' I said. 'Three CC, leap out at me!'

Outside, in reception, Lauren said a sweet goodbye to her client, who praised her for a job well done. 'I could barely move my neck, and now look,' I heard him say.

'My pleasure,' Lauren replied. 'See you soon?'

'Every week forever,' he said, chuckling.

The heavy front door closed.

I looked back at the key rack and began turning them over as gently as I could. 'Come on! Come on!' I pleaded. I was at the last set now, and I held my breath as I reached out for it. I closed one eye, then checked. 'Three CC! Yes! Success!' I squealed with delight.

The internal door to Hazel's office swung open, as I thrust the keys into my pocket. I put my head down and stepped forward.

'What you doing?' asked Lauren. She cocked her head and flicked her chin towards the fields. 'Why aren't you riding?'

I followed her gaze to see Margot on Bellamy as they trotted round the paddock. Josie walked next to Hazel, but stared in our direction.

'I'm on my way to the toilet, innit?'

'Hmmm,' she said, an eyebrow raised.

I threw my hands in the air. 'What, a boy can't pee? Please, be serious, Lauren,' I said, pushing past her.

NIGHT FIVE

1

I put my hands behind my head and sat back in my seat. 'And I was like, I need a wee, Lauren – move.' I shrugged. 'It was easy really. No sweat.'

'Taking the keys was a good idea,' said Margot, nodding. 'We might need to get back in the house.'

'My thoughts exactly. That front bedroom –' I pointed to my head – 'was front of mind.'

'Yeah, it was a good idea,' said Josie quietly.

'But . . .' I could sense one coming.

'I just . . . need you to be careful.'

I waved her and her worries away. 'Nah, congratulate me instead. Actually, well done to all of us. I got Caroline's number and Rachel's new keys and you both got on a horse. Where's the problem?'

'Don't forget about the Lauren–Hazel connection clear-up,' said Margot. 'Families can be *so* weird.' She leaned forward. 'It reminded me of me and my mum.

She seems fabulous, cool and fun, but when you scratch the surface it's . . . not. Not really.'

I nodded. 'I hear you, but at least you have a surface to scratch. I've got nothing to scratch with Craig unless you count his eyes. And I've got way too many siblings – three too many.'

Margot laughed. 'Don't say that! At least you'll never be lonely.'

'Girl, take your only-child sob story somewhere else; it doesn't work on me.'

Josie smiled. 'I know my parents are still together, so I can't complain and never would, but I can relate.' She sighed. 'When I found out I was going to be a big sister, I took it badly.'

Margot and I looked at each other and laughed.

'Yeah, we know. We remember,' I said.

'We were there.' Margot smiled.

'All right, all right, give me a break.' Josie nudged me in the ribs and pointed to my phone. 'Right, focus. This number?'

I looked at Caroline's number. 'Who's doing it, and what we doing? Call or text?'

'Call,' said Josie. 'Older people don't reply to text messages quick enough.'

'Even if it is Caroline at the other end, she didn't look that old to me.' I tutted. 'Ageist.'

'I'm not, but calling's quicker either way,' Josie replied. 'And you know what? You should do it.'

'Yep.' Margot nodded. 'You found it; you do the honours.'

'Wow, what a prize,' I said. 'But fine.'

'You need to be quick because we're getting off soon,' Josie said. 'Two stops until home.'

'Use your nice voice, OK?' Margot pleaded. 'None of your gruff stuff.'

'Just read the numbers for me, yeah?'

Margot read the digits slowly and I punched them in. I swallowed as I pressed the green button and put the phone on loudspeaker.

Margot peeked between her fingers. 'Eeek, it's ringing!'

'Phones do that,' I replied.

'But remember Hazel thought this one was disconnected since that person stopped answering it,' said Josie.

'Well, she clearly got blocked –'

The phone stopped ringing.

Margot covered her mouth to stop herself screaming.

'Hello?' said the gruff deep voice at the other end. 'Who's this?'

I took a deep breath. 'Can I speak with Caroline Nicholls, please? This is Wesley Evans.'

There was nothing but silence at the other end of the phone. Dead silence.

'Hello?' I shouted. 'You there, mate?'

'Wesley?' the voice asked, weak and soft, but with a clear Welsh accent. 'Wesley, it's me, Dad.'

My jaw fell off my face and rolled down the aisle. My

heart busted free from my ribcage and pulsated on the floor. Josie and Margot's eyes bulged.

I threw my phone down the bus and gulped down the deepest breaths I've ever taken in my life. They didn't help. I was still drowning.

2

They couldn't keep up with me. I stormed down Copsey Close. I swore repeatedly, rhythmically, out loud, and I couldn't give a heck who heard.

'Oh my God, oh my God!' said a breathless Margot behind me. 'I can't believe this!'

'We have to break this down before he breaks something!' Josie replied, jogging next to her.

I came to a stop in the doughnut, the houses of the close spinning around me. I pulled at my hair and squeezed my eyes shut, keeping the world out for a moment. 'This is not happening!' I screamed. 'This isn't real!'

'Come on, calm down –' Josie said gently.

'*Calm down?* You have *no* idea what this feels like, Josie! I haven't spoken to that man for years, and, and . . . now he's back on the scene? He's involved? We've got each other's numbers?'

Margot touched my arm. 'We get why you're angry, we promise. Let's work this out – together.'

I pushed her away, glaring at them, panting. This wasn't their fault. I opened my mouth to speak, but nothing came out. I had no words, not yet. I just guppied and furiously fought back tears.

'OK,' Josie started softly, palms out to placate me, 'let's be logical.' She breathed out. 'Hazel said that was Caroline's number. We saw Caroline's name on Rachel's contract, so that's true. So why did Rachel have your dad's –'

'Craig!'

'Sorry, Craig's number?'

'And why is it attached to Caroline's name?' asked Margot, her hands pulling and pushing her cheeks around her face. 'How are they connected?' She looked at me. 'Are they related?' she asked. 'Do you have aunties in Canada?'

I shook my head. 'Nah, Craig's like you, an only child,' I said. 'Grandad Alan said he was too naughty to have a little brother or sister.'

'OK, no family connection,' said Josie.

'When did you last speak to him?' Margot shook her head. 'Before now, I mean.'

'Haven't heard a peep out of him since he left. I was, like . . . five? Christmas 2017.' I thought back to that time and shuddered. 'Mum was a *wreck*. She took to her bed with a puffy face – just like she did yesterday.'

Wait.

I stared at Rachel's house. The lights were on. Nine night had begun.

A slow panic rose from my feet and tied my stomach into complicated knots when it got there.

Pieces were starting to put themselves together, but I didn't like the look of this puzzle, not at all.

I blinked at my friends. 'Mum's been bad since Molly got back . . .'

Margot nodded. 'Since Molly saw Rachel's photo on Ella's phone and recognized her.'

'Recognized her from where, though?' Josie wondered. 'School? Maybe they all went together, and your mum forgot Rachel?'

'Would that be such a shock, though?' said Margot.

It wouldn't.

I felt utterly sick. I was literally about to puke on the concrete. I swallowed it back and it tasted like betrayal.

'Molly didn't recognize Rachel from school,' I whispered. I dug my nails into my palm and bit on my trembling bottom lip. 'She recognized Rachel from seeing her in town around Christmas 2017 –'

'OK . . .' said Margot.

'Walking hand in hand with – and kissing on – Craig.'

They instantly turned to stone.

Josie held her arms in the air, her eyes darting back and forth, like she was accessing files from the inside of her forehead.

Margot grabbed her elbows behind her head. 'Wait, wait, wait.'

Josie gulped. 'Auntie Molly seeing them makes sense. Your mum wouldn't have met her, and Molly would definitely have remembered her face. Rachel moved to London around that time too, didn't she? That's what Apollo said.'

'Oh my gosh,' said Margot, her hand at her mouth. 'It makes sense why Ella would be so sad now – her new best friend being involved with your family breaking up.' She looked over at Rachel's house. 'Are we *sure* about this?'

'Rachel was doing that terrible Welsh accent,' I said, hands trembling. 'Craig's Welsh.'

'And Lauren said she had a Welsh boyfriend,' Josie whispered.

'I think I'm going to be sick,' said Margot. She held her stomach. 'Hang on – Ella said that before Rachel died there was some distance between them, didn't she?'

I nodded weakly. 'Yeah.'

'We thought she had a boyfriend? That's why she had less time for Rachel, but was also so cheerful.'

'Smiling at her phone, getting messages from Boulder Bae –'

I stopped speaking and stared at my friends. 'Washing grey hoodies that belonged to no one.' I looked down the close. 'Not to Lauren. No one but that person I chased down last night. Craig.'

'And you saw him the night of Rachel's party too, looking up at her house,' whispered Margot. 'Then heard him celebrating downstairs with Ella.'

Josie drummed her chin. 'So maybe Craig was dating both your mum *and* Rachel?' She took a step back. 'Boulder

Bae . . .' said Josie. 'Oh no, Wes, could that boulder have been a rock emoji?'

'As in "Rocky",' whispered Margot. 'Oh, oh!' She pointed and stood on her toes. 'Ella did have a strange reaction to that name when we were talking about Apollo's play. Is that Craig's nickname? That he's had for ages, since school?'

'I dunno!' My voice cracked.

Josie grabbed her phone. 'I'm googling.' Her hand flew to her mouth. 'Wes . . . "Craig" means "Rocky" in Welsh.'

Gut. Punched. Vomit? In mouth.

Margot gasped. 'You are *lying*!'

Josie shook her head. She put her phone down and stared at me. 'Was it him on the phone with Rachel? Why would he do this?'

'Because he's disgusting – and so is Rachel,' I said, my voice trembling with white-hot rage. 'Together, they broke up my family, then she came back to Luton, to the close no less – directly opposite where we live – to rub it in Mum's face! For an encore. *This* was the role she was talking about. Acting like she was friends with Mum, but really a comedienne, laughing in our faces. We've been utterly played! Played like puppets and she's still pulling our strings – look at us now, doing her duppy a favour! Why?' I burst into hot tears.

Voices shouted and screamed from Rachel's house as it plunged into darkness. All the lights went out.

3

Whisper opened Rachel's front door. His chunky old man's phone was in his hand, and its torch beamed brightly. He flashed it at us and we flinched away.

'Don't!' Josie hissed, shielding her eyes.

'Sorry, sorry. Electrics finally gone.' Whisper tutted, leaving the door ajar. He walked back into the shadows. 'They need me – turn on your own torches.'

We loitered in the doorway. 'I can't do this tonight,' I said hoarsely. 'I'm gonna lose it.'

'Whatever you want to do, we support you,' said Josie.

I rubbed my heavy eyes, then leaned into the house. 'Mum?'

'Yeah?' she replied from the living room.

I needed to check on her. She was my priority tonight, not Rachel – even though I could feel her dark spirit swirling around her house. I stepped in and over Whisper, who was looking at the fuse box in the cupboard under the stairs. Hazel stood in the kitchen, giving him instructions.

'Very dramatic,' said Apollo, holding his torch under his chin. 'I quite like this,' he said. He raised his voice. 'Whisper!'

'What?'

'Don't hurry, darling – this lighting suits me.'

Lauren laughed as she sat at the dining-room table, eating crisps in the dark.

Mum was sitting on the sofa with no light on her, her arms folded. Her eyes glistened as she looked out of the window. Without words, I sat next to her and squeezed her lemon-tight.

'What's this about? You want to be my baby again?' She laughed and softened into the hug. 'That's nice. I needed that,' she whispered as she tried to break away.

But I didn't let her go, not yet. I held her tight until I sensed eyes on us. I didn't want them in our personal business.

Mum smiled. 'What happened?' She sniffed. 'Why do you smell like farm? What did you lot get up to?'

'We went to see Hazel's horses, Ella,' said Margot from somewhere in the house. I couldn't see her.

I leaned in close. 'Mum?' I whispered.

'What?'

'I know why you're sad, like *really* sad. It's Craig, isn't it?'

Mum gasped and tried to cover it with a cough.

'He's . . . mixed up in all of this, isn't he?'

Mum sat still and stared at me.

'Molly saw Rachel in town with him all those years ago, didn't she?'

Mum bit her lip.

'And you were –' I shuddered – 'seeing him again? It was his grey hoodie?'

Mum didn't reply, not with words anyway. Her forehead wrinkled and her eyes glistened as she fought back tears. Her face said it all.

I silently got up from the sofa and left that house.

4

I took my clothes off where I stood, leaving them in a puddle next to my bed. I pulled the covers back and got in with my phone – and Rachel's duppy.

I just *knew* it was there. I felt it wrapping itself round me. Poking at my eyes, whispering in my ears.

Jayden, home from holiday club, sat on his bunk, while downstairs Kayla and Jordan rowed over the remote control.

'Heavy day?' he asked. 'Those girls tiring you out?' He chuckled.

I looked blankly at him, then put a pillow over my face.

I squeezed my eyes shut beneath it and tried to shake the duppy off me while my mind swirled with questions. Why did Craig have to be in this? Exactly how long had he been with Rachel? Do I get details from Mum and/or Molly? What do I tell my sibs? Anything? Nothing?

The biggest question I asked myself was why? Why was I still helping Rachel when she'd ruined Mum's life?

I swear the duppy laughed, mocking me.

I shuddered. I knew the answer. I always did. She'd haunt me forever, hang around forever if I didn't fix this.

I screamed silently into the pillow. Rachel had well and truly stitched me up. In life and in death.

The duppy nodded in agreement.

I had to keep going.

When I pushed the pillow off my face, I felt the duppy float away. I reached for my phone. A message from Margot. *Are you OK?*

Brown thumbs-down react emoji.

I opened my other chats and looked at the messages I'd shared with Molly. I took a deep breath and began typing.

I know you saw Rachel in town with Craig.

A bubble with three dots instantly appeared. She was typing.

I sat up, waiting for her response. But as quickly as those dots arrived, they left. Just like her sister, the silence was enough – if it wasn't true, she would have straight up denied it.

I left my messages and looked at my call list.

I stared at Craig's number, feeling my breaths get deeper and angrier. For a second my finger hovered over it, but instead I threw my phone on the floor.

THE COPSEYS' INVESTIGATION INTO THE
~~MURDER~~ LIFE OF RACHEL KOHL

VICTIM: Rachel Kohl

AGE: 40

OCCUPATION: ~~actress?~~ homewrecker

CAUSE OF DEATH: ~~TBC. Something she ingested or inhaled?~~
~~Potato skin, sorrel tea, oils? Complications from~~
~~cancer.~~ Who cares?

DATE OF DEATH: ~~between 10:00 p.m. on 9 April and 9:00 a.m.~~
~~on 10 April.~~ Whatever

FACTS (?) AND EVIDENCE:
- Lived at 3 Copsey Close – opposite Wesley
- Liked shopping – lots of deliveries, a spare room full of empty boxes (but her house was pretty bare??)
- Has a locked front bedroom (code set to 0666) – mentioned something about cars behind it??
- ~~Had IBS?~~ Whisper not sure?
- ~~Cast for a role in a new play? Only Hazel and Lauren~~ ~~aware.~~ Playing with our lives

INVESTIGATION QUESTIONS:

- ~~Who killed Rachel?~~ No one
- ~~How?~~ Natural causes
- ~~What time?~~ That doesn't matter now
- What's the lock's code?
- Who was Rachel on the phone with when she arrived at the party?
- Who was outside Rachel's house? ~~Lauren?~~ Craig?
- ~~Why did that person come again on Thursday night?~~ To see Wesley's mum
- ~~Who is Rachel's next of kin? Her sister(s)?~~ Caroline Nicholls
- What does Molly know?
- WHY IS ~~WESLEY'S DAD~~ CRAIG INVOLVED IN THIS?

INVITED GUESTS AKA SUSPECTS	RELATIONSHIP	MOTIVE BEEF	BIRTHDAY GIFT	QUESTIONS
APOLLO FORTUNE	Old friend – lived together in London	Selfishness? Wanted her to return to London . . . or else?	A collection of his plays	• Why did Rachel have a negative reaction to her present? • Who really wrote Close? • What was Rachel like in London? Apart from not famous?
CAROLINE NICHOLLS	Unknown	?? Did not attend the party Believed to be in Canada	Did not send one	• Who are you? • ~~What is your relationship to Rachel?~~ Rachel's next of kin? Her sister??

INVITED GUESTS ~~AKA SUSPECTS~~	RELATIONSHIP	~~MOTIVE~~ BEEF	BIRTHDAY GIFT	QUESTIONS
ELLA EVANS – WESLEY'S MUM	Neighbour and close friend	Elimination? Rachel was being a bit much recently Ella needed a break . . .	Throwing the party with us and trying to set her up with Auntie Molly	· ~~Why did Rachel not tell you about the play?~~ Privacy and distance · ~~What's in your potato skins?~~ Vegan cheese · ~~Who were you really with on the night of the murder party~~ Craig
FITZROY 'WHISPER' JENKINS	Knows Rachel from their IBS support group	Elimination? Doesn't trust her; thinks she's faking her IBS?	Home-made sorrel tea	· What exactly is in your tea? Clove, orange, hibiscus. Hazel still alive. Not poisoned · Why are you so suspicious of Rachel?

HAZEL WILSON	Landlord	Gain? Did Rachel owe her money?	A riding helmet	• ~~Did Rachel owe you money?~~ Maybe — Rachel didn't pay her rent on time. YES • ~~Why the horse-riding helmet?~~ Rachel tried to horse-ride • ~~What is the deal with you and Lauren?~~ Secret sisters
LAUREN ROBERTS ~~**CHIEF SUSPECT**~~	Masseuse – and maybe in a relationship?	Jealousy? Was Rachel cheating on her? Upset that Ella was trying to introduce her to Molly?	Aromatherapy oils	• ~~Why were you so upset at the party?~~ Because she knew she was going to kill Rachel? • ~~Were you dating Rachel?~~ No. Massages only • ~~What's in the oils you gave her? What do they do?~~ • ~~What is the deal with you and Hazel?~~ Secret sisters

DAY SIX
SATURDAY 15 APRIL

1

'Wake up, Wes!'

I wasn't sure what time it was, but I knew it was way too early for this.

I turned to face my little sister, as she shook my arm. 'What do you want?' I grumped. 'Get lost – go to holiday club, Kayla.'

'It's Saturday, silly.' She laughed, jumped on the bed and rested her face on mine. 'I miss you – haven't seen you all week. I've come to say hello.'

'Hello!' I grinned sarcastically. 'Happy now?'

Kayla recoiled. 'Ew, your breath!'

'Yeah, well, that's what you get for being an annoying alarm clock.'

She laughed and sat at the end of my bed. Across the room, Jayden was on the top bunk, hands behind his head, staring at the ceiling. His twin, Jordan, below, read his book. I squinted to look at the title. *Ghost* by Jason Reynolds. Great. I groaned and turned away.

'Why so snappy, Wes?' asked Kayla.

'Well, he tried to suffocate himself last night,' Jayden smirked. 'He's heated cos he's alive.'

'Don't joke about things like that,' Jordan said without looking up. 'Not cool or funny. You doing OK, bro?'

Honestly? I wasn't.

Kayla nudged me. 'Talk!'

I sighed. 'I'm just tired.'

'Having too much fun at the daily death party, are you?' Jayden shuddered. 'You wouldn't catch me over there, not even for a minute.'

'It's tradition, though,' said Jordan, turning a page. 'It's kind of cool.'

'I dunno about cool,' I said. 'But Whisper, the man who arranged it, says Rachel won't rest if we don't do it. She'll haunt everyone. Forever.'

Jayden snorted. 'That is some ish.'

I sat up. 'You don't think it's true?'

'You do?' Jayden shook his head. 'You've gone soft, Wes. Too much time with those girls. You're being swept into sorcery and scammery.'

'You ain't wrong about that last bit,' I muttered.

Jordan put his book down, eyes full of concern. 'What do you mean?'

'Nothing,' I said. 'Keep reading.'

'Well, I won't haunt you, I promise,' said Kayla.

'That's kind of you, Kay.' I patted her knee.

324

'You know why? Cos I'm never gonna die!' She laughed. '*Never!* That'll be fixed by the time I get old.'

'Unrealistic.' Jordan smiled. 'It's a nice dream, though.'

Jayden sat up and dangled his legs over the edge of his bunk bed. 'Speaking of dreams, I had a weird one last night.'

'What happened?' I asked. 'You were kind and nice, and now you're shook?'

'Funny,' he replied flatly. 'No, it was about Mum. She had a boyfriend and was super happy.'

Oh no. Had I shared secrets in my sleep? Did Rachel's duppy pay him a visit too? Maybe Craig had been in touch? I lay still, a bit scared to move. 'Erm . . . how did you feel about that?'

Jayden shrugged. 'Fine, yeah.'

I looked at Jordan and then Kayla. 'What do you reckon? Would that be cool?'

Jayden shook his head. 'It's none of my business – whatever Mum wants, I want.'

'Same,' added Kayla with a nod. 'We might get extra presents too. I'm into that.'

The bedroom door opened and Mum poked her head through the gap. 'Oh, the party's up here, but no invite for me?' She smiled at me. 'Wes, can we borrow you for a second, please? Downstairs?'

'Ooooh!' my sibs sang in unison.

Kayla laughed. 'Wes is in trouble!'

2

Molly sat on the sofa with a cup curled in her hand. If the snake sisters were planning on putting me under the spotlight, they had another thing coming. Tables were gonna get turned today.

'Morning.' I folded my arms and stood by the television.

Molly smiled as she sipped her tea. 'Morning, Poirot.'

Mum shut the living-room door. A shut living-room door normally spelled trouble.

'You're not in trouble, Wes,' Mum said gently.

'I know,' I said. '*I'm* not the one keeping important secrets.'

'We just want to know how . . . how you –'

'Found out about Craig?'

Mum nodded. 'Because I never said anything to you about your dad –'

'Don't call him that. The big question is why? Why didn't you say anything?'

Mum sighed. 'I . . . I –'

'He's been in the house. I heard you laughing with him after Rachel's party. Now you're washing his clothes –'

Molly wrinkled her nose like she'd smelled something bad. 'You're what?' She shook her head. 'Ella . . .'

'It was one time, one jumper, OK?' said Mum. 'But, Wes, how did you find out?'

'Because neither of you are slick.' I sighed. 'You think I don't see things because I'm a kid. But I see *everything*. You don't have to use words because your faces and the way you move give you away.' I turned to Mum. 'You were all giddy and skipping before Rachel died, and a bit after, which was weird. And, Auntie Molly, when you saw Rachel's photo on Mum's phone, you were all like –' I clutched my chest and gasped.

They both laughed, but I wasn't trying to play the joker.

'It's not actually funny to me,' I snapped. 'So it turns out Craig left you for Rachel, then she ended up living opposite us? That ain't funny – it's sick and weird.'

Mum bit her lip and nodded.

'Did she do it on purpose?'

'I don't know,' Mum whispered.

'Was Craig still going out with her when she died?'

Mum shrugged. 'I haven't spoken to him since Molly saw the photo. I don't know.'

'Are you gonna talk to him?'

Mum stared at the carpet.

'And, like, I feel sorry for you, Mum – what's happened is *wild* – but I also feel sorry for the sibs – and me.'

328

Mum's eyes filled with tears.

'Like, where's Craig been all this time? All these years we could have known him in some way. He could have been helping when you were sick last year.'

'That's when we started speaking again,' said Mum quietly. 'You know, in case something . . . happened.'

'Wow, so for ages then!' I shouted. 'When were you gonna tell us?'

Mum started to cry.

'She was going to tell you,' said Molly, putting her tea down. 'When the time was right – *if* he proved he'd changed, like he said he had. *If* he'd stopped cheating and she could trust him.'

'And then what? We'd be one happy family. Like in the movies?' I said sarcastically. 'Because that's exactly how that works in real life, isn't it?'

'Wes . . .' Molly began.

'Nah, don't "Wes" me! Don't treat me like an idiot.' I could feel the tears coming. I pointed at the ceiling. 'You know, we were just talking about how nice it would be, and what it would mean – for all of us – if you had someone –'

Mum's eyes got big. 'You didn't tell them, did you?'

'Of course I didn't!' I snapped. I took a deep breath and put my hands on my head. 'Look, I know you lot are always going on about privacy. I get it, you have a right, but this affects all of us. He's our . . . Craig's our . . .'

I couldn't bring myself to say 'dad'.

'I'm sorry, Wes,' Mum whispered. 'I thought I was doing the right thing. I thought I was protecting you.'

She looked so sad, shoulders all slumped, face glum. I had to give her a hug.

Molly's phone beeped. 'Ah, work.' She sighed. She groaned as she stood up. 'I'll leave you to it.'

'On a Saturday?' said Mum from somewhere near my shoulder.

'Cyber security never sleeps,' she said 'TTYL.'

'TTYL?' I said, turning to look at her. 'What you on about?'

'It means "talk to you later".' Molly rolled her eyes. 'God, you make me feel and look so old and uncool.'

I shrugged. 'That's because you are.'

3

After brushing my teeth – which made Kayla happy – and taking a shower, I shuffled over to the doughnut in my slides to meet Margot and Josie. They stared and stayed silent.

'It's OK, you can talk. You can say "morning" at least.'

'We wanted to check on you,' said Margot.

'That thumbs down on our message didn't tell us much,' added Josie.

'Yeah, that was the point. I wasn't in the mood to chat last night.'

'Understandably,' said Margot.

'I miss anything at nine night?'

Josie shook her head. 'Not a thing. We pretty much left after you.'

'It's not the same if we're not together,' said Margot, putting a hand on my shoulder. 'Whisper fixed the lights, though – Rachel was really coming through, wasn't she?'

I nodded. 'I think we're getting closer to knowing her truth, that's why. It's a shame I prefer her lies.'

Margot and Josie looked at each other and then at me.

'So . . . ?' Margot shuffled nervously. 'Do you want to update us?'

I sighed. 'Craig *was* in the house that night. All confirmed. Molly and Mum just tried to tag-team me, but I rowed with them instead.'

'Gosh,' said Margot. 'How are you feeling?'

'I'm on top of the world, over the moon,' I said, smiling. 'Thrilled.'

'What now?' asked Josie. 'What next?'

'Are you going to call Craig again, since he's officially Rachel's next of kin?' Margot wondered. 'You should. We have to.'

'But, before you do anything, do some deep thinking,' said Josie. 'Find out the best way to talk to him because you might get hurt. It could be bad, and we don't want that for you.'

They were so kind and sensible, they really were. Mum should have taken lessons from Margot and Josie.

'You know, my finger hovered over his number last night.' I pulled my phone out. 'I was well tempted. He's definitely gonna have answers to our questions. If I do reach out, and he asks to meet up, will you come?'

Josie snorted. 'As if you needed to ask.'

'Whatever you need, we've got you,' said Margot. She paused. 'Should we tell Hazel?'

I narrowed my eyes. 'What for?'

'If Craig really is Rachel's next of kin, Hazel can start giving out Rachel's things and the police can know. Maybe Rachel can get to the other realm quicker.'

I paused and thought. 'I mean, I hear what you're saying, but then she'll know I was snooping around her office.' I sighed. 'I also don't want people in Mum's business like that, not yet. How do we explain this without Mum looking like a mug? I can't let her go out sad like that.'

'I think we need to talk to Craig first anyway,' said Josie. 'To confirm what he knows and what exactly happened with Rachel.'

Margot nodded. 'OK.'

Someone's phone beeped and it wasn't mine.

Margot pulled hers from her pocket. 'It's Apollo,' she said.

'What does he want?' I grumped.

Last night the lights made me feel like I was onstage! How do you three fancy performing the school disco piece for everyone else tonight? Nine night is apparently a celebration, and, well, it hasn't been. Besides, we deserve an audience, darling – don't you think?

'I think absolutely not,' I snorted. 'Not now we know his little plays are the origin stories of Rachel and Craig's . . . romance. How could I do that to Mum? Rub it in her face like that? And also, gross. When we went to Apollo's and stepped onstage, I –' my body cringed in horror – 'I was acting Craig's part? I feel dirty, hoodwinked.'

'Yeah, I get that,' said Margot. 'I'll tell him no.'

'Thanks. If it weren't for Rachel's stupid ghost, I wouldn't go tonight. I'm sick of it,' I said.

'We have to go, though,' said Margot. 'To end this.'

'I know.' I sighed and looked at my phone. Maybe Craig could get us there sooner? I tapped the envelope next to his name. I knew he could. I took a breath.

Craig. It's Wesley. Can we meet tomorrow? Don't tell Mum, please.

Three dots.

Yes.

I nodded at Margot and Josie. 'We're on.'

NIGHT SIX

RACHEL STARTS HER JOURNEY TO THE OTHER REALM – WHETHER SHE LIKES IT OR NOT

1

Here we were. Again.

I sat on the sofa by Rachel's front window, close to Mum, like her little guard dog. I felt protective tonight. I put my arm on her elbow, then we linked arms. She kissed my head.

Margot and Josie saw this from the floor where they were sitting, sharing a bowl of chips with so much vinegar it stung my nose. Margot smiled and made a heart shape with her fingers.

'Easy, Mum,' I said. 'Don't mess up my curls. It takes a lot to look this good, you know?'

Mum laughed. 'It's worth it.'

I wondered if being there was worth it. I was torn between absolutely hating Rachel and having to help her. I looked at Mum. 'Is this worth it? To you?' I whispered.

She sighed. 'I'm not . . . loving it, but we started it, so we have to see it through, don't we?'

Eurgh, did we?

'I always say don't make promises you can't keep, don't I?'

She did. I really should've listened.

Hazel came in from the kitchen and dropped a plate of custard creams that clattered on Rachel's dining table. 'Sorry.' She sighed. 'I'm just tired.' She glared at Whisper, who sipped at a hot cup of tea. 'Look, is there any way we can chivvy this thing along?'

'What thing?' he said.

'These . . . nights,' she said.

'Why?' asked Lauren, who sat on a chair at the table. 'It's important. I enjoy it.' She picked up a biscuit. She smiled and stared at Hazel as she ate it.

Whisper shook his head. 'No,' he said. 'I've told you. Night six is another crucial night.'

'Go on then, tell us why,' said Hazel, tapping her foot.

'I'll tell you,' I said. 'Because there's no way back now – the duppy's starting to leave, for real. Home stretch.'

Whisper smiled at me proudly, like I was his grandson or something. 'That's right! Rachel's transition really begins. The struggle to let go really starts. It's the *worst* time to stop.'

'Hear that, Hazel? The *worst* time.' Lauren laughed. 'You have to see it through now.'

'Look, Whisper,' said Hazel, 'some of us have . . . lives.'

Oof, where was her spade because that was a major dig.

Whisper sat up in his chair, and put his mug on the

floor. He stared at Hazel, straight in her eyes. 'You're saying I don't have a life?'

Hazel's lips flapped. 'Well, *if* you had things to do, more things, this wouldn't be a priority.'

'*This?*' Whisper spat. 'The commemoration and remembrance of a woman who lost her young life years too soon? This thing here?'

Hazel's head hung down. 'OK, Whisper. I understand. You've made your point.'

'Good,' said Whisper. He picked up his mug and sat back. 'I've never heard anything so *despicable* in my life. You should be happy we're doing this, so she doesn't come after you for eternity.' Whisper kissed his teeth and twisted his body to face the window. 'These people think I have no life,' he muttered. 'See what happens when you put yourself out?'

Mum leaned over and touched his arm. 'It's OK, Whisper, we'll see it through.'

'I'll show them,' he grumped. 'I'll show them who I was.'

I spotted Apollo approaching through the window and we made eye contact. Instead of knocking on the door, he tapped on the glass and threw up jazz hands.

'Places, children!' he shouted, clapping his hands.

2

'No? I didn't get your message,' Apollo pouted. He put his hands on his hips.

Margot looked down at her phone, then up at him. 'But it says you've seen it.'

He waved his hands. 'OK, OK. Fine, I saw it – I just thought I could change your minds.' He looked around the room. 'Don't you want to see the kids act?'

They didn't. The room stayed silent – apart from Lauren, who laughed to herself.

'I'll take that as a yes.'

'No, it's a no. A firm no.' I glared at Apollo.

'But why?' Apollo whined. 'Let's liven up these long evenings.'

'We're not in the mood, all right?' I warned. 'Leave it.'

The last thing I wanted to do was rub Rachel and Rocky's . . . love in Mum's face.

'But you were when you came to rehearsal,' he pleaded. 'You were an excellent Rocky. Wasn't he, girls? Morgana – back me up, darling.'

I glanced over at Mum, who was looking in her lap. My temperature rose twenty degrees.

'He *was* good –' Margot folded her arms – 'but now's not the time.'

'Because?' Apollo laughed. 'It's not like we're going anywhere.'

'Because the writing was crap, OK!' I shouted. 'Absolute dog poop, yeah? Happy now?'

Whisper and Lauren both chuckled.

'And now you know,' said Lauren.

'Please, no shouting. I can't take this.' Hazel shook her head as she left the room.

Apollo looked gutted, but it's what he deserved. We had told him not to push and now look at him, over the edge. 'Is that what you *really* think?'

I nodded. 'Yeah. It is.'

'What's the writing about?' asked Whisper. He sat forward, eager to know just how bad it was.

I grabbed Mum's hand. 'Not much, just some sad girls thinking about talking to a wack boy at a school disco. It ain't that deep – in fact, it's shallow. Empty. Hollow. Trash.'

'Gosh, you don't hold back, do you, darling?' said Apollo. He nodded at Margot. 'Morgana, surely you don't agree with him?'

Margot glanced at me before speaking. 'I wouldn't use those words . . . but yes. Kind of.'

Apollo, wounded, clutched his chest. '*Et tu, Brute?*'
Eh?

'It's just that the other one, *Close*, was much better.'

'What happens in that one then?' Lauren asked.

Margot looked at Mum and me. 'It still . . . has the same kids in it – Rocky, Rachel and Naomi. But it's more . . . poetic.'

'But what happens? They still at the party?' Whisper wondered.

'No,' Margot continued. 'They're in some kind of shop after school, and they're talking about the boy, yes. But it has more heart – and it ends in a real interesting way.'

'How?' asked Lauren.

'It just . . . ends,' said Margot. 'Abruptly.'

'It's not finished?' Whisper sat back in his chair and blinked. 'Hmmm.'

I shook my head. 'Nah, I think it is. Like, that's what's supposed to happen – in the story anyway.' I raised an eyebrow at Apollo. 'Well, you tell us, since you wrote it?'

We locked eyes, daring each other to speak, but there was no way Apollo was gonna win a staring contest against me.

His eye twitched and his nostrils flared. He threw up his hands. 'Fine!' he shouted. 'I *didn't* write it, OK? Happy now?'

'Well, well, well,' said Lauren, laughing into a glass.

Margot made a fist. 'We *knew* it.'

Apollo grabbed his drink from the mantelpiece and gulped it down.

3

Whisper was troubled by what had happened. 'This bickerment is beyond me, Ella. Let me leave the night in your capable hands.' He trembled as he stood up.

'You really don't have to,' Mum replied. 'Really. You don't.'

Whisper stared at Apollo but continued to talk to Mum. 'You can clean up this mess. I have to run home, something to do.' He leaned forward and directed his voice to the kitchen where Hazel was. 'I also have life things to do.' He looked back at Apollo. 'Goodnight, liar.' He addressed the rest of the room. 'Goodnight, everyone else.'

Lauren put her head down and laughed so hard her shoulders – and the table – shook.

'It's really not that funny,' Apollo grumped.

'You know what else isn't funny?' said Josie. 'Taking credit from your friends!'

'Your dead friends at that,' I added, twisting the knife.

'You gave Rachel a copy of "your" book for her birthday – but it had *her* writing in there?' Margot shook her head. 'How could you do that? That's weird!'

'No wonder she hated it. We saw her face,' I said.

'The kids are right,' said Mum. 'That's a very strange thing to do. I don't understand.'

Apollo took a sip and sighed. 'I . . . I just wanted us to both make it. Have a good go at our goals and our lives. I encouraged her to write – believe me. I really pushed her. She was *so* good, as you have read. And, darling, let me tell you, she could direct!'

That I could well believe. Look at her directing me, even in death.

'But for some reason, some inexplicable reason, she wanted to come back to Luton and act. Said she needed to, and I-I couldn't understand it. Well, fame, glory, money, I get *that*.' He chortled. 'But she wouldn't have got that in this town –'

Hater.

'But she could have got somewhere, by playing to her strengths, by writing. And, you know, I just thought . . . if she's not going to write, *I'll* write for her.' He looked up through his eyelashes. 'I actually thought putting *Close* in the collection would encourage her, get her back on track, back to doing what she loved.'

I snorted. 'Yeah, right! You want us to believe you stole her work for her benefit? That's complete toilet.'

'It does sound scammy,' said Margot.

Apollo straightened up. 'Listen, OK,' he said, his voice suddenly serious. 'I wasn't always Apollo Fortune, this fun guy.'

'You're fun?' Lauren smirked. 'That's news to me.'

'When I was just regular old Dev Kartik, I was *nothing*,' he said. 'Nothing! Do you know how hard I've had to work? The money I've spent staging my shows? How much I've had to prove to my family? To show them all of this is worth it? Trying to make them proud? Do you know what that's like?'

The room was silent apart from the sound of Apollo panting, catching his breath post rant. Lauren didn't laugh this time.

I felt kinda sorry for him.

But not that sorry. 'Yeah, that's sad and all, but it doesn't mean you should steal, though, does it?'

Apollo picked up his jacket and swung it round his shoulders, nearly swiping Margot's eye out with it. 'I'm not a thief,' he snapped.

4

We left Mum with Hazel and Lauren at Rachel's to catch up. We watched Apollo – or should I say 'Dev'? Nah, I'd let the man keep something; he had no dignity now – stomp up the close on his way to the station.

'He tried it.' I shook my head and laughed. 'He really tried to spin stealing into good vibes.'

'Good job for calling him out, Wes.' Josie folded her arms. 'That was a bit tense.'

'It had to be done,' I said. 'I couldn't talk about the play in front of Mum. He should've just taken no for an answer.'

Margot nodded. 'Right. It's interesting what he said about Rachel being good at writing, though.' She put her hand to her chest. 'As a writer myself –'

I laughed. Margot *was* a writer, but she was so dramatic about it.

'I wouldn't just give it up – I could never. I love it too much. Apollo said Rachel decided to come home and act, but why? What was the rush?'

'Maybe because she found out she was sick?' said Josie.

'I guess.' Margot twirled a curl round her finger. 'But act in what? Why?'

'Act like a best friend to Mum,' I griped. 'To laugh in her face?'

Margot stared at the sky. 'Maybe there's something in that play she was supposed to be in after all,' she whispered.

Josie's nose wrinkled. 'What do you mean?'

Margot shook her head. 'I don't know yet. Just, like . . . Rachel said she wanted to act, but was really good at writing; she tried to ride horses when she was allergic. I –'

Rachel's door opened and Lauren stepped out. She nodded a goodbye before getting in her car.

'She was enjoying herself,' Josie muttered. 'You know, I think Lauren's all right. She's funny.'

'She's got some quick quips, that's for sure,' I said. 'I think she likes mess and drama.'

'Her sister doesn't,' said Margot. 'Hazel's really over this. She spent most of the night in the kitchen.'

'Well, she's counting the money she's losing.' Josie crossed her arms. 'Every day the house isn't up for rent –'

I tutted. 'The fewer pounds she's making. I know.'

We were quiet for a moment, as we ran the evening back in our heads. 'Whisper made a break for it pretty early,' I said. 'After all his talk about tonight being one of the big ones.'

'Hazel saying he had no life really got to him,' added Margot.

'It was rude,' said Josie. 'I'd be offended too if I was trying to do something important and meaningful.'

I looked over at my house and through the front window I could see Kayla dancing in front of the telly. I then saw Jayden reach up and pull her to the floor. I laughed, but I knew I had to go before that got serious.

'So tomorrow then,' I said. I sucked air through my teeth.

'I've got church, then I'm ready for anything.' Margot rested her head on her shoulder. 'How are you feeling about seeing Craig?'

'Sick, scared, angry, nervous?' I replied truthfully. 'I can't actually believe it's happening.'

'Does Ella know you're going?' asked Margot.

I shook my head. 'If I tell her now, everything will go left. I can't.'

'Have you heard from him?' said Josie. 'Is there a plan?'

I looked at my phone. There was a message.

We still on for tomorrow, son? Wardown Park, 11 a.m.?

I glanced up at Josie. 'There's a plan.'

I replied to Craig. *I'm not your 'son'. See you there.*

DAY SEVEN
SUNDAY 16 APRIL

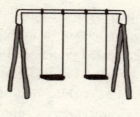

1

I know this is turning into my sleep diary and I'm sorry, but I hardly got any last night.

Craig kept creeping into my brain. On the bright side – if there was one – at least it wasn't Rachel or her duppy.

So, instead of sleeping, I listened to my brothers gently snoring in their bunks. On the other side of their wall, Kayla was up late – way beyond her bedtime – giggling at something on her phone. She took after her mum.

Clueless, the three of them. Unaware of how terrified I was to see the man formerly known as Dad today. They didn't know he had a way back into our lives, and it was me holding the door open.

All because of Rachel. This was all her fault.

Man, if Mum or Molly knew what I was about to do, I'd be deader than Rachel. We'd be morgue mates.

Later that morning, I met Josie in the doughnut and while we waited for Margot she tried walking me through little scenarios to prepare me for how it might play out with Craig. I couldn't tell you a word of what she said because I wasn't listening. I pretended I was – but I wasn't there. Like, my body was – I could feel myself tapping my toes, clenching and unclenching my fists – but my mind was already at Wardown Park. I was fully concerned and consumed by Crap Dad Craig, Raggedy Rachel and their slimy shenanigans.

When Margot skipped down the close towards us in her frilly white church dress, Josie and I walked to meet her. She didn't say a word; she just put her hand on my shoulder.

Wardown Park was pretty empty when we got there minutes before eleven; just a few walkers with their dogs off their leads. The park's overgrown grass glistened as it caught the late-morning sun. My trainers slid across it, flicking green flecks over their white toecaps as we got to the best part of the park, the bit with the swings and stuff.

Margot and Josie ran towards a rusting roundabout. Josie jumped on and tightly gripped the flaky bars, while Margot pushed and ran, the hem of her white dress flapping as she made it go quicker and quicker, which in turn made Josie scream louder with each spin. Once Margot couldn't run any faster, she jumped on and Josie grabbed her. They clung to each other and laughed in each other's faces – in a good way. I'd never seen them act like that before – like have pure actual fun without Post-it notes or a PowerPoint presentation. It was a bit weird, to be honest. Unsettling.

When they shouted at me to join in, I shook my head, leaving them to their moment. Even though it felt like I was on death row, freaked out by who and what was to come, it was nice being still, being outside. I sniffed in as much morning air as I could, and you know what? It burned my nostrils a bit. I spun away to dab at them.

When I turned back, a man stood directly in front of me. A tall man wearing a hoodie. He had one hand on his hip, and another on his head.

'Wesley?' he said. 'It's me. Dad.'

2

Craig looked different, but it had been years, so, duh, of course he did. He seemed larger, greyer, sadder. He was still tall, still white, still had the same rough beard with two random patches of ginger. He was wearing a navy hoodie today – it must have been a special occasion – and those green army shorts, ones with pockets everywhere. He had on sandals with two thick straps and silver buckles. It definitely didn't seem warm enough to show toes in the park, but Craig's bad footwear choices were a Craig problem, not mine.

He coughed. 'Wes?'

'I know who you are,' I whispered. He awkwardly put his arms out and walked towards me.

Imagine going in for a hug when you haven't seen or smelled me for six years? The audacity.

I ducked and stepped back. 'First things first, Craig.' I raised a trembling finger, desperately trying to be brave, to

359

show him who was boss. 'I ain't calling you "Dad" because you aren't one. Secondly, don't you touch me.'

Craig's face crumpled. He was wounded, like *pow, pow* – I'd shot him straight in his swollen gut. 'Yeah, that's fair, that's fair.' He looked past me to the playground, where Margot and Josie stood like statues on the still-moving roundabout, staring at us.

'That's Josie, isn't it?' he asked.

I nodded. 'Yeah, it is.'

'Wow,' he whispered. 'You're both so big. Same faces, though.' He squinted. 'Who's the other one?' He turned to smile at me. 'That other one your girlfriend? Looks like she's ready to get married in that white dress.'

I scowled. 'Don't make jokes with me. That's my friend Margot. Craig, where have you been?'

Craig opened his mouth to speak, but I cut him off.

'I saw you in the close, didn't I? Thursday night? You ran away? Typical,' I spat.

'Wes . . .'

'*And* you were in our house, weren't you? On Sunday?' I looked at his chest and sneered. 'That's why you've got on your blue jumper today, because Mum's got your grey one. She even washed it – you've got her doing your dirty work, literally.'

Craig winced, not knowing what to do or say. He took a deep breath. 'I've missed you,' he said quietly, voice wavering and wobbling. He bent over for a moment, his hands on his knees. As he stood up, he wiped his wet red eyes.

That's right, you cry, Craig. Cry more, I thought. But, the longer he stood there staring at me, studying my face, the more I felt a pang of pity.

Only a little one, though. Tiny.

'I'm just glad to see you, son,' he said. 'Properly see you. I've been hoping, praying, wishing for this moment to come true. I've thought about you all every day for the last six years –'

'OK, but instead of *thinking*, why weren't you *doing*? Six years is forever!'

Craig began to stammer. 'Your-your mum didn't want me around you at all . . . at first.' He reached out to touch my shoulder, but I recoiled. 'I'm sorry, I'm sorry,' he said. His hands shook. 'But things were changing – last week she told me you might change your mind about seeing me –'

'So it *was* you texting her?' I said. 'It was you making her grin at the screen.'

Craig smiled. 'She was happy? I knew it.'

I scowled so hard he had to change the subject. He bit his lip. 'How are your sibs?' he asked. 'I hoped they'd be here too. I thought we'd have a reunion and we'd be –'

'Be for real,' I spat. 'They dunno you, and they know nothing about this. And neither does Mum – you haven't said anything, have you?'

He firmly shook his head. 'No, no – not a word. I couldn't mess up my one chance with you. This means everything, *everything* to me.'

I narrowed my eyes. 'If that's the case, and you care so much, where've you been? Luton ain't that big and phones are a thing, as we've found out. Letters exist too. Like . . . come on, Craig.'

Craig scratched at his neck. 'I . . . I made one mistake – a huge, stupid one – one I regret with my whole heart.'

'You cheated on Mum, didn't you? That's why you've been gone?'

Craig stared at the grass, then nodded.

'So because things didn't work out with Mum, you just decided to ditch us and dip?'

'But your mum –'

'But Mum nothing!' I screamed. 'You're supposed to be our parent too.' I dug my nails into my palm. 'Yeah, cheating's bad, but is going AWOL better? Going with the woman Molly caught you in town with?'

'You know the details?' Craig's eyes bulged. 'Listen, you're not wrong – me and your mum have been trying to work it out for a while –'

'Yeah, I get that. I saw how many hearts you sent in your message.' I shuddered. 'Gross.'

Craig blushed. 'Yeah, well, I love her. Always have, always will. Never stopped –'

'So why cheat on her then?' I stomped. I was beyond frustrated. 'Make it make sense!'

'It doesn't. It was stupid – I was stupid.' He paused. 'I . . . when Kayla was born, everything was so overwhelming. Your mum was so busy with all of you, and I felt . . . I felt neglected, sort of.'

'Aww,' I snarled sarcastically. 'You didn't get enough attention? Got jealous of a baby? How sad for you! That's pathetic, man!'

'I know, I know. I am so ashamed. So embarrassed of myself.'

I folded my arms. 'So what happened then? With this . . . woman.' I was so mad with Rachel, I couldn't even say her name.

'Well . . .' Craig began slowly, 'I met her in a pub. She told me we used to go to school together, but I didn't remember her at all. I liked talking to her, we hit it off, but it was never serious. It lasted about a month, then I never saw her again. We didn't even –'

'Stop,' I said, putting my hand out. 'TMI. Also, that's a lie – it must have been serious for her to put your number on her lease, as her next of kin. I dunno why she called you Caroline, though? Did you even meet her sister?'

Craig stood up straight. 'What? No, I never met her sister. What do you mean "lease"?' He held his chin. 'You know, I *did* have to block someone calling me, asking for a Caroline, talking about unpaid rent –'

I snorted. 'Come on, Craig! You were in love with Rachel. She trusted you – just admit it! I know it was you talking to her on the phone last Sunday.'

'Wait, no! What? Who's Rachel?' Craig was well confused.

'What?' I hissed. 'Stop lying and wasting my time!'

'I don't know any Rachel, Wes. I was talking about Naomi. Naomi Baxter-Banks?'

3

Do eleven-year-olds have heart attacks?

The way my heart was giving bass line, I thought it was over for me. I screamed for Margot and Josie. They jumped off the roundabout and sprinted over. Josie looked at Craig and nodded a cold, sharp hello. Margot thrust her hand forward for him to shake.

'Tell them the name of the woman you cheated on Mum with,' I panted, staring at Craig.

Craig looked between Margot's hand and me. 'Wes, this is a family matter –' he said quietly.

'Tell them!'

'Naomi Baxter-Banks,' he said quickly.

Margot and Josephine gasped at each other.

Margot put her hands up. 'Wait, wait, wait. Naomi . . . Rachel's friend from the play?'

I shrugged. 'I dunno. Maybe?'

Josie looked at Craig. 'You don't know Rachel Kohl?'

Craig shook his head. 'Never heard of her.'

I put my hands on my head. 'Did people call you Rocky at school?'

Craig smiled. 'Yeah, they did! Everyone did. How do you know that?'

Margot jabbed her finger at my pocket. 'Show him the picture!'

I grabbed my phone and flicked through the photos. I found the one I was looking for. The one of Rachel and her friend from her room. I then showed it to Margot and Josie before holding it in front of Craig. 'Which one's Naomi?' I said, my heart doing hurdles.

He stood back, squinted, then put his finger on the screen. 'That's Naomi. She looks young there, but, yeah, that's her.'

Craig was pointing at Rachel.

I stumbled backwards and pulled at my curls. 'Oh my God. Rachel was not even *Rachel*; she was Naomi.' I stared at Margot and Josie. 'We've been completely scammed.'

'Was?' said Craig. 'What do you mean?'

Oh, he didn't know what had happened. I made the picture longer on my screen. 'This woman? Naomi? We knew her as Rachel. Rachel Kohl.'

'*You know her?*' His eyebrows met his M-shaped vampire hairline. 'How?'

'She lived on the close; she was friends with Mum –'

'What?!' Craig's eyes darted from left to right and his head wobbled on his neck as he tried to understand what we were saying. We hadn't even got to the important part yet. Here it came . . .

I took a deep breath. 'And she died. Last Sunday. Complications from cancer.'

Craig's chin trembled. 'I . . . I never told her about your mum. How did she —'

'Did she have sisters or say anything about her family?' asked Josie.

Craig looked through Josie and stared at the swings. 'I . . . She said she had a sister, I think.' He looked at me. 'She didn't say much about family. She talked about moving to London, being an actress.'

Margot nodded. 'That sounds right.'

'Did you call her Sunday night?' I asked.

Craig shook his head. 'No, I blocked her years ago.' He looked pointedly at me. 'I've been trying to get my life together.'

'Do you know why your phone number is on her lease?' asked Josie.

'No . . . I, we —'

I didn't like him calling them 'we'.

'— weren't that close. I told Wes, we only saw each other for four weeks or so.' He put his hand to his chin. 'I said I'd help her out, where I could, but it was just something I said. I didn't mean next of kin, not necessarily.' He shook his head. 'Naomi lived on the close and now she's . . . dead?' He blinked while his hands trembled. His mouth opened and closed and his brow wrinkled. 'Your mum never said. She stopped answering my messages on Wednesday night —'

'When Auntie Molly came to nine night,' I said to my friends.

Josie nodded. 'That tracks.'

'Nine night?' he asked.

I waved my hand. 'A ghostly gathering for Rachel, Naomi – whoever.'

'We're making sure she gets to the other side,' said Margot.

'What?' he said, gawping at Margot in complete confusion. He turned to me. 'Maybe I should come and talk to your mum.'

'Absolutely no chance.' I put my hand out to stop him speaking. 'Craig, seriously – this is *not* the time. And not a single word of this to Mum – don't call her, don't come creeping, because I will block you quicker than you can blink if you try anything. This little door I've opened here will close. I'll lock it forever. You get me?'

Craig swallowed hard. 'I get you.'

'I'll deal with it, all right?'

'OK, OK.'

I looked at Margot and Josie. 'Let's go and figure this out.' I side-eyed Craig. 'Thanks,' I grunted. 'This was . . . helpful.'

We nodded our goodbyes and left the playground.

As we walked across the grass, I looked behind me. Craig was staring, watching us leave.

4

You know how people look well awkward when they try to speed-walk? All janky elbows and knees? That was us the whole way home, all the way along Copsey Avenue and up Copsey Close.

'So not only was "Rachel" a husband thief, she was an identify thief too?' I panted. 'Wild, wild behaviour. Why was Naomi cosplaying Rachel? Was she a stalker or something? Wait.' I stopped suddenly. 'What if Naomi killed Rachel and took her life?'

Margot shivered. 'Don't say that.'

'Why not?' I shrugged. 'It could be true. Caroline did say her sister was dead. I thought she meant dead to her, but now I ain't sure.'

'Maybe,' said Josie. 'But, Wes, husbands can't be stolen. That's not a thing. Naomi playing a role? The role of "Rachel"? That makes some kind of sense.'

'Like I was with my Morgana Foxley Facebook,' Margot added. 'We know from Apollo that she wanted to get into acting. Perhaps "Rachel" was Naomi's biggest, most important role.'

'But you were Morgana Foxley for safety,' Josie replied. 'What's Naomi's reason?'

'Identity theft and stalking. I done told you,' I said.

Margot twisted her hair. 'Speaking of Apollo and the play, if Naomi wrote it and Naomi is Rachel, she didn't even like Craig, did she?'

'God, maybe she was just a weirdo? It could be why Whisper was iffy about her,' I said. 'He knew something was off the whole time.' I thought for a moment. 'Yo, it's why she sometimes didn't reply when you called her name –'

'Or spoke about herself in the third person!' Margot grinned. 'Ooh, it just gets *better*!' She rubbed her hands together.

'Margot, what you smiling for? How's this better? Like . . . what the heck is going on here? We're running round town, riding horses, sniffing oils in hippy health shops, thinking Mum was a murderer and for what? If . . . Naomi wasn't gonna haunt me, I'd quit all this with a quickness.'

'But the intrigue . . .'

I snorted. 'Intrigue? What if this woman was mixed up in mob business or up to spy shenanigans? I know you love all that, but I don't want to be involved in that mess *and* hauntings. It's too much.'

'Be serious.' Margot rolled her eyes.

'I am!'

'What we need to do,' said Josie, looking down at her phone, 'is find the real Rachel Kohl and the real Naomi Baxter-Banks.'

I made my eyes bulge. 'Wow. Really? You don't say?'

Josie sighed. 'I'm searching both, but nothing relevant is coming up. I need to get to my laptop and open some tabs – this is not a phone job. We need a plan too,' she said quietly, 'to get into Rachel's locked room. It's not breaking in if we already have the key, is it?'

'Oh, look who wants to break the Copsey Code now.' I laughed. 'But, yeah, I agree – we need to get into her house when it's empty.'

'How about a lie angle?' Margot asked. 'I'll say I'm staying with you, Josie, so you tell Nia you're with me. Wes, tell Ella that you're also with me. I don't think they'll check with each other, so it should work.'

'Wait, why do we need to lie about where we're sleeping? I ain't staying there,' I said.

'But we might need to,' said Margot. 'We'll need time to work on that lock, try different combinations. It's not going to be quick or easy.'

She made a good point. Cool. We'd stay at Haunted HQ, no biggie. Absolutely fine . . .

'Where will we sleep?' asked Josie. 'Not that we'll get much, but you know.'

'Not in Rachel's bed, that's for sure.' I shuddered. 'I ain't sleeping on no dead lady duvet.'

'I have sleeping bags, don't worry,' said Margot. 'After we . . . let go of the last set, Mum got some new ones.'

The last set got lost when we went camping in The Outback, the wooded wasteland behind our houses. Guess what happened? We got scared by a ghost and ditched them.

I looked up at Rachel's house, at that front bedroom, hoping history wouldn't repeat itself.

NIGHT SEVEN

1

We sat cross-legged on the floor of Rachel's? Naomi's? Raomi's? Yeah, that will do: Raomi's living room, looking at and nudging each other, making sure we held in our biggest secret.

It was gonna be the longest night of tongue holding ever. The Guinness World Record for not telling the adults that everything they knew about their friend was a big fat lie went to the Copseys.

Mum leaned by the window and gently pulled back the net curtain. 'It's not like Whisper to be late.' She turned to the room. 'I haven't heard from him today. I hope he's all right.'

'Well, he wasn't in a good mood yesterday, was he?' I directed that at Hazel.

'All that talk about not having a life probably got to him,' Lauren added, fuelling the fire.

Hazel stiffened in her chair. 'Well, that's not exactly what I meant.'

Lauren shrugged. 'It's exactly what you said, though.'

Margot leaned over and scratched the carpet to get our attention. 'Listen,' she whispered, 'the sleeping bags are in my porch. We'll grab them and let ourselves back in later.' She smiled at me. 'You feeling good about this?' The way her eyes were wide, I knew she was. Margot was McDonald's about this. Loving it.

To answer her question, though, no, I didn't feel good. About Raomi or breaking and entering. But I liked ghosts even less, so it had to be done. I wasn't going to be followed by a phantom for my whole life.

'I'm fine,' I lied. 'All good.'

Margot turned to Josie. 'Anything on the internet?'

Josie shook her head. 'Nothing of note – and I even went past page four on Google, which means I *really* researched.' She nudged me. 'Did you say anything to your mum about this morning?'

I tutted. 'Have you lost it? Course not!'

When there was a knock at the door, Lauren stepped over us to get it. 'That's OK – keep hissing between yous, I'll go.' She opened the front door with a chuckle. 'Oh, it's you.'

Apollo narrowed his eyes at us before heading to the dining-room table. He placed an orange shopping bag on it and began unpacking bags of crisps and tubs of treats. 'A contribution.' He sighed. 'And an apology.'

'An apology for what?' asked Lauren, biting back a laugh.

Apollo closed his eyes. 'My behaviour last night.' He crouched down next to us. 'Hey,' he said gently.

We looked up at him. We had no choice: he was right in our faces.

'On the way home last night, and all of today, I thought about what you said.'

'Yeah?' I said. 'And?'

'And . . . while I was angry – incandescent, actually – I've taken what you said on board. I'm making life changes. Big ones.'

'Like what?' asked Josie.

Apollo stood up. 'Well, darling, I've decided to hone my craft – and to do that I'm taking a playwriting course. I've found one at City Lit, starting Wednesday.'

'That's a great thing to do.' Mum smiled. 'It's never too late to learn.'

Apollo beamed and clutched his chest. 'Thank you. That means a lot. I agree.'

'And the plays?' I said, looking at my friends. 'Rachel's plays. Are you taking them out of your little book?'

Apollo snorted. 'No! They're brilliant; they must live on. I'll tweak them and thank her for the inspiration in the acknowledgements.' He returned to the table and opened a bottle of white wine.

I threw my hands up. 'He ain't learned a thing! If we don't get Rach– I mean, Naomi – to the other realm, I'm setting her on him. Josie, plot a new destination for the duppy on Google Maps, ghost edition.'

Mum moved from the window. 'Ah, here's Whisper now. I'll get it.'

When she opened the front door, Mum and Whisper shared their hellos. He followed her into the room, groaning as he dropped his heavy backpack on the floor.

'I have something to show you,' he said.

2

'You said I don't have no life.' Whisper wouldn't look at Hazel, but we all knew who that shot was aimed at.

'I really didn't mean it,' she muttered to the carpet.

'Well, look at these!' He crouched and unzipped his bag. From it, he pulled four thick books and laid them out on the floor. They were covered in dust and he swept their cobwebs on to the floor. 'Sorry for the mess, Rachel,' he said. 'These have been hiding in the attic a long, long time.'

I leaned over. 'What are they?' I asked, reaching out to touch them.

The adults in the room tittered like bitter birds.

'What?' I said. 'I dunno what's in these books, do I?'

'They're photo albums,' said Mum. 'You know, from the old days, when we had to print pictures.'

'You had to be so serious when taking photos, didn't you?' Apollo laughed. 'You only had one chance because it was all so expensive to print. What hassle!'

'Wasn't it?' Hazel smiled. 'School photos, anyone? We would stand like this –' She stood soldier straight, opened her eyes wide and made her lips sit in a totally straight line. She relaxed, then held her arm out towards Whisper. 'Can I have a look?'

'Please do,' he replied flatly. 'I haven't checked them; just brought the four I could carry. So no laughing.' He handed one to her. 'Be careful, please! They're fragile – so no foodie fingers on them.'

'Awww,' she said as she opened it. 'Is this baby Whisper?' She pointed to a black-and-white photograph of a frankly ugly baby. Whoever said all babies are cute was capping. Bruh, this baby looked like a scrunched-up bag.

'Yes, that's me. Back in Saint Vincent.'

Margot leaned forward and chose one herself. It had a slightly puffy pink cover and inside the photos were covered in brittle plastic film. The once-sticky paper round the photographs had yellowed. There weren't baby pictures in this one but snaps of Whisper smiling, putting his thumbs up by various landmarks. There were plane tickets, receipts and business cards from people with telephone numbers that didn't make sense any more. There were newspaper cuttings and postcards too.

I mean, it was cool, but I was also like, why do you care so much, Whisper? Honestly, it was a bit sad.

'You've travelled a lot,' said Josie.

'I tried to.' He smiled. 'I like getting around. Meeting people, knowing places.'

We turned the page and there was Whisper with his thumb up outside a shop. His shop, the one near Wardown Park. I swivelled the page towards him. 'I recognize this.'

Whisper nodded proudly. 'The day I got my key. Anyway, I just wanted to show you my life.' He gestured at Margot for his book. 'Enough about me. Let's return to Rachel.'

Rachel? I laughed to myself; they knew *nothing* about Rachel.

'Yes, let's,' said Josie. She thought for a moment while a plan was brewing in her brain. 'I know. We've talked about . . . Rachel a lot these last few days, of course, and it was funny because you couldn't agree on some simple things about her, like her smoking.'

'Because she was lying!' Whisper tutted.

'I know . . . but can you tell me a time when you thought, "Oh, now *this* is Rachel"?' asked Josie.

The adults were confused, but Margot knew what she meant. She sat up. 'Like, was there ever a time you thought, "Ah! This is her being her true self"? Not acting or playing – just being genuine?'

Mum, understandably, snorted and folded her arms. When everyone – excluding us – turned to stare, she fiddled with her fingers. 'Come back to me,' she mumbled.

'I have something!' said Apollo. 'When we shared a house for a while, she was *very* particular about her things – she liked everything to be in their exact places and she had a story for every trinket – they all meant something.' He looked around the room. 'It's why I was a bit . . . puzzled by her place.'

'OK,' said Josie, taking notes. 'What about you, Whisper?'

'Well,' he replied, 'she was up and down, but she was very caring. When I had a big flare-up, and Thelma went back home, Rachel came round every day to help – she didn't have to. This was before I saw her eating those biscuits on that bench, though.' He pursed his lips.

'Mine was when she told me she was sick,' said Lauren quietly. 'There was *nothing* fake about that. I'm so glad she shared that with me – even though we weren't that close.'

'Yes.' Hazel sighed. 'We only met a few times, but it was a joy to see her with Bellamy – especially now I know she was allergic. She really tried so hard.'

All eyes were on Mum now. She sighed and unfolded her arms. 'She was fun. She was. And even though I thought she was a bit stuck in the past, she really did love the nineties.'

'It was her era,' said Apollo. He took a sip of his wine while we sat in silence.

Hazel yawned and clapped her hands together – the international sign for 'get the hell out of my house'.

We sat up straight. It was time to spring into action.

'Oh, before I forget,' Hazel said, rummaging through her handbag, 'I'll be late tomorrow. Horse stuff.' She handed a key to Mum. 'Let yourselves in. That's a new key – I had to change the locks, then I misplaced one of my spares, so I had to get a new one cut.'

Misplaced it? Ha! It was burning a hole in my pocket. I bit my lip and made sure I didn't glance or breathe in Margot and Josie's direction. I turned round slowly to look at the dining-room table instead.

Lauren was smirking back at me, one eyebrow raised.

'That's fine,' said Mum. 'I'll do that.'

Whisper rubbed his hands together. 'Good. I have a likkle something planned.'

Hazel stood up. 'OK . . .'

Margot nudged me and flicked her head towards the front door. 'Tell Ella we're going,' she muttered.

I nodded. 'Mum, I'm staying at Margot's with Josie, if that's cool?'

'Yeah, fine with me,' said Mum. 'Have a good time – don't stay up too late!'

Whisper shook his head. 'Boys *and* girls at a sleepover? Together? Now I know I'm old because that would *never* be allowed in my day. Too much potential for trouble.'

Mum waved Whisper away. 'I trust those three. They're the most responsible kids I know.'

Lauren snorted. 'You must not know many kids then.'

Apollo laughed. 'Who sleeps at sleepovers anyway?'

Whisper chuckled. 'Now *that* makes sense – they're up to something.'

'Who, us?' said Margot, firmly shaking her head. 'Absolutely not.'

3

We huddled, hunched over in Margot's cramped and now pretty chilly porch. Margot was crouching, looking through her letter box. 'Right,' she whispered, 'I've seen everyone leave; the coast is clear.' She stood up and pointed to three rolled sleeping bags. 'We've got our kit. You got the key?'

I patted my pocket.

We opened and closed the porch door slowly, then rushed to Raomi's, each of us gripping a sleeping bag. I pulled out the key, my hand trembling a bit. I checked the close to see if anyone was coming.

Josie did not like that. 'Concentrate!' she hissed, physically turning my shoulders to the door. 'Margot's keeping watch. All you have to do is get us in!'

'All right!' I said. I pushed the key in the lock, turned it, but the door didn't open. 'It's not working!' I hissed.

'Try it again, try it more!' Margot pleaded. 'It has to!'

I twisted it once more and thankfully it clunked open. 'Yes!' I pushed it and we jumped inside the house. We slammed our backs against the hallway wall, sighing with relief.

'Was that you trying to be funny, Wes?' asked Josie.

I shook my head. 'Nah, this ain't the time for jokes.'

'It's the time for ghosts!' said Margot, shining her phone's torchlight under her chin.

I slapped her phone out of her hand, on to the hallway carpet.

In the living room we laid our sleeping bags out on the floor and sat on top of them, using only the lights of our phones to see. Turning on the main light would be way too risky.

Josie shuddered. 'I've given this some thought.' She looked around the room. 'Maybe we *don't* need to stay here?'

'Yeah, we do!' Margot shouted. I shushed her, and she lowered her voice. 'It's closer to the action. Plus, we can't be sneaking around the close after midnight, not really. What if we get caught? Then we'd be really in it.' She shook her head. 'Nope, we need to stay until around five – that's when Dad gets up and goes to work. Once he's gone, we'll go there. That's not that long.' She looked down at her phone and checked the time. It was eleven thirty-one. 'Only seven-ish hours.'

Her happy chuckle faded into a sad one, which cracked me up.

'Look at you two! I thought *I* was the wimp?'

'Don't make this about you, Wes,' said Josie, staring at her phone. 'It's about Rachel and/or Naomi. Right, what's the plan exactly?'

I pointed above us. 'We need to get in that bedroom. Right now.'

'And if we can't break the code? What do we do?'

'Then we look for more clues.' I shrugged. 'We have to – this might be our last chance in here, alone.'

'Wait!' said Margot. 'What will we do when we get in? What if it's worse than we could ever imagine?'

I stood up. 'I thought you liked intrigue, Margot? Let's take it one step at a time – now we move.'

When I opened the living-room door, the sound of keys jangling echoed in the hallway.

'Oh my God,' I mouthed. 'Someone's here!'

I closed the door and threw my back against it. The girls jumped up to join me.

We held our breaths and each other's hands.

4

Someone crept up the stairs, metal clanging together with each step. We didn't dare move or talk, because if we did, surely it would be the end of our little lives. As I tried to remember how breathing worked, I wondered who it could be.

Apollo searching for more scripts to steal?

Lauren doing Hazel's dirty work to keep a roof over her head?

Hazel herself because she couldn't rely on Lauren any more?

Whisper coming for . . . Nah, it wasn't Whisper.

Maybe it was Mum – she had a new key too. Maybe she was looking for her own clues, clues to why Raomi did what she did? Crap Dad Craig had probably snitched and told her.

What if it was Raomi herself? Nope, I was being stupid. Ghosts don't need keys, do they? They can float through walls and flicker lights, so they're good on that front. Security means nothing to the spooky.

Upstairs, the person fiddled with the lock on Raomi's bedroom, then sighed deeply.

Margot opened her mouth, but I slapped my hand over it – gently – and shook my head. Whatever she had to say was not worth it. It could definitely wait.

Then . . . drilling. The sound of drilling, minutes to midnight. Josie pressed her ear to the living-room door and waited. Waited for the sound of a door being put on a floor, then footsteps walking above us, but there was nothing. Nothing like that.

Nothing but the sound of a frustrated person kicking wood, then a muffled, frustrated scream. The disappointed person plodded down the stairs. We didn't move a single muscle, but we hoped, prayed and begged that we'd be safe. That they wouldn't attempt to open the living-room door.

Whoever it was stood in the hallway for what felt like forever before closing the front door gently behind them.

We immediately crawled to the front window, desperate to see who it was, but keen not to get caught.

Green wellies pounded the pavement towards a car.

Hazel put her toolbox on the passenger seat before slowly driving away.

THE COPSEYS' INVESTIGATION INTO THE ~~MURDER~~ LIFE OF ~~RACHEL KOHL~~ NAOMI BAXTER-BANKS

VICTIM: ~~Rachel Kohl?~~ Naomi Baxter-Banks?

AGE: 40

OCCUPATION: ~~actress?~~ homewrecker

CAUSE OF DEATH: ~~TBC. Something she ingested or inhaled? Potato skin, sorrel tea, oils? Complications from cancer~~ Who cares?

DATE OF DEATH: ~~between 10:00 p.m. on 9 April and 9:00 a.m. on 10 April~~ Whatever

FACTS (?) AND EVIDENCE:

- Lived at 3 Copsey Close – opposite Wesley
- Liked shopping – lots of deliveries, a spare room full of empty boxes (but her house was pretty bare??)
- Has a locked front bedroom (code set to 0666) – mentioned something about cars behind it??
- ~~Had IBS?~~ Whisper not sure?
- ~~Cast for a role in a new play? Only Hazel and Lauren aware.~~ Playing with our lives

INVESTIGATION QUESTIONS:

- ~~Who killed Rachel?~~ No one
- ~~How?~~ Natural causes
- ~~What time?~~ That doesn't matter now
- What's the lock's code?
- Who was Rachel on the phone with when she arrived at the party?
- Who was outside Rachel's house? ~~Lauren?~~ Craig
- ~~Why did that person come again on Thursday night?~~ To see Wesley's mum
- ~~Who is Rachel's next of kin? Her sister(s)?~~ Caroline Nicholls
- What does Molly know?
- ~~WHY IS WESLEY'S DAD CRAIG INVOLVED IN THIS?~~ He had an affair with Naomi

INVITED GUESTS AKA SUSPECTS	RELATIONSHIP	MOTIVE BEEF	BIRTHDAY GIFT	QUESTIONS
APOLLO FORTUNE	Old friend – lived together in London	Selfishness? Wanted her to return to London . . . or else?	A collection of his plays	• ~~Why did Rachel have a negative reaction to her present?~~ Apollo had stolen her story • ~~Who really wrote Close?~~ Rachel • What was Rachel like in London? Apart from not famous?
CAROLINE NICHOLLS	Unknown	?? Did not attend the party Believed to be in Canada	Did not send one	• ~~Who are you?~~ • ~~What is your relationship to Rachel?~~ Rachel's next of kin? Her sister

INVITED GUESTS AKA SUSPECTS	RELATIONSHIP	MOTIVE BEEF	BIRTHDAY GIFT	QUESTIONS
ELLA EVANS – WESLEY'S MUM	Neighbour and close friend	Elimination? Rachel was being a bit much recently Ella needed a break . . .	Throwing the party with us and trying to set her up with Auntie Molly	• ~~Why did Rachel not tell you about the play?~~ Privacy and distance • ~~What's in your potato skins?~~ Vegan cheese • ~~Who were you really with on the night of the murder party?~~ Craig
FITZROY 'WHISPER' JENKINS	Knows Rachel from their IBS support group	Elimination? Doesn't trust her; thinks she's faking her IBS?	Home-made sorrel tea	• ~~What exactly is in your tea?~~ Clove, orange, hibiscus. Hazel still alive. Not poisoned • Why are you so suspicious of Rachel?

HAZEL WILSON	Landlord	Gain? Did Rachel owe her money?	A riding helmet	• ~~Did Rachel owe you money?~~ ~~Maybe - Rachel didn't pay her rent on time~~ YES • ~~Why the horse-riding helmet?~~ Rachel tried to horse-ride • ~~What is the deal with you and Lauren?~~ Secret sisters
LAUREN ROBERTS CHIEF SUSPECT	Masseuse – and maybe in a relationship?	Jealousy? Was Rachel cheating on her? Upset that Ella was trying to introduce her to Molly?	Aromatherapy oils	• ~~Why were you so upset at the party?~~ ~~Because she knew she was going to kill Rachel?~~ • ~~Were you dating Rachel?~~ No. Massages only • ~~What's in the oils you gave her? What do they do?~~ • ~~What is the deal with you and Hazel?~~ Secret sisters

DAY EIGHT
MONDAY 17 APRIL

1

Sleep update – absolutely none had.

We sat on those bags all night, not talking much, definitely not moving and barely breathing. What if Hazel came back and broke into that bedroom, like we wanted to?

Great minds thinking alike would have got us into a gigantic mess.

But, as dawn's light filtered through the net curtains, we decided, through tight-lipped nods, it was time for one last try.

We tiptoed up the stairs.

'Hazel's such a menace,' Margot hissed behind me. 'I know it's her house, but still!'

Josie agreed. 'It is technically, but she still can't move Rachel's stuff without permission, remember? It's almost like Hazel was trespassing.' She stuck her tongue out. 'Poor form.'

'That's a bit rich, isn't it, Josie?' I scoffed. 'Like, I ain't Hazel's biggest fan, but we can't call anyone out for trespassing, can we? I mean, look at us. Look at where we are, what we're doing?' I laughed. 'Be serious.' I leaned against the wall and touched the lock. 'Right. Any ideas?'

'Hmm,' said Josie. 'Only one.'

'Go on, share.'

'Well, last night when everyone was talking about "real Rachel" moments –'

'That was genius, by the way,' Margot said, patting her own back.

'Her love of the nineties came up again. So let's try one, nine, nine, zero?'

'And every year in between that and two thousand,' added Margot.

It was a good idea; I'll give Josie that. So I tried it, but bad news – it didn't work. The lock stayed stuck. I put my back flat against the door, so tempted to just kick it like Hazel had, but thought I'd better not. 'What else is there?' I said, desperate for ideas. 'Tomorrow's day and night nine; we're seriously running out of time.'

'Let's look for more clues,' said Margot. 'You suggested that last night – let's check now, before Dad wakes up and wonders where we are.' Her eyes drifted to Rachel's bedroom.

We jumped across the landing and opened the door. The room looked just like it did on Wednesday.

I turned to my friends. 'Now what?'

'We'll go in and just check,' said Margot. 'In the wardrobe, under the bed –'

'You take the wardrobe.' I shuddered. 'I know ghosts *definitely* live in those.'

'Yep, I totally believe Bobby now,' said Margot. 'Right, Josie, we'll look in it, OK?'

Josie bit her lip. '. . . OK.'

You know what? I'm glad she was scared. It showed me she really believed now. I was proud, in a weird way.

But enough thinking. I had a job to do. I crouched down by Rachel's bed, just like I did when I found her body. Now, instead of flinching away, I focused. There was mostly dust, crumbs and cobwebs under there, but there was something else. I squinted at a scrunched piece of paper towards the head of her bed. I groaned as I lay down on my stomach and stretched my arm out as far as I could to get my fingers near it. I rolled it towards me and, once it was in my palm, I leaned against the bed to have a long look at it.

'Oh my gosh,' I whispered, my eyes widening as I took in its words. 'Margot, Josie! I've blinking found Rachel's bucket list!'

Rachel's List

5 FEBRUARY 2018

~~Move to London~~ ←

9 APRIL 2023

~~Live alone~~ 18 FEBRUARY 2023

~~Have (or throw) the BEST surprise party~~

Step onstage and <u>shine</u> ★ ★ ★

~~Ride a horse~~ 21 JANUARY 2023

Paint our portrait

♡ ~~Rocky <3~~   16 NOVEMBER 2017 ♥ ♡

Be best friends forever

2

'I'm telling you,' I said as we sat on our sleeping bags, 'Naomi killed Rachel – why else would she have her list?' I shuddered. 'Naomi has got to be the *creepiest* person I've ever come across.' I side-eyed Margot. 'I thought you were weird, but Naomi takes the entire pack of chocolate digestives. We've been doing the dirty work for a murdering, cheating, scamming identity thief!' I scratched my neck. It was starting to get hot in here.

'Wait,' Josie replied. 'We don't know that.'

'Yes we do! Look at the list!' I shouted, jabbing it. 'Have or throw the best surprise party? It's crossed out, and look at the date! Same day as our party! Naomi was actively working on this until the day she *literally* died. Not us aiding and abetting!'

'These dates do work out with what we know,' Margot mused, holding the list close to her face. 'Moved to London in 2018 – Apollo said that.'

'She lived here alone since February,' added Josie. 'The horse riding checks out with what Hazel said too. And . . .' Her voice trailed away.

'And?' I snapped. 'What?'

'And she kissed Rocky,' said Josie. 'Way back in 2017. The November.'

'Before Christmas, before . . . Craig left,' whispered Margot.

Josie took a breath. 'There are three things she hasn't done —'

'So? Who cares?' I was raging now.

'*Step onstage and shine, paint our portrait* and *be best friends forever*. That last one's a little difficult to measure,' she said, rubbing her chin. 'How long is forever?'

I walked circles round the living room. 'This just gets worse,' I groaned.

'Naomi wanted you to paint something for her, didn't she?' asked Margot, drumming her lip.

'It's why and how I found her,' I said, flopping into a chair by the dining table. Next to Whisper's photo albums was a bag of prawn cocktail crisps. I gladly stuffed a handful into my mouth. 'It's the reason this whole thing started.'

'All the dates on this are recent, Wes. She'd been working hard to finish it, even though she was seriously sick.'

'Well, that's guilt for you,' I mumbled.

'It must have meant a lot to her,' said Josie.

'Guilt!' I shouted, spraying damp crisp crumbs over Whisper's photo albums. 'Now look what you made me do,' I said, waving my hands over his books. I wiped the covers clean, then opened one up. 'He was right not to trust her.' I sighed. I shook my head at the thumbs-up picture of him outside his shop. 'Whisper was happy before Naomi came into his life, and so was I!' I angrily flipped the page.

'Careful!' Josie warned. 'They're fragile.'

'Not as fragile as me,' I replied, reading a faded newspaper cutting in front of me. I scanned the headline.

LOCAL GIRL KILLED IN CAR TRAGEDY.

When I looked past the words and over to the pictures, I thought I was going to die too. I choked on my crisps.

'Yo,' I coughed. 'Yo, you have to come and see this.' I spun in my seat. 'Now!'

3

I pulled up the picture of Naomi and her friend and put my phone next to the newspaper article. 'Look!' I said breathlessly, blood rushing around my ears. 'It's the same photo! It's them!'

Josie read the caption over my shoulder. '*Victim Rachel Cole and her foster-sister Naomi Baxter-Banks.*' She took a deep breath and held her stomach. 'Oh my gosh,' she said. 'They were sisters.' She looked up at me. 'And Rachel died.'

Margot pulled the photo album towards her with shaky hands and began reading. Her voice trembled and tripped over the words. '*L-local Girl Killed in Car Tragedy.*' Her lip quivered. '*A normal afternoon turned to tragedy as a fifteen-year-old girl was killed in Luton. Rachel Cole –*' Margot looked up – 'spelled C-O-L-E not K-O-H-L *of Old Bedford Road was pronounced dead on Alexandra Avenue on Thursday afternoon. The investigation into the cause of the crash is ongoing, but eyewitnesses have said that Cole had failed to check the road before she crossed it.* Oh wow.' Her eyes filled with tears. *'Cole was with her best friend and foster-sister Naomi Baxter-Banks at the time.'* Margot started sobbing.

I pulled the photo album towards me and continued. *"'This is tragic. The children who come here every day are funny, kind and bright. It is very sad and a deep shame that this happened to a young lady who had her whole future ahead of her," said Fitzroy Jenkins, owner of Fitzroy's Fine Foods.'* I looked up. 'Whisper.'

'It's why he has the cutting,' said Josie, holding Margot's hand.

'Cole is survived by her parents, Lynda and Benn Cole, and sister, Caroline.'

Josie leaned forward. 'What's the date on this?'

I pointed to the top of the page. 'Eighteenth of May 1998.'

Josie quickly counted on the fingers of her free hand. 'Twenty-five years ago,' she whispered.

Margot shook her head. 'It's awful,' she whispered. 'I couldn't cope if this happened to one of us.' She turned round and fanned her face. 'It's too tragic. I can't.'

I patted her gently on the back and took a deep breath. 'Let me get this straight.' I looked at Josie. 'So Rachel K-O-H-L, who we all knew, was Naomi Baxter-Banks. Craig confirmed that.'

Josie nodded. 'Rachel C-O-L-E was Naomi's foster-sister and best friend. She died when she was fifteen.'

'So "our" Rachel, Naomi, was living as her, right?' I asked. 'She changed the spelling of her name to cover her tracks?'

Josie shrugged. 'It seems so. I think so.'

Margot spun round. 'That cold, awful message from Caroline makes sense now. *I know my sister is dead.* She did know – the Rachel she knew has been for years.' She covered her eyes. 'We must have scared her or brought up awful memories for her.'

I rubbed my head. 'Oh my God – remember the park bench with that tribute to a Rachel Cole? After we went to that health shop? It was for her, wasn't it?' I jabbed the photo album. '*That's* where Whisper saw Naomi sitting munching biscuits on Mars.'

'His shop was directly opposite the park,' said Josie. 'And remember he said he felt a lot of guilt about an accident?'

'No wonder he thought he knew our Rachel from somewhere!' I shouted. 'He did.'

'Don't forget the play,' said Margot. 'Not Apollo's one, the good one? *Close*? It's set in Whisper's shop, isn't it?' She paused for a moment, and her eyes once again filled with tears. 'It ends really abruptly.'

'Like real Rachel's life,' said Josie quietly.

'That could be why Rachel –' I stopped and shook my head – 'Naomi – I have to get used to that – was funny about cars. Remember that weird thing she said about speeding vehicles behind the locked door.'

'Trauma because of tragedy,' said Margot.

I paused. 'Was it an accident, though?' I asked. 'We dunno that. Maybe she pushed her?'

A controversial question, I know, but I had to pose it.

Margot and Josie gasped in unison, and Josie stepped backwards.

'Wesley, what are you *saying*?' Margot shouted. She waved the paper in my face. 'We just found Rachel's bucket list – and now this cutting. Isn't it clear that Naomi was doing this list to honour Rachel, to help her pass through? *Exactly* what we've been doing?'

'Keep your voice down, yeah?' I warned. 'Look, all I'm saying is, I don't know. I just don't trust Naomi. Not after I found out what she did to my family.'

4

'I cannot believe that you just said that, Wes,' Margot growled. She snatched her sleeping bag and stomped to the front door. 'That's beyond – even for you!'

I followed her. 'Well, you best believe it,' I said flatly. 'Because, while this is sad and all, we still dunno exactly what happened. Josie, thoughts?' I stepped into the close and into the doughnut. The early birds tweeted and twittered overhead.

'There are two scenarios at this point,' Josie muttered in her lowest voice. 'Well, one scenario – two different motives.'

'Go on,' said Margot.

'Well, it's clear Naomi stole Rachel's identity. That we can agree on, correct?'

Margot and I both nodded.

'The question is, did she do it for a good reason –'

Margot jumped in. 'To honour her best friend, when she herself was dying.'

'Or for a bad reason.'

Josie and Margot stared at me, waiting for me to say something.

I sighed, and it turned into a wide yawn. 'All I'm saying is we dunno. Like why is Naomi going around kissing her best friend's crush –'

'Because Naomi wanted to finish Rachel's list!' Margot snapped. She stamped her foot, like a toddler having a proper temper tantrum.

'I haven't even mentioned Mum yet.' I pointed my thumb at Naomi's house. 'What if she moved there on purpose? To laugh at Mum while she bodysnatched her bestie?'

Margot kicked at the pavement.

'See? I have a point, don't I?' I was on a roll now. 'Craig's number with Caroline's name on her lease? It makes no sense. What if Naomi grave-robbed, and Rachel's body's behind the locked door, eh? That wouldn't be cool and poetic and lovely, would it?'

'Wesley!' Margot shouted, raising both her arms and voice. 'Too far! What's *wrong* with you?'

'Shhh!' I hissed. 'I'm just saying.' I turned to Josie. 'You get me, don't you?'

Josie shuffled her feet. 'I don't like or agree with what you're saying –'

Margot took a triumphant bow. 'Thank you!'

'But he's right. We don't know, and I want the facts.'

I took that as a win. 'Thank you,' I whispered, gloating in Margot's direction.

'Either way, we now have not one but two restless spirits to settle tomorrow night.' Josie sighed. She pushed her hands apart. 'We have to understand Rachel and Naomi as separate people.' She drummed her lips with her fingers. 'That article said her parents lived on Old Bedford Road, right?'

I said yeah, but I didn't remember.

'Then I'll find out if they still live there. If they do, we visit them maybe?'

'Great idea.' I grinned. 'Yeah, let's spring up and ask them about not one but two dead daughters without warning. Just a pleasant Monday in spring thing to do to two, I'm guessing, old people. Lovely.'

Margot shook her head. 'Wes, please . . .'

'Look, I'm sorry,' I said. 'I'm just tired, stressed, betrayed and hungry. Don't start.'

Margot spun on her heel and addressed Josie. 'Let's contact Caroline again.'

'If she hasn't blocked us already,' I muttered. 'But, yeah, that's worth a try.'

'If we do, we should just tell her about Naomi, and what we think we know,' said Josie. She looked at me. 'Consider calling Craig too? We're running out of time.'

My mouth opened as Margot's porch door did. Her dad stepped out into the close in a sharp suit and shiny shoes. He waved and smiled, but that cheerful hand and warm grin quickly fell when he realized the time and our place. He rubbed his forehead with his palm. 'Margot . . .' he began, 'why do you have sleeping bags?'

'Great, just great,' Margot muttered through a fixed, fake smile. She skipped over. 'Nothing to worry about, Daddy,' she sang, pulling him into a tight hug. 'We're just up early, ready to start the day, like you.' She looked back at us, determination in her eyes. 'We've got a lot to do.'

5

I went straight to bed when I got home. The sibs had gone to holiday club and Mum was at work. I had peace, quiet and some duppy-free sleep for the first time this week. When I woke up, feeling like a new man way after lunch, Margot was blowing up my phone with messages.

Come over! We've had an idea and I've got everything you need to do it!

Eh?

Wake up, Wes! Come on!

And now Josie too? Great. A two-pronged attack.

I showered and headed over. I knocked and knocked on Margot's front door, but no answer. These girls were playing me. Payback for this morning, maybe. I pulled out my phone.

Erm, hello? Are you even home?

From somewhere at the back of her house I heard Margot giggle and shout, 'Coming! When she finally opened

her door, she was slightly out of breath. 'Sorry,' she panted.
'I was outside.' She swung her hands in the direction of
her hallway. 'In the garden, setting up for you.'

'Setting what up for me? A trap?' I knew it. I narrowed
my eyes. 'What are you up to?'

'You'll see.' She grinned. 'Follow me.'

I nervously stepped into her house, suddenly afraid of
the Anderson abode, even though I'd been there loads of
times. I decided not to cross Margot again, the dread was
too dreadful.

'Ta-da!' Margot shouted with her arms outstretched
when we reached her garden.

Margot and Josie had clearly set up something, that was
for sure. They'd pushed Margot's polished wood loungers
and garden table to one side of her patio and put up a
racing-green parasol. There was a jug of juice, packets of
crisps and a plate of square sandwiches on the table
beneath it. A large clear plastic sheet mostly covered her
lawn and on top of it was a canvas, pots of paints and
brushes of various sizes. There were three cushions
scattered round the sheet for us to sit on, and next to one
of them was one of her dad's shirts.

'What's this for?' I asked, eyeing everything up.

'It's for you,' said Josie, leaning out of Margot's bedroom
window above. We heard her run down the stairs, then she
joined us in the garden. We each sat down on a cushion.

'You gonna tell me what's going on?' I said, reaching for
a sandwich. Smoky cheese, so good. Margot had the best
food. It's partly why I could never cut her off, not really.

Margot leaned on her elbow and pulled Rachel's bucket list from her pocket. 'When we got home, I couldn't sleep – I just looked over this list. I am certain, one hundred per cent, that we have to finish it – *that* will get both Rachel and Naomi over to the other realm.'

Josie nodded. 'Remember when Naomi was talking to Apollo about coming back to Luton to tie up loose ends?' She jabbed the paper. '*These* are the loose ends.'

I took the list from Margot and stared at it. The tasks, the dates. It made sense. They made sense. Josie and Margot had a point.

'Of the three things left – *step onstage and shine, paint our portrait* and *be best friends forever* – we completed the first one when we went to see Apollo,' said Josie. 'We did that, for them.'

'Rachel wanted you to paint something, Wes. It's why you went over with your paintbrush,' added Margot.

I nodded. 'And why she bought the frame and canvas, the one Whisper and Hazel had a scrap about. Yeah, makes sense.'

'"Our" portrait *has* to mean Naomi and Rachel. The one in Naomi's bedroom, the one in the newspaper, the one on your phone,' said Josie, tapping my screen.

I found the picture in my camera roll and peered at it.

'What are you thinking?' Margot whispered.

I sighed. 'I'm thinking that you make good points and real sense. If portrait painting gets Rachel and Naomi to rest, and out of my life, of course I'll do it.'

'But?' said Margot.

'But I have to know *exactly* what the deal was between them; I can't paint a portrait full of bad vibes and energy. You know I don't trust Naomi, and these two don't look pleased in this photo. It doesn't give happiness and harmony, does it?'

Margot nodded. 'I hear you, but we've got to try.'

'We?' I looked round. 'You're painting too! Look at you, skilling up.'

She smiled. 'You know what I mean.'

'Yeah, I do.' I stared down at my phone, wondering how this was gonna work. 'You heard anything from Caroline Nicholls? She could really help here.'

Margot shook her head. 'I haven't messaged her. I was waiting for you.'

'All right,' I said. 'Let's do that first.'

We huddled closely together.

'What are you going to tell her?' asked Josie.

Margot took a deep breath. 'Just the truth. *Hello Caroline –*' she talked as she typed – '*I'm sorry to bother you again. I understand that my message was insensitive.*'

Margot glanced at Josie and me for approval. We gave it to her with encouraging nods.

'*I now know that your sister, Rachel, died twenty-five years ago. It was your other sister, Naomi Baxter-Banks, who recently passed away. We're sorry for the confusion and very sorry to share this sad news. Can we talk?*' Margot looked up again. 'Send?'

'Send,' I said. 'Hopefully she'll have something to say. Any luck stalking her parents, Josie?'

Josie shook her head. 'It's not stalking. I looked at freely available data, OK? I found a house on Old Bedford Road that was sold by Benn Cole in 2000 – that's all I know.' She shifted on her cushion and sat forward. 'Listen, I know it's a big ask, but . . . Craig?'

'He might know something. Think about it?' said Margot.

Outwardly I groaned, but inside I knew I had to.

When my phone beeped, they gasped. 'Don't get excited – it ain't fate or him; it's Mum.'

'What's she saying?' asked Margot.

'When are you coming home? Did you come home?'

I replied with a brown thumbs up.

My phone beeped again.

'You coming to the nine night? Whisper is going ALL out and wants everyone to be there.'

'As if we'd miss it!' Margot rubbed her hands together. 'Seven nights down, two to go.'

NIGHT EIGHT

NIGHT EIGHT

1

No, but when I say the music coming from Raomi's was loud it was loud loud. We could feel the bass in our bones from Margot's house. We stood in the doughnut and stared at the house. From here, we could see the living room was jam-packed, absolutely rammed full of people. The house was bouncing.

Margot took in the scene with wide eyes. 'Where did they all come from?'

'And do they all know Rachel or Naomi?' asked Josie.

'I doubt it,' I said. 'I do know Hazel is absolutely gonna hate this, though.' I grinned; this was gonna get messy.

The front door was ajar, and as we walked in we could hear Whisper laughing, even over the thumping tunes.

'We're never getting facts from these people!' Josie shouted.

'What?' Margot pointed to her ear.

Josie shook her head. 'Forget it!' she mouthed glumly.

Naomi's living room had been completely transformed into a club. Someone had set up big booming speakers, and people stood around them, drinks in hand, smiling and laughing with each other. Whisper leaned near the patio door with Apollo, who had his arm round Whisper's shoulders. Shockingly, Whisper didn't seem to mind. 'Now *this* is what a nine night is supposed to be!' he shouted over the reggae music. 'You see? Not us sitting around, sniping – a celebration! Tomorrow is serious – but tonight is fun.' Whisper beckoned us over. 'Come, come! Make sure you eat!'

'This is certainly a celebration, darling!' Apollo shouted back. 'So many people . . . Where are they from?'

'Ah!' said Whisper. 'This is everyone from stomach group. Plus old friends.'

'Did they all know Rachel?' asked Apollo.

Whisper shook his head. 'But I'm mourning, so they are too.'

A tall, thin older Black woman with long grey hair walked over to Whisper and stood by his side. 'This is my Thelma!' Whisper shouted proudly. 'See? I do have a life.'

I pulled Josie close, to talk in her ear. 'That comment about him not having a life really bit his butt.'

Josie nodded. 'Massively,' she mouthed back. She pointed at Margot, then grabbed her and whispered in her ear.

Margot started laughing and looked at us. She did the cheesy thumbs-up pose Whisper did in his pictures, which made us crack up.

My shoulders relaxed. This was a good party. Fun. I'd almost forgotten what fun felt like.

'Thelma!' said Whisper. 'These are the kids I told you about.' He pointed at me. 'This one's Ella's boy.'

Thelma leaned over and shook my hand. 'Thank you for making him laugh,' she said in my ear. 'You've really cheered him up. He hasn't been around kids for a good twenty-five years, so thank you.'

2

We looked back at the house from the end of the concrete yard. Lauren raised her cup in our direction while she talked to Thelma.

'How can we investigate with this going on?' Josie grumped.

I shrugged. 'We're just gonna have to do our best. I dunno? Earwig into conversations?'

'How?' she snapped, pointing back at the house. 'With all this noise?'

'The main thing is getting through the locked door,' said Margot. 'It might be a good time to try again, what with all the people in here.'

Josie shook her head. 'Bad idea *because* of all the people in here.'

I agreed. I took a sip of my drink. 'Right? Who knows what we'd unleash if we did that now? That could go extremely left, quickly.'

Mum and Molly stepped out of the house and into the yard. Mum grinned and gave her sister a huge hug.

I wondered what that was about. Something Craig-related maybe?

'I'm *so* proud of you,' Mum said, pinching Molly's cheeks when they broke apart.

Maybe not.

'Stop!' Molly smiled. '*I'm* the big sister, not you. But thanks, thanks,' she squealed.

I wanted to know what that was about, so we walked over. 'Why are you hugging? What did you do, Auntie Molly?'

Molly nodded. 'Well, hello to you too, Wes. I'm fine, thanks for asking.'

'You're welcome.' I smiled sarcastically. 'Go on then, tell us what happened.'

'Big day at work. Huge. We launched a stable beta of the app.'

A what now? This meant nothing – to me at least.

Margot rubbed her head. 'Wait, you work in cyber security, don't you? Ella told us last week, at Rachel's party.'

As Mum nodded proudly, Margot stood taller. 'So you know about codes and . . . lock combinations, right?' She quickly looked at us, then towards the top of the house and Naomi's locked room.

Josie started to smile.

'Well.' Molly sighed. 'I know a little – I just do the marketing.'

'I have some questions!' Josie bit her lip and tapped her foot against the concrete. 'Margot's dad –'

Margot snapped her head in Josie's direction.

'He's got one of those locks, you know, with four silver spinning number dials, which he uses at the gym. That's right, isn't it, Margot?'

'Yeah, he's forgotten the code, and his kit's all in there, festering.' Margot slapped her forehead. 'What's the most common code for those locks?'

Molly puffed her cheeks. 'Pfft, honestly, it's normally zero, zero, zero, one, or something easy to remember – which is why so many people get hacked or have their stuff stolen.'

'You need one really strong password,' Mum said, like she knew what she was on about.

'I have that for my Google apps,' said Josie. 'But the problem is trying to remember it.'

Molly smiled. '*Exactly!* You should come and work for us, Josie. *That's* the problem we're trying to solve.'

Josie beamed as if Molly was really offering her a job.

'How are you doing that?' asked Margot, biting at her fingernail. 'Can you give us – I mean, my dad – any tips?'

'Well, we're trying something based on old codes we used to use when the internet was an infant.'

'Like in the nineties?' Ooh, this was getting good.

'Yeah,' said Molly. 'For oldies like me and your mum.'

'And Naomi,' Margot whispered.

'What do you mean? Give us an example?' asked Josie.

Molly turned to Mum. 'Els, remember we used to say one, four, three –'

Mum nodded. 'For "I love you". The number of letters in the word made the code. I one, love four, you three.'

'That's cool, but how did that catch on?' said Josie. 'How did all the people in the world decide that was a thing, and agree to it? Before the internet helped you spread it?'

Mum shrugged. 'Not sure, but they did.'

'By actually talking to each other.' Molly laughed.

'Were there any other ways to make codes?' asked Margot.

Molly thought for a moment. 'Erm, that was the big one.'

'OK,' said Margot. She stared at Molly and nodded.

'OK . . . ?' Molly replied, looking around nervously.

'So how does your app actually work then?' asked Josie. 'Just so I know, if I were to accept an offer from your company.'

See? I knew she had taken it seriously.

'You use your voice to say your code – one, four, three – and it shows you your little phrase, then you say the phrase – I love you – then you're let into your secure passwords.'

Josie wrinkled her nose. 'That doesn't sound very . . . efficient to me. That's a lot of steps.'

'It's meant to be fun.' Molly sighed.

And, just like that, Josie had talked herself out of her imaginary job.

THE NINE NIGHT MYSTERY

The music stopped suddenly, and a chorus of 'awwws' and 'boos' rang out from the living room.

'What in the living *hell* is going on?' roared a voice from the beyond.

Hazel.

3

People filed out of the house, some kissing their teeth, some laughing as Hazel shook in the middle of the room, her hands balled into tight fists, her cheeks bright red. 'What is the meaning of this!' she spat, actually spat – water was flying out of her mouth. It was gross, but so engrossing. I couldn't look away.

Whisper shrugged. 'This is what a nine night is *supposed* to be like. I told you I had something special planned. You said it was OK.' He turned to his wife. 'See what I mean, Thelma?'

'A *celebration*?' Hazel said, her words stuffed with spite. '*Something special*? This is disrespectful to the dead. I didn't OK this!'

Thelma stepped forward. 'Sorry for any confusion, but I must say that in our culture, when people pass, this is what we do.'

Hazel stared at her. 'And you are who now?'

'This is my Thelma!' Whisper snapped.

'Oh.' Hazel took a surprised step back.

Lauren tutted and laughed. She smiled in Thelma's direction and rolled her eyes.

'Oh, well, it's nice to meet you,' Hazel said, her tone turned to nice. She appealed directly to Thelma with a semi-apologetic chuckle. 'You see, I'm not used to all this. I don't like too many people in my house – in Rachel's house – while all her things are still here.'

I narrowed my eyes.

'I think people were upstairs, forcing their way into that locked room. The door's loose on its hinges.'

My mouth hung open. The liar! She did that! I glared at Margot and Josie, who begged me to stay silent by shaking their heads.

'That might just have been the bass, darling,' said Apollo. 'And the treble. Look, I went to the bathroom several times and saw no one there. Besides, they were all Whisper's friends. I don't think they'd do that.'

'They wouldn't,' Whisper snarled. 'They would have never been invited if they were troublemakers. I would never –'

Hazel had her hands to her head. 'This has just got to stop!' she shouted. 'I just want my house back! My house! Mine!'

The room felt vacuum-packed. Air sucked clean out.

'And there it is,' said Whisper, as the living-room light pulsed furiously above us. 'It's not about Rachel. It never was. It's all about her. Just like I said, Thelma – but now everyone knows.'

Mum dug into the pocket of her jeans and pushed the house key into Hazel's palm. 'You'd better have this back.' She pursed her lips and turned away.

'Just one more night,' said Whisper, 'and all of it comes back to you. Everything. All of it.'

Hazel gulped, and so did I.

The living-room light dimmed.

4

We were back in Margot's porch, but no lie angles or sleeping bags this time.

We had a plan. The lock would give up its code tonight. Then we'd actually stay and sleep at Margot's.

I scanned the close – I was keeping watch this time. Everyone had left, except Lauren and Hazel. Both their cars sat outside.

I flipped the letter box shut and turned to my friends. 'I cannot believe she tried to pin her late-night DIY doings on the guests. That's some low-down, dirty behaviour.'

'Very uncool.' Margot nodded. 'Whisper really got to her.'

'Yeah,' Josie agreed. 'She thinks she's going to be haunted forever now.'

'Fingers crossed,' I said.

Somewhere, a door closed, so we shut up immediately. I resumed my position, which I now call the Copsey Crouch. I could see two pairs of legs, one wearing wellies, the other in white trainers, walking to separate cars. 'That's them leaving!' We waited in silence until we heard two engines start, then fade into the distance.

I took another look just to be sure. They'd gone. It was time.

I turned to Margot and Josie. 'The lock and the lock only?' They confirmed with nods. I opened the porch door. 'Let's go.'

The cool evening air calmed our nerves a little as we raced to the house. I put the key in the door and we piled into the hallway, closing the door softly behind us. Before heading up the stairs, I peeked into the living room – it was as if the party hadn't even happened. There were no cups on the floor, no half-eaten plates of food lying around; it was completely clear.

The only things left were Rachel's canvas leaning against the wall and the pair of giant speakers in the corner. I guess Whisper couldn't wheel those home on his bike. Not with old Thelma on the back.

I tiptoed up the stairs, half expecting the door to be missing, poof, gone, but, no, it was there. Josie turned on her phone's torch and lit up the lock. Four zeroes. Hazel was *still* trying it, because I'm certain I left it on 1999.

But that didn't matter now. 'Right, what we gonna do then?'

'Part of me wonders if we do what Hazel was trying to do,' said Josie. 'Take the door off and just put it back on.'

'With what tools?' I said. I patted my pockets. 'Oh, wait a minute! I have a screwdriver in my pocket.'

Josie gasped. 'Are you serious?'

'No! Do I look like a handyman to you?'

I tutted and checked my phone. Almost midnight: the last day was nearly upon us. I looked over at Margot, who was staring into space. 'I know you're thinking about the code, but say something, OK?' I snapped my fingers in her face to bring her back to this dimension. I wanted Rachel and Naomi in the realm, not Margot.

'What did Molly say?' Margot whispered. 'One, four, three?'

'You think the code is something like that?' I asked.

Margot nodded. 'I do, but I don't know *what*.'

'Let me try zero, one, four, three in the meantime,' said Josie.

I shone my phone's torch over her hands while she worked.

But no luck, no unlock.

Margot held her head in her hands. 'Remember, at the party, Ella and Naomi were talking about creating codes with their friends – she said Rachel loved one and wrote it everywhere –' She stopped talking and thrust her hands into her pockets. She pulled out Rachel's bucket list. 'Look, this has "IDST" on it – that is the code!'

She was right. It made sense.

'OK,' I said, tapping my foot. 'We're closer – but what does it mean again? How many letters in each word? God, *what* was it . . . ? "I Don't Sleep Tonight", "I Don't Steal Things", except husbands –'

Josie pursed her lips. 'Stop it.'

'I'm joking. I agree with you.'

'It means "If Destroyed, Still True".' Margot grinned, her eyes bright, her face shining blue from her phone's screen. 'That's it – that's the key!'

DAY NINE
TUESDAY 18 APRIL

1

I checked my phone. One minute past twelve. Day Nine had officially begun.

'IDST,' Margot whispered. 'If Destroyed, Still True. Two, nine, five, four.'

I kneeled next to the lock and looked up at her hopeful face. 'If this works, I will owe you forever.'

I wasn't lying. I would. Whatever she wanted – within reason – I would do. I shone my torch at the lock and her trembling hands.

Margot took the deepest breath. 'My palms are properly sweaty.' She laughed nervously and wiped them on her skirt. 'OK, this is it. I'm doing it.'

I squeezed my lips tight and hoped my heart would jump for joy rather than race in fear.

Margot spun the dials on the lock. She muttered the numbers under her breath. 'Two . . . nine . . . five.' She stopped to look up with shining eyes. 'I swear it's getting looser!' Margot closed her eyes. 'Four, please be four, *please* be four,' she prayed and begged. She flicked the last dial to four. The lock slipped off the door, into her hands.

Stunned silence.

Margot looked up at us and her eyes got bigger and bigger.

I let go of my breath. 'You did it, Margot,' I whispered with shock. 'Oh my God, you actually went and blinking did it!'

Josie put her hands on her head. 'I . . . we . . . we really unlocked it?' The girl was shell-shocked.

'I knew we would!' I said. 'I just *knew* it.'

Those duppies better have been packing up their bags on the other side of that door because the jig was very close to being up.

Margot rubbed the back of her neck. 'I'm not saying I'm scared –'

'I'll say it. I'm bricking it,' I said.

'Same.' Josie nodded. 'Me too.'

I stepped forward. 'But we have to open the door – whether there's a body behind it or not. I've already seen one now. I can handle it.'

'Don't say that, Wes. That is not helping!' Margot grumped, folding her arms.

'We can't wait any longer.' My fingers crawled towards the door handle. My stomach flipped right over, giving Pancake Day energy when I slowly pushed it down. As I closed my eyes, bracing myself for whatever lay behind it, I felt something – or someone – touch the back of my hand. 'Holy Moly!' I said, jumping out of my skin, leaving my birthday suit behind.

'Wait, it's just me!' Josie whispered. 'What are we going to do about light?'

Josie . . . please, was that question worth scaring the stuffing out of me? 'Our phones obviously?'

'But we won't be able to see properly,' she said.

'Yep, and three torches at once is too much,' Margot added. 'The police might come, thinking we're intruders.'

'I mean, that's *exactly* what we are, but I get it – I don't want to be busted for burglary either.' I thought for a moment. 'OK, how's this? We flick on the main light for, like, thirty seconds max. That way we see as much as we can, take it in, get some photos and get out. Deal?'

'It's intense,' said Margot, drawing a breath through her teeth. 'But let's do it. I'll set a timer.'

Josie nodded. 'OK.' She put her hand on top of mine on the door handle, then Margot added hers. Together, we pushed the door open into the dark beyond.

The first thing that hit us was the sweetest scent. Very much like fresh daisies and definitely not death. This was a good start and I took that as a win.

I fumbled along the wall for the light. 'I can't find the switch!' I hissed. 'I'm gonna have to use my phone for one second.'

'But not the torch, just the screen!' Josie pleaded.

'Yeah, fine.' I turned the brightness up and shone my phone against the wall. I tutted when it turned out the switch was basically next to my face. I flicked it without warning the girls. The light grew warmer in the room.

I was shook by what I saw. 'Wow. Wow. So *this* is where all Naomi's deliveries went, eh?'

2

Margot stumbled around the room, mouth agape. 'It's *incredible.*'

It was incredible all right – incredibly creepy.

The room was night and day, truly chalk and cheese compared to the rest of the house. It was like dipping through a portal into a different dimension. The walls were painted a fresh light pink, and the beige carpet was thick and soft. A Spice Girls poster was Blu-tacked to the wall, next to one that said Nirvana, which had a naked baby swimming in a pool towards a dollar bill.

Weird flex, but OK.

Two single beds on opposite walls faced each other. One of the beds was covered with stuffed horses. A big desk was pushed against the wall that faced the window and a small grey television with a big back. It had, like, a letter box attached underneath it. I pointed. 'You send post through that?'

'No,' said Josie. 'That's for videotapes, I think?' She looked at the little rectangular boxes next to it. 'These things! Oh, wow, *Clueless* is here!'

'That's what Ella was watching!' Margot smiled.

'It's real?' I said, walking over to check. 'Huh. I thought Mum was pulling my leg.' There was a collage of photos, notes, tickets and trinkets pinned up all over the wall behind the television. A return to King's Cross, a ticket for *Twister*, a faded library card and a friendship bracelet. My eyes zeroed in on a photograph. When they focused in that one second everything made total sense.

'I've found something,' I gasped. 'Well, two things.'

Margot and Josie jumped over. 'We've got to be quick,' Margot said, panicking.

The bedroom light sparkled and shone.

Rachel and Naomi had arrived.

'That's them,' Margot said softly, checking the ceiling. 'What did you find?'

I pointed to half a gold necklace, with a pendant hanging from it. Half a broken cracked heart, with 'friends' written on it in letters that cascaded down. 'Naomi had the other half. Remember when she said she was her own best friend? She really was. It's in her room, isn't it? The other piece?'

Margot nodded. 'It's still on her bed –'

'If Hazel hasn't put it on eBay yet, you mean,' I said.

'What was the second thing?' asked Josie. She waved her hand to hurry me up.

I tapped a photo on the wall. 'This is *exactly* what I needed. I get it now.'

Margot stood on her tiptoes to see. The picture was like the one in Naomi's bedroom and Whisper's article, but instead of looking sad and solemn, Naomi was grinning at the camera, her perfect teeth on display, her eyes gleaming. Rachel was laughing. She had her arm round Naomi's neck and was kissing her cheek.

They radiated pure joy. They, thankfully, didn't know the woes that were quickly coming their way. 'I can paint now,' I whispered, wiping away a tear. I took out my phone and snapped a picture.

'See? They *did* love each other! I told you!' Margot gloated. Her phone buzzed in her pocket.

'The timer!' I reached up to turn off the light.

We jumped out on to the landing and I relocked the door, making sure all the dials were set at zero.

'That wasn't my timer,' Margot said. Her phone buzzed and flashed. '*That's* my timer. The other beeps were from Facebook.'

I froze. 'From her?'

She nodded. 'Caroline Nicholls.'

'And?' asked Josie.

'She's left a number. Caroline wants to speak to us. As soon as possible.'

3

We stood in the dark hallway by the front door. 'We can't call her here,' I said, holding Rachel's canvas under my arm and shaking my head. 'It's way too risky – Hazel could spring up any second, and so could the cops. We've gotta bounce.'

'Agreed,' said Josie.

Margot shrugged. 'We'll just call her from my house?'

'And if your dad wakes up?' said Josie. 'He'll be mad and you'll be in trouble.'

'Doubt it.' Margot snorted. I couldn't see it, but I felt her wave us away. 'He's a deep sleeper anyway. It's not like we can go to either of your houses and do it. Let's go.'

'All right,' I said, opening the door for them, then shutting it quickly behind me.

I glanced at my house – Mum's bedroom light was on. I hoped and prayed she was lying down and not looking out of the window.

Margot unlocked her porch, then her front door. She pointed up the stairs, but we knew the drill; we knew where to go. Margot softly walked up the stairs behind us. As she was about to close her bedroom door, her dad's face appeared in the gap like something out of a slasher film.

I gasped, clutched my chest and nearly rolled off her bed in sheer shock.

'Where have you been?' he said flatly. He didn't seem angry; her dad was calm – and that made it much creepier.

Margot smiled and dropped her shoulders. 'We went for a little walk before bed to decompress, Daddy.'

'Don't "Daddy" me, Margot. It doesn't work. It's especially broken after midnight.'

I stared at the floor. I didn't want to be here, in this. I glanced over at Josie. She shook her head.

'We only walked round the close, Dad, I promise,' Margot said. A fully brilliant half-truth. 'The nine night was *intense* – loud music, lots of people, an argument. It was overwhelming.' She snuck a look back at Josie and me, seeking support.

I stepped up. 'Oh yeah, it was wild. I-I'm looking forward to tomorrow, well, tonight, when it will all be over.'

Margot's dad raised an eyebrow at me, then looked at Josie. 'They're telling the truth.' She sighed. 'The nine night was exactly like that.'

'And what about this morning? With the sleeping bags? Going to London by yourselves? Don't think I don't know about that!'

Margot shrugged but stayed silent. So did Josie and I.

'You're going to end up in trouble,' he warned. 'Margot, you're grounded.'

Margot smiled. 'Starting when?'

'Starting now. Your friends have to go home.' He looked over at us. 'Sorry, kids, it is what it is.'

'Wait!' said Margot. She touched her dad's arm. 'Permission to negotiate?'

My jaw dropped, and I looked over at Josie. Negotiate? Bruh.

I knew her dad was a lawyer, but, my gosh, if I tried this even once with Mum, there'd be no second time. I'd be hanging out with Rachel and Naomi, haunting the close.

I stared at Josie, who shrugged. 'This is what she does.'

Margot's dad sighed. 'Permission granted.'

'OK, how long were you thinking of grounding me for?'

'A month, starting right now,' he replied. He crossed his arms.

'A month?! That's way harsh. I haven't even done anything!' Margot touched her chin. 'How about you make it ten days, but it starts after nine night's finished? I can't miss that; I won't. Actually, wait, it can start after we go back to school, so next Monday.' She paused to think. 'Also, my friends can stay because we're working on some things. A memorial for Rachel.' She pointed at Naomi's canvas. 'Important stuff.' Margot put out her hand. 'Deal?'

Margot's dad looked at her hand. 'No deal. Two whole weeks, starting as soon as the nine night's over. Your friends can stay – but you keep it down! Deal?'

'Deal.' Margot smiled, shaking his hand.

4

We huddled round Margot's phone. I glanced at her closed door, then back at her. 'I can't believe you did that,' I hissed. 'And it worked? What?'

'Meh,' said Margot. 'Dad cares, of course – his bald head makes him look tough, but he's marshmallow soft.' She shrugged. 'It's just chat. Speaking of which . . .' She touched her screen. 'Let's call Caroline.' Margot nudged Josie. 'What time is it over there?'

'It's twenty past midnight here, so –' Josie looked up as she ran the numbers – 'seven twenty in the evening. It's still yesterday there.'

Margot nodded. 'And what's the plan?'

I sat up. 'We need to know a few things. One, why was her first message to us so cold? I mean, I *think* we know – Rachel was her sister and Naomi was using a variation of her name, but why not just say that? Two, what were Rachel and Naomi like together? I've seen that nice photo,

I think they were friends, but I want to be sure. Three *and* four, I guess – what were they like individually? We think we know a lot about Rachel, and a few facts about Naomi, but are they right?'

'You're so on it, Wes,' said Margot proudly, like she was Mum. 'I'd also ask if Caroline knew Naomi was sick and, if so, for how long?'

'And the connection to Craig,' added Josie. 'What happened there?'

'We'll also have to tell her we're sorry – for both of her losses,' I said.

'Of course.' Margot nodded. 'Good thinking.' She copied and pasted the number and pressed call.

The dial tone rang loudly in her room. Margot winced and quickly lowered the volume.

There was a click, then a voice.

'Hello? Morgana?' said the voice.

'Hi, Caroline,' said Margot in her smartest, most mature voice. 'My name's actually Margot.'

Caroline chuckled wearily at the other end. 'Using another name? How . . . ironic.'

How . . . rude, no?

Margot gulped. 'I'm here with my friends, Josie and Wesley. Thank you for reaching out.'

'I had to, after your message.' She lowered her voice. 'I'm sorry to hear about Naomi – I take it she was your friend?'

I screwed up my face and gestured at the phone.

Caroline was so strange – her sister had died and *she* was saying sorry to *us*?

'Yes, she was – and we're sorry too,' said Margot.

'Thank you, thank you.' Caroline sighed. 'We had an inkling it was getting worse –'

'Sorry, who is we?' asked Margot, cutting in.

'Our parents,' Caroline replied.

Josie jumped in. 'Lynda and Benn, right?'

Caroline paused. 'Yes . . . They live with me in Canada. We left England.' She took in a deep breath. 'Twenty years ago now? A long time.'

'What did you mean you had an inkling it was getting worse?' asked Josie, leaning over the phone. 'Was Naomi sick for a while?'

'I'd say so,' Caroline said coldly.

This woman was so frosty. What was her problem? I shrugged in my friends' direction.

'Did you speak to Naomi recently?' Margot asked, nibbling her nails.

'I did,' said Caroline. 'Last Sunday – it was tense to say the least.'

I looked at my friends. So Naomi was on the phone to Caroline at her party. Confirmed.

The whole truth was in touching distance.

5

It was my time to talk.

'We heard some of that conversation – Naomi's side anyway. What happened?'

'She wouldn't let us help her, as usual – *I* was getting sick with worry and frustration!' Caroline raised her voice. 'Look, we knew Naomi had cancer, she had told us, but she wouldn't let us do *anything* to help – she was committed to remembering Rachel! She had Rachel's bucket list apparently and had to complete it! Those two made a pact – and Naomi couldn't break it.'

The three of us looked at each other. Margot cocked her head smugly.

Caroline continued. 'We told her over and over and over that it wasn't her fault – it was an accident. Forget the list. Move on! But she wouldn't. When Naomi got sick, it made her focus sharper. To her, time was ticking.'

A baby cried in the background. Caroline took deep breaths.

'Listen, I have to get off this call soon, so I'll say this quickly – Naomi and I had a . . . difficult relationship. I was jealous of their closeness – their shared jokes, their love of chocolate digestives. They were best friends and they . . . always left me out?' Caroline laughed. 'It sounds so stupid and petty – I'm a grown woman. I have kids. But that's how it felt then. I'm still annoyed now, clearly.'

'Is that why you were cold with us when we told you Rachel died?'

'Yes,' Caroline whispered.

We stayed silent, taking that in.

'You still there?'

Margot nodded – not that Caroline could see. 'Yes,' she said. 'Just a couple more quick things? Through Naomi we've got to understand a little bit of what Rachel was like. She wanted to act, loved horses, had a crush on someone –' Margot caught my eye – 'called Craig Evans.'

Caroline laughed. 'Oh God, Rocky? From school? That's a blast from the past!'

'Did Rachel like him?' I asked.

'Like him? She was obsessed. She thought she was going to marry him!'

'What did Naomi think?' said Margot.

'She wasn't a fan, thought Rachel could do better.'

I winced hard. Listen, Craig's an idiot, but I didn't like that comment, coming from her. I leaned forward. 'Are you friends with him?'

'With Rocky?' She laughed. 'No!'

I didn't know what was so funny.

'Do you know why his number was on Naomi's lease then, with your name?'

'She used his number?' Caroline sounded shocked. 'She really did it?'

'Did what?' we asked in unison.

Caroline sighed. 'When she was getting that place in Luton, she asked to put me down as next of kin – of course I said yes. I wanted to help. The conversation turned to Rachel, then rolled into an argument. I snapped and said something like "Put Rocky instead", because in Rachel's mind he was her "husband".'

Margot and Josie stared at me.

'Naomi shouted something like, "Fine, I have his number – he blocked me years ago, so I'll do just that," and slammed the phone down. That was the last I heard on that. I thought she was just joking.'

I sat back. I felt . . . now this is weird . . . warm inside? Part of me was proud that Craig really had blocked her. He wasn't lying. Maybe he was actually telling Mum the truth?

Caroline snorted. 'Who cares about Rocky anyway?'

That warm feeling suddenly ran hot and boiled over. 'I do!' I snapped. 'That's my dad!'

Everyone – *everyone* – fell silent. I couldn't believe I'd blurted that out, but I couldn't take Craig getting cussed by outsiders. That's *my* job.

'Wow, OK,' said Caroline. She coughed. 'I'm sorry.'

'For laughing at him or because he's related to me?' I said.

Caroline paused. 'The first one, obviously.'

It wasn't obvious. She was obviously trying it on.

'Listen, I do have to go – do you need anything else?'

'One more thing – can you tell us a bit more about Naomi?'

Caroline took a deep breath. 'Well, she was a wonderful writer.' She laughed. '*Loved* the Spice Girls – called herself Allspice. She was thoughtful, kind, funny. I can admit that now. It's the truth.' Her voice wobbled. 'I just wish she'd spent more time being herself – not Rachel.' She sniffed. 'Anyway. There's things to wrap up over there, I'm sure – send me her landlord's number. I'll talk to our parents and handle the arrangements. OK?'

'OK!' said Margot, who stared at me. 'We'll do that first thing tomorrow, our time. There's some things we have to do here. For both Rachel and Naomi.'

NIGHT NINE

'RACHEL' GOES TO THE REALM . . . BUT DOES HER DUPPY REMAIN?

1

I kneeled on the plastic sheet in Margot's garden, putting the finishing touches to the portrait. I looked at it through one eye, then the other. It wasn't bad at all, even if I said so myself. I put my paintbrush down and turned to my friends.

Margot walked in circles round her lawn, talking to herself.

Josie sat opposite me, staring at her phone. She glanced up. 'How's it going?' she asked. 'Because we don't have much time – it's starting soon.'

'Well, come be a critic,' I said.

Josie stood up and peered over my shoulder at the painting. 'Wes, that is so good.' She literally and figuratively patted me on the back. 'I don't know how you do it.'

'Magic,' I said. 'It's magic.'

'Yeah, maybe it is.' She laughed. 'Margot, come look!'

Margot walked over, muttering under her breath. 'And something that started as a murder mystery morphed into something much different.' She opened her arms wide then looked at us. 'How's that sounding? Dramatic enough?'

'Apollo will be proud.' Josie laughed. She pointed down at my painting and raised her eyebrows.

Margot tapped at her chest, as her eyes began to water. 'That is *amazing*,' she said. She fanned her eyes. 'Oof, it's hit me right in the feels!'

'Hey, please don't weep on my work. I'm trying to dry it, not rewet it!'

'Sorry, sorry,' she said, stepping back. 'You've just . . . captured them perfectly. It looks just like the photo.'

I looked up at Josie. 'So, *paint our portrait* . . . we can tick it off their list, right?'

'Right,' Josie replied. 'We're done. Is it dry enough?'

I tilted the canvas towards me. 'No drips – we're good to go.'

2

I cautiously carried the canvas, its portrait side facing the street. It was dry enough, but you can't be too careful. I couldn't ruin it now by being careless. No one needed The Banner of Doom Part Two.

Margot knocked on the door. She turned to us and drummed her fingers together. 'I'm nervous – and I hope Whisper doesn't mind our interlude. He has this whole thing planned.'

'We'll take ten minutes max. He can have the rest of the time. But you know what? I think he's gonna love it – it is the point of the nine night after all.'

Lauren opened the door. 'All right?' She looked down at my hand and pointed. 'What's that then?' She stepped outside to look.

'Can you not?' I asked, protecting the painting. 'I'll show you, but give it a minute, yeah?'

'All right, touchy.' She laughed. 'You know what? Pop it in Rachel's room, away from everyone else.'

Look at Lauren being helpful.

'That would be great!'

She smiled and moved out of the way.

I ran up the stairs and opened Naomi's bedroom door. Her belongings were, thankfully, still on her bed. My chest tightened looking at her Spice Girls T-shirt. It was all so sad, so tragic.

These last nine days had been a lot – to put it mildly. And, even though I still had slight beef with Naomi, I felt terrible for her, and for Rachel. I felt a bit of pity for Mum too. I even had a sea-salt sprinkling of sadness for Craig. I propped my portrait against the wall and glanced at Naomi's half of the shared gold necklace, the word 'best' cascading down its cracked heart. I snatched it, pushed it into my pocket, then ran down the stairs.

The usual suspects were in the living room, plus new recruits Thelma and Auntie Molly. Hazel sat on the sofa with her head down.

Apollo leaned on the mantelpiece. 'You know what? I'm actually going to miss this.' He raised his glass. 'The train fare not so much!' He chortled and the others chuckled along with him. He leaned over and put his hand on Whisper's shoulder. 'Come on then, tell us what we're in for tonight.'

Whisper sat forward on his dining-table chair. 'Well –' he rubbed his chin – 'this is the ninth night, the night when the duppy comes home.'

Hazel sat up. 'Rachel's coming here?'

Whisper nodded. 'She'll go to her room and take whatever she wants. We need to prepare.'

'How?' asked Mum.

'By putting her mattress and bedframe against the wall, so she has a clear path to pass through.'

Hazel pinched the bridge of her nose and groaned.

Whisper waved his hand over the covered dishes of rice, meat and fried dumplings on the table. 'This food that Thelma prepared?'

'Thank you, Thelma,' Apollo mouthed, reaching for her hand.

'It's not to be touched until after she arrives.'

'When's that then?' asked Lauren.

'Midnight,' said Thelma with a solemn nod. 'That's their usual time.'

'But it's only eight!' Lauren whined. 'It looks so good.'

'How will you know when Rachel's here?' Margot asked. 'How can you tell?'

'Someone will see her in a doorway, and they will let me know,' said Whisper.

Apollo drummed his fingers on the mantelpiece. 'So what do we do now?'

'We wait,' said Whisper. 'Unless anyone would like to share a story about Rachel?'

I looked over at Margot and Josie and nodded.

We were ready.

It was time.

'We have a story.'

Whisper waved his hand to give us the floor. 'Please. Go ahead.'

Mum reached out to grab Auntie Molly's hand. 'You sure about this, Wes?'

'We're certain.' I coughed, then took a sharp breath. 'There's something we need to tell you about Rachel. She wasn't who you thought she was. At all.'

3

'I'll start at the beginning, and I'll be straight – we thought all of you, potentially, had something to do with Rachel's death.'

'*I knew it!*' Whisper shouted, slapping his thighs. 'I told Thelma – didn't I tell you they thought we were murderers?'

Thelma nodded. 'He did.' She smiled proudly, which was super weird to me, but anyway. Old people, I guess.

I continued. 'I found Rachel in her bed the day after her party with some of her birthday gifts around her.'

'What do you mean?' said Lauren.

'Exactly what I said – the sorrel tea Whisper made was spilled on her bed and on the floor. Apollo, your . . . plays –'

He hung his head in shame, like he should.

'– were by her side. Lauren, your oils were mixed in the burner –'

Lauren put her hands up. 'I didn't put them in there! I'd left by then!'

'We know,' said Margot. 'But Wesley thought he saw you in the close later that night, remember?'

'Haven't forgotten, never will,' said Lauren. She glared at me, but a smile twitched at the corners of her mouth.

I kept going. 'Very close to her hand was one of Mum's potato skins – the special ones she'd made for Rachel and Rachel only.'

Mum looked surprised and a bit panicked. 'They were special because of the vegan cheese – I know you think it's nasty. I didn't want you to waste them.'

Hazel sat forward. 'So everyone's gifts, but not my riding helmet?' She smiled smugly. 'I wasn't in the frame?'

Josie shook her head. 'Oh no, you were *very* much in the picture. Just not yet.'

Lauren creased up, as Hazel's cheeks turned cherry red.

'What did you think killed her? At this point?' asked Auntie Molly, stroking her lip. Yes, she was 'Auntie' again. I was over our fight.

'A poison,' said Margot with a nod.

'It seemed logical,' added Josie. 'We researched your tea, Whisper, and went to the shops to check out your oils, Lauren.'

Whisper smiled. 'The investigation started right away?'

Josie nodded. 'That same night – well, we had notes from the party the night before. It was so weird and awkward; we knew something was strange when everyone's stories about Rachel didn't make sense when you put them together.'

'Did she smoke or not? Was she allergic to horses or not?' Margot said, counting on her fingers.

'Was she in a play or not . . . ?' Apollo added.

I tutted. 'We're coming to that!'

Margot looked at Whisper. 'Once you told us about nine night, our investigation had a definite deadline. We believed everything you said about duppies and spirits, so it was a race against time to find evidence of Rachel's murder —'

'Because there was no way I was gonna spend the rest of my life haunted by her.' I pursed my lips and shook my head.

Whisper nodded. 'Good kids. You learned something from me!'

'We did,' I said.

'Why did you think they did it?' asked Auntie Molly.

'You asking about motives?' I asked.

'*Motives!*' Whisper clapped his hands together. 'These kids are so serious.'

Apollo's arm shot up. 'What was mine? What was mine?'

'Selfishness,' said Josie. 'She was a better writer than you, and you couldn't take it.'

'Ooh, burn!' said Lauren.

'Yours was jealousy, Lauren — we thought you were in love with Rachel,' said Josie. 'Hazel, yours was money and/or getting your house back. Whisper, yours was harder —'

'Because I didn't have no reason?'

'We thought you didn't trust her, and you needed to eliminate her maybe,' said Margot.

'And what about your mum?' asked Hazel, turning to her.

I sighed. 'Well, Mum, it was looking *really* bad for you.'

4

Mum squirmed in her seat.

'Mum was really happy before Rachel died.' I sighed. I looked at her out of the corner of my eye. Auntie Molly gripped her arm, on edge, waiting for the next bit. 'Mum said Rachel could be a lot sometimes and that she had needed a bit of a break.'

'A . . . permanent break?' Apollo asked, his eyebrows raised.

'Maybe,' I whispered. 'She was being well weird, getting strange messages, suspicious items of clothing turning up where they shouldn't have been.'

'Wes,' Mum warned.

Yeah, she was right. That was enough details for them.

Lauren put her hand up. 'Wait, but you all knew Rachel had cancer by the third night –'

'We knew that morning, actually,' said Margot, trying not to be smug and failing. 'We called the police and they told us. We knew before most of you.'

Whisper gasped.

'Yep, Hazel was the first to know,' Josie confirmed. 'PC Stevens told us – in not so many words.'

'I don't get it,' said Lauren. 'Why didn't you bin your binoculars once you knew Rachel had cancer? Investigation over at that point, no?'

'Nope. The goal was to make sure Rachel crossed into the other realm, regardless,' said Margot.

I looked at Mum and Auntie Molly. 'That night, my auntie arrived. When she saw Rachel's picture on Mum's phone, she was shook – and so was Mum. Mum was *gutted*.'

Whisper wagged a finger. 'I remember that night very well.'

'It was jarring because Ella had been so happy in the days before,' said Margot. She turned to Mum. 'I'm sorry.'

'It turns out Rachel and Mum had some . . . shared history – but they didn't know it.'

Mum gulped.

'That's vague,' Hazel mused. She tucked her hair behind her ears and peered at Mum.

'It wasn't vague for long.' I stared at Hazel. 'When we went to your stables, we didn't come for the horses – well, I didn't anyway.'

'We had to know who Rachel's next of kin was,' said Josie. 'To make sure she could have a proper burial.'

Margot pointed at Lauren. 'Your sister directed us to your office.'

Apollo's jaw dropped. 'You're *sisters*? Well, well, well. Why didn't you say?'

Lauren shrugged. 'Wasn't sure I wanted to claim her.'

'Fair enough,' said Apollo, nodding slowly. 'Totally understood.'

'You went through my files at the office? You *trespassed*?' Hazel's hands balled into tight fists. She glared at Lauren. 'And you let them?'

'I didn't know that's what they were doing! Besides, they threatened me.' Lauren scowled. 'Said they would give me bad reviews if I didn't tell them what our deal was.'

Auntie Molly stared at me. 'Really, Wes?'

Mum groaned and buried her face in her hands.

'I'll ask again, did you trespass?' Hazel demanded. She stood up.

'We did, yes,' said Josie. 'I'm sorry, but it was worth it.'

'How so?' Hazel shouted.

'Because we called the number and found Rachel's next of kin,' said Margot.

Hazel gasped. 'They answered you?'

I nodded. 'He blocked you for blowing up his phone too much.'

'He?' asked Mum. She sat forward on her seat. 'And who was he, Wes?'

She totally knew who 'he' was. I knew she hoped she was wrong.

I took a deep breath. 'It was Craig Evans.'

'You are joking!' screamed Auntie Molly. 'That . . . rat!'

I put my hands up. 'It's bad – but not as bad as you think, Auntie Molly!'

'Who's Craig Evans when he's at home?' asked Lauren.

Mum turned to her with wet eyes. 'Wesley's dad.'

When I tell you the room fell silent, believe me. It was like the whole house had been pulled off Earth and hurled into space, where no one could hear us scream – except Naomi and Rachel maybe.

Apollo looked between Mum and me, his eyebrows high, his chin tucked into his neck. 'No!' he whispered. 'No!'

'Sadly, yeah,' I said. 'I haven't spoken to him for ages either – six years – so it was a shock to me too. Like, I was spinning, couldn't sleep. Felt sick. Wanted to hug him, wanted to fight him. All the feelings.'

'So what did you do?' Auntie Molly wagged her finger. 'Do not tell me you went to see him?'

'We went to see him. Obviously.'

Mum stood up, fear all over her face. She trembled as she walked in tight circles round the room. She bit her lip. 'Do I even want to know what happened?'

'I do,' Thelma said quietly. 'It's getting good now!'

'We met him in the park,' said Margot. 'He was really sad about what he had done.'

'He told you?' Mum whispered.

'Oh yeah, he did.' I nodded. 'But here's the kicker. He didn't cheat on you with Rachel, not really.'

'Now hold on a minute,' warned Auntie Molly, 'I saw the photograph; I saw them in town. I'm not stupid – I don't forget a face.'

'Rachel Kohl, K-O-H-L, never existed,' said Josie. 'The woman you saw was actually Naomi Baxter-Banks.'

5

Eyes, tongues, jaws. All on the floor. Auntie Molly stood to catch Mum. Whisper dribbled his drink down his shirt. Hazel and Lauren stared at each other, just shook. Apollo spoke first.

'Naomi?' he whispered. 'Naomi from . . . my plays?'

'Naomi from *Naomi's* plays, Apollo.' I tutted. 'And Rocky was Craig – that was his nickname at school, wasn't it, Mum?'

Mum nodded weakly. 'I caught that.'

'Nope, I don't believe this,' said Hazel, shaking her head. 'These children are spinning us a story.'

'*I* believe them,' said Whisper quietly. He jabbed the air. 'I always said there was something about that girl that didn't add up.'

'There were three things that helped us put it all together,' said Margot. 'One, we found a bucket list that belonged to Rachel. Two –' she turned to Whisper – 'your photo

481

albums.' She pursed her lips at Apollo. 'And, three, *Naomi's* plays.'

'How?' said Mum. 'How did you do it?'

I looked around the room. 'Are your photo albums still here, Whisper?'

He pointed. 'Yes, on that dining chair.'

I grabbed the one I was looking for, the one I spat crisps on. I opened it and found my page. I held up the book. 'There's a news cutting about an accident outside Fitzroy's Fine Foods – Whisper's shop in the 1990s.'

Whisper jolted back in his chair. Thelma grabbed his hand.

'The girl who passed away was Rachel Cole. C-O-L-E,' said Josie.

'She was Naomi's foster-sister. Naomi was there, at the time of the accident.'

Whisper's face contorted as the sad memories came flooding back in waves that washed over him, through him. 'Thelma,' he croaked, as he gripped her fingers tight, so tightly his knuckles lightened and the bones beneath threatened to break through. His eyes watered. A teardrop ran down his face.

Thelma put her arm round him. 'There was nothing you could have done, my love, *nothing*.' She looked up at us with the saddest eyes I've ever seen.

I paused, and shuffled on my feet, not knowing if continuing was the right thing to do. All eyes in the room were on Whisper now, his sorrow onstage. He wiped his eyes with the back of his hand. He wagged his finger at me. 'Carry on. Finish your story. Let us know – let the girls pass through.'

'We also knew this from *Close*, the play Naomi wrote,' said Margot very quietly. 'That was set in a shop and it ended abruptly.'

Whisper gulped down a loud breath.

'There's a bench dedicated to Rachel in Wardown Park, near the shop,' said Josie. 'The bench where you saw Naomi eating chocolate digestives, Whisper.'

We watched Whisper weep on his wife's shoulder.

'Wow,' Apollo murmured. 'Wow.' He paused. 'I don't know how to feel. On one hand – well, both hands, actually – this is tragic, awful. But I have to admit, deep down, I feel duped. Did I know Rachel, I mean Naomi, at all? Where does one personality end and the other begin?'

I nodded. 'I felt scammed too at first. Up until this morning, I was, like, nah, I'm not about it.'

'What changed your mind?' asked Hazel, sitting forward.

'We spoke to Naomi and Rachel's real next of kin – their sister Caroline.' I turned to Mum. 'She told us Craig blocked Naomi years ago, before she moved back to Luton.' I shrugged. 'If you wanted to drop him a message, I know he wouldn't hate it.'

Mum and Auntie Molly looked at each other and instantly started whispering. Mum smiled up at me, and I grinned back.

Hazel wasn't so happy. She nearly fell off her perch in shock. 'You found her?'

'We did, in Canada – she was invited to the party all along. She's going to get in touch with you tomorrow to make arrangements,' said Josie, folding her arms. 'You can have your house back soon. No need to drill doors off their hinges in the middle of the night. For example.'

'What?' Hazel scratched at her neck, eyes darting around the room. 'I don't know what you mean.'

'Why would you?' said Josie. 'Like I said, just an example – an illegal example. That's not your style, is it?'

Hazel glared at Josie. 'Not at all, but I'm interested to know what's behind that door.'

'Which door?' asked Josie innocently, staring at her.

Hazel talked through her tight mouth. 'Rachel had locked her front bedroom and I'd be interested to know what was in it.'

I looked around the living room for the frame Naomi brought to her surprise party. It was tucked just behind the sofa where Mum and Auntie Molly were sitting. I pointed to it, and then to me. 'I'll need it in a minute,' I whispered.

'Oh, you want to know what's behind the door?' Margot smiled. 'We know the code; we can show you.'

'You *know* it?' said Lauren, leaning forward. 'How? Did yous guess?'

'Nope, we worked it out.' Margot looked at Auntie Molly. 'IDST mean anything to you?'

'If Destroyed, Still True!' said Auntie Molly immediately.

'Come on then,' said Margot. 'We'll show you her room.'

6

'At her party Naomi said Rachel's favourite code was "IDST" – we also saw it written on her bucket list,' Margot explained, as she fiddled with the lock. 'And, Molly, once you started talking about your job, it began falling into place. We counted the number of letters and –'

'Two, nine, five, four!' Auntie Molly shouted like she was on a game show.

Margot nodded. 'Two, nine, five, four.'

The lock clicked and Margot pushed the door open. When she flicked on the light, everyone gasped and filed in.

'Oh my God,' said Mum, amazed, rubbing her eyes, then looking at her sister. 'Is this or is this not like our bedroom from back in the day?'

'Uncanny,' Auntie Molly replied. 'It's not *like* the nineties – it *is* the nineties.'

I popped the frame down and ran to Naomi's room to pick up my portrait. It was just the thing, I hoped. The thing that would tie the room together, the thing that Naomi wanted me to do, the thing that would send both Naomi and Rachel to the other realm. I brought it into the room and propped it on top of its frame.

'There,' I whispered to Margot and Josie. 'It's in the right place, almost. We did it.' I bit my lip. 'I hope.'

'We did our best,' said Josie, patting my shoulder.

Margot reached for my hand. 'And that's good enough. It has to be.'

I looked up at the light. 'Let's see what the spirits say first, eh?'

'Erm, who painted that?' Apollo asked, pointing at my portrait. 'Not you, darling?'

I nodded. 'Yeah, I did it today. It's Naomi and Rachel when they were about fifteen.'

'Well . . .' Apollo put his hand to his chin. 'It's *stunning* – and created so quickly. You know, if you ever want to get into set design . . .' He smiled, his eyes twinkling.

I would never work with him. What? Would he take credit for my work too? Get out of here.

'Thanks, I'll think about it,' I lied.

Apollo nodded and glanced at Naomi and Rachel's desk. '*Clueless*!' he said.

Yeah. Exactly like him.

Mum tapped me on the shoulder. 'The portrait's incredible' She smiled. 'So's this room – and everything you three did to open it for them, and us.'

THE NINE NIGHT MYSTERY

'It's what Naomi's worked on the whole time; it's what she was getting all those deliveries for,' I said.

'A tribute and promise to her best friend, her sister,' said Margot, leaning over. 'On that journey to keep Rachel's memory alive, Naomi lost herself, but we got who she was and why she did it. They were incredible friends.'

'We did this for both of them,' added Josie.

'Right.' I nodded and put my hand in my pocket. I felt a sharp edge on my finger. I looked at the desk. 'Oh! There's one more thing to do!'

I pulled Naomi's part of their pendant from my pocket and hung it next to Rachel's half. 'Best' and 'friends' back together. Forever, hopefully.

Rachel's list was complete.

The bedroom light flickered loudly and brightly above us – brighter than ever before. There was a snap, then silence and the room was plunged into a peaceful darkness.

Rachel's List

5 FEBRUARY 2018

~~Move to London~~ ←

9 APRIL 2023

~~Live alone~~ 18 FEBRUARY 2023

~~Have (or throw) the BEST surprise party~~

~~Step onstage and shine~~ ★ ★ 13 APRIL 2023

~~Ride a horse~~ 21 JANUARY 2023

~~Paint our portrait~~ 18 APRIL 2023

♡ ~~Rocky <3~~ 16 NOVEMBER 2017 ♥ ♡

~~Be best friends forever~~ 18 APRIL 2023

LOVED *THE NINE NIGHT MYSTERY?*

SHARNA JACKSON

AUTHOR OF THE BESTSELLING *HIGH-RISE MYSTERY*

'Brilliant – a joy'
Katherine Rundell

'I love it!'
Elle McNicoll

THE GOOD TURN

'Sharp, witty,
entertaining'
Alex Wheatle

'An intriguing
mystery adventure...
bold and brilliant'
Sophie Anderson